T0196000

Cassies Ruler

A BERTRAND MCABEE MYSTERY

Joseph A. McCaffrey

authorHOUSE®

AuthorHouse™
1663 Liberty Drive
Bloomington, IN 47403
www.authorhouse.com
Phone: 1 (800) 839-8640

This book was originally published in 1999 by Jamic, Ltd

Published by AuthorHouse 01/17/2020

ISBN: 978-1-7283-4172-9 (sc)
ISBN: 978-1-7283-4171-2 (e)

Print information available on the last page.

This book is printed on acid-free paper.

Cover Design: Sally Paustian

DEDICATION

For my son David, always true and ever sure.

 **CHAPTER 1**

Erin Tobin finished washing down the strapping standardbred, placed a blanket over him and began walking him. It had been a big effort, his being parked out in the Saturday Open at the Quad Cities Oval harness track. The mile went in one minute and fifty seven seconds, and he had been sucking air and taking extra steps for three quarters of a mile. Cassies Ruler lost by a length to the front-running Ice Palace, made $750 for trainer/owner/driver Tobin, and came out of the race undamaged as far as Tobin could tell.

She worried about the nine-year-old horse who in his heyday was a dominant, high-claiming pacer at the Chicago harness tracks - Maywood, Sportsman's, Hawthorne, and Balmoral. He had gradually slipped out of the top tiers when Erin approached the Chicago trainer, Jim Slade, about a purchase. She thought Cassie would be better suited to the less-strenuous racing in downstate Illinois- the Quad Cities Oval in East Moline during the spring and summer and Fairmount Racetrack in Collinsville during the fall and winter.

He was a handful, a kicker and a biter. Her groom, the incessant talker, Brian Sligo, refused to work with Cassie, having been missed by a back leg kick three inches from his head that would have killed him instantly. But Cassies Ruler was a pro; once he was harnessed to the race bike, he was all business. It was as if the hellish attitude was only meant for leisure time. Erin figured that he just didn't know how to relax, a condition that she could relate to herself.

Erin was the only child of Thelma and Orville. Her mother died when she was four. Orville had a 500- acre spread near Aledo, Illinois, and besides the requisite corn and cattle, he had as his pastime the breeding and racing of standardbreds. He had gone as far as circling part of a corn field with a three-eighths mile track. Orville raced at the numerous county fairs throughout Illinois summers and would send some of his better pacers onto the parimutuel circuit in the state.

Already a tomboy, with the death of her mother, Erin's crossover into the very masculine and arduous world of standardbred racing was a choice without any meaningful obstacles. When she graduated from high school in 1985, she took the exam given by the United States Trotting Association (USTA) and became a trainer and also acquired a provisional harness driver's license. She went up to Quad Cities Oval with two horses, an eighteen-year-old woman into a culture that was still debating women's suffrage.

Erin was 5 feet 10 inches tall and weighed 130 pounds. Her eyes were a stunning blue and her face ruggedly handsome. Bettors knew Erin easily because her long, blonde, helmeted hair would fly in the wind as she aggressively circled the five-eighths-mile track.

After two years, she had established a stable of seven horses, lost the (P) which indicated a provisional or neophyte driver in the racing program, and was called, in a puff piece on the front page of the April 29 program, "one of the top drivers/trainers at the Quad Cities Oval."

Cassies Ruler was her favorite. She knew that he was a mean son of a bitch, but what an animal to drive. He never quit - he had the soul of a warrior. Bettors never knew the problems that he presented in the backstretch - all they saw was a horse who gave everything each time he raced. She loved the smell of him - the drying skin freshly soaped and washed off with a gentle hosing. She held the rope attached to his halter and walked around the perimeter of Barn Q at the Quad Cities Oval backstretch. It was Saturday night on May 23, 1987. The distant lights of the track were turned off, and since Cassie had been in the last race on the card, things were delightfully quiet, most backstretchers having gone home or to The Stretch Tavern located about a quarter mile up the road.

"Erin, tough race tonight - he's one helluva stalker." Omar Johnson was another trainer and driver in Barn P. He was headed to his car. He patted Cassies Ruler on the back haunch.

"Yeah, I wish I could have gotten him to the rail-he didn't need to run an extra 200 feet. But nobody'd give me a hole. Oh, well."

"See ya around," Johnson said.

She continued to walk Cassie until he was relatively dry. She took him to his stall, walking in with him, removing the rope from his halter, and swiftly moving out of his stall, which was for this possessive horse, his territory.

She went back to the hosing area of the barn where she filled up a pail of water which she placed in Cassies' stall. As usual, his ears were pinned back, which indicated a preparedness to attack, but she was out of there with alacrity.

She turned around and found herself facing a man who was vaguely familiar. He was extremely wide but not fat; it was hard for her to see beyond him. His brown eyes were hard and watchful. She surmised that he couldn't be more than twenty-five years of age. She figured he was a groom from some other stable.

"What can I do for you?" she asked.

He didn't say anything, but he advanced another few feet, which brought him to within a yard of her. She sensed danger and edged back slightly. Erin was seventy-five feet from the stable door when she heard it slam. She turned to find Rickie facing her. Rickie was a groom in Tom Barley's barn. He was good hearted but pretty severely retarded, an innocuous track pet, taken seriously by no one, patronized by everyone.

"Listen you two," speaking loudly enough for Rickie to hear also, "what the fuck do you think you're doing? You get your asses out of here right now." She reached back to grab a loose tie to the right of Cassies' stall. But just as her fingers curled around the chain the wide guy swung at her with his open hand and knocked her against the steel gate of Cassies' stall. She tripped and fell to the ground, the quickness of the man's hand startling her.

She tried to scream, but the wide son of a bitch was now sitting on top of her as she lay prone on the stall floor. She was petrified and knew that she was had. There was no one around and these two assholes had already committed a serious crime.

The wide one, all too calm, crooked and waggled his

index finger at Rickie who stumbled over and looked down on Erin with red eyes and some drool coming out of the right side of his mouth. The wide guy said, "Go in the trunk and get me some tape and rope." It was obvious to Erin that Rickie was drunk. She cursed her luck at being at the mercy of a psycho who sat on top of her with a hand on her mouth and a severely retarded drunkard who was rummaging through her training trunk, which had every manner of gear and equipment for horse training, and with a little imagination, human bondage.

Rickie came back with some electrical tape that is used to secure a variety of equipment to horses, some rope which is used for stringing up lines on which to dry blankets, as tethers for horses, and assorted other potentialities.

The wide guy now looked at her with a sneer and said, "Bitch, listen to me. If yuh scream, I'll knock every tooth out of yuh goddamned head within a second of yuh trying it. I'm gonna fuck yuh and yuh'll go along with it or else." To which Rickie said, "Yeah do it, do it, Tommy Lee, do it. Then I want a shot." He started to rub his groin in anticipation.

Erin calculated her odds. They were bad. She nodded her consent. Tommy Lee took his hand off her mouth but kept it about six inches from her lips, testing her, as it were. He reached out for the roll of tape, tore off a piece and put it over her lips. He took ten more pieces and deliberately built a tape pyramid of sorts so that Erin could not open her lips. He then got off of her, knelt to her side and started to unbutton her denim shirt. Erin was becoming catatonic even though she was using every skill that she could summon to remain in control.

When her shirt was unbuttoned he took her by the hair and brought her up to a slouching position. He unsnapped her bra and removed both articles of clothing at the same time, throwing them on the ground next to her. Her shame was enormous. He pushed her back to the ground. He looked at her with a filthy sneer. He then went to her feet and started to untie her tennis shoes while Rickie knelt down beside her and started to finger her breasts.

It was too much. She kicked Tommy Lee in the balls and sent him back falling and grunting. As she made a move to sit up, she tore the tape off of her mouth, but Rickie fell on top of her and made it hard for her to scream or to maneuver, his being an amorphous 200 pounds or so. He then turned and lay on top of her, holding her arms down. She could feel his dick getting hard as she struggled to free herself before Tommy Lee could recover his wind from her well-placed kick.

She leaned into Rickie's shoulder and bit as hard as she could. He let out a yowl and fell away from her as she scooted back and in one move was on her feet. She turned to run to the stable door, reached for it, but just as she was about to pull it open she was brutally slammed against the stable door as Tommy Lee hit her full force with a flying tackle. It was her turn to deal with wind being knocked out as she knelt on the ground grimly gasping for air through her nose.

She could smell the bad breath of Tommy Lee as he looked at her from a distance of six inches and growled:

"You'll pay extra for this yuh cunt!"

She tried to tear the tape from her mouth so as to get more air and was slapped viciously sending her sprawling away from the barn door. He grabbed her by the hair and yanked her heaving, partially upright body back to the area near Cassies' stall. He said, "Lie down on yuh tits bitch." She did. He took her arms and snarled at Rickie, "Bring me the rope." He tautly knotted her arms behind her. Then he turned her over by way of a kick in the ribs to which Rickie, rubbing his bitten, bleeding shoulder, said, "Good, kick the bitch again." He was ignored.

Tommy Lee then went up to her ear and whispered - "If yuh kick me again I'll beat yuh to an inch of yuh life. Shake yuh head if yuh understand me." Through tears, she nodded. He stood up and hatred found hatred. Cassies Ruler was leaning over his gate with his ears pinned, defying Tommy Lee to come close. For several seconds they stared at each other, Erin sensing the pervasive hate that hung in the environment.

"What horse is this, bitch?" Realizing that her mouth was taped, he jerked his head toward Rickie. "That's Cassies Ruler - the meanest fucker on the track," Rickie said with an awe that even surpassed that which he had shown to Tommy Lee.

"Yeah," Tommy Lee laughed, "I have a surprise for him." He took the metal tie that Erin had previously reached for, curled it in two and swung it at Cassies' face, just missing the horse's left eye but catching him near the ear. Cassie leapt against his gate in anger and anguish as he was hit again by Tommy Lee. Blood flowed from his brow into his eyes. His nostrils were flared and his ears were pinned back. As Tommy Lee wound up again, Cassie backed away from the gate. Erin watched in disbelief.

He threw away the chain and spat toward the horse

before he reassumed his position of standing in front of Erin. He picked up her right leg, now unresisting and pulled off her tennis shoe and a sock, likewise for her left foot. He then unbuckled her belt, unbuttoned the pants button, unzipped her jeans and took off jeans and panties in one prolonged move. Erin was in shock watching the event now as almost a disinterested observer.

Dumbfounded, Rickie stood and watched as Tommy Lee spread her legs, took his pants half way down to his thighs, and forced his way into Erin. He rammed and rammed at her now unresisting and broken body. His grunts signified his epiphany and his slap across her face when he was finished as his resolution.

"Go ahead, yuh retarded jerk, yuh can have at her. She's a frigid bitch!" Rickie came just as he entered her. Her tears flowed incessantly as Tommy Lee decided to have another go at her. His arousal correlated with her subjugation. He slapped her and kicked her in the ribs when he was done.

Erin lay sprawled with her arms tied behind her, her mouth taped, and her entire inner psyche straddling sanity. She tried to focus on one thing- saving her life. If she could do that perhaps she could mend the rest of herself over time. But life was the essential. Between the tears, her confusion, her anger, her shame, she saw the two of them high-fiving each other.

Tommy Lee came over to her and said, "I'm gonna cut the rope. If yuh try anything, I'll smash yuh face to pieces. Do yuh hear me bitch?" He kicked her just below the hip. She nodded her head.

He turned her over and cut the rope that held her hands.

He slapped her ass and said, "Nice ass yuh got there baby." They laughed. "Now, put yuh clothes on, whore!"

She reached for her panties and jeans. She was bleeding from her vagina; he had torn her up pretty badly. The pain seared through her. She reached for her bra and shirt, and put them on. Tommy Lee and Rickie just stood there watching, quiet. She didn't like that composure; she saw it as a quiet before a storm. Even the idiot Rickie should realize that he was in big trouble. She sat on a director's chair that was nearby and started to put her socks on. She put on her shoes so that the left shoe was on her right foot and her right shoe on her left foot. Just in case they kill me, she thought, some clue might tip off an alert investigator. The two of them, full of themselves, never noticed. She reached to take the tape off of her mouth. Having done so, she felt a gush of blood flow into her mouth from her nose. She used every control she could muster to maintain her wits as she spat out a mouthful of blood. She looked at their unsmiling faces and saw hatred in one, and perhaps a slight look of remorse in Rickie's, the bastard's primitive conscience finally kicking in, she thought.

"So what are yuh going to do about it baby?" Tommy Lee asked.

Through swollen lips and a blood-drenched mouth, she responded awkwardly, "Nothing. You got me fair and square. Let's just forget it and go on." Like hell you filthy pigs. I'll kill both of you if I get the chance.

"That's more like it. Right, Rickie? Looked to me like the slut wasn't enjoying it. Whaddya think, should we let her go?"

"Sure, sure, she's going to keep quiet she just said she would."

"Yeah, right, and yuh teachers told yuh, yuh was normal, yuh dumb shit," he laughed meanly.

That comment sent shivers through her. He wasn't done yet. She tried to remember things that she had seen on television and read in newspapers about not allowing threatening situations to get out of hand. Keep talking and remain as calm as possible.

"I really won't say a word to anyone. I don't need this getting around," and more blood was in her mouth. "Did someone put you guys up to this or are you on your own?" A risky question, she thought, but she needed an answer.

"I've been scoping yuh for two weeks, babe. I almost took yuh Wednesday night by myself, but I figured that dildo-head could be a help, especially since he's got the big time hots for yuh. Right, Rickie?"

"Yeah, yeah, right."

She figured that she'd give it one more run. If someone was behind it, she needed to know so that she could add him to her list.

"So it's just you on a lark?" she asked as unthreateningly as possible.

"Yeah, a lark baby, but there's also a message here, and this is it. Don't blow off the suits around here. When yuh asked to help with a race- yuh do it. Don't yuh be so highfaluting. Yuh hear me, bitch? And when they are trying to treat yuh like a woman and buy yuh a drink and pay some attention to yuh, don't piss on them. Don't play dike; those are the messages bitch!"

"Who are you talking about?" There were really only three suits employed by the track on a full-time basis. Two of them had made a play; one of them seriously, a fat, greasy, middle-aged, drunken bastard up in the track bar. So, now what, she thought.

"Yeah," Rickie said, "you don't play games with big Eddie Fox. He'll ..."

"Shut the fuck up, yuh jerk! Yuh dumb piece of shit!" Tommy Lee screamed at Rickie.

Erin had it rightly guessed- Eddie Fox, pig of pigs. A likely poster boy for carrying any venereal disease that ever existed. She saw Tommy Lee put a finger up to his mouth and rub his chin.

The bitch never really saw the right crossing fist that broke her jaw and knocked her unconscious. Tommy Lee looked at Rickie and said, "Go in that mean fucker's stall and hold him still."

Rickie opened the gate of Cassies Ruler's stall, then with quiet talk and a quick hand managed to get his halter and quiet him. Tommy Lee dragged Erin into the stall and laid her near the gate, which swung inward into the stall.

Rickie said, "What are you gonna do?"

"Yuh'll see, just hold the fucker." He then closed the gate, placed the lock on it and proceeded to reach under the gate, which had about a two-feet opening between it and the floor. He grabbed Erin's body and placed it in an upright sitting position, with her upper back serving as a brace against the gate. Cassies Ruler became more and more difficult to hold as he began to rear up and battle Rickie who was holding on tightly to him. This was the maniac's stall and it was as if the people in it were in total violation of his space.

"OK, get the hell outta there asshole," Tommy Lee barked at Rickie who let go of Cassie and scrambled on all fours under the gate and between the unconscious Erin and the wooden wall that held the gate in place.

Tommy Lee went to the training trunk, found a spray bottle of Windex, looked into Cassies' stall and sprayed the animal in the eyes. Cassie raced to the back of his stall and charged the gate, stepping on Erin's right thigh. Cassie became all too aware of her and reared up, coming down on her chest area with both of his aluminum-shod feet. Her body fell to the left side at a 180-degree angle. Cassie was sprayed again. Rickie reached in with a broom and poked at the animal, who now frenzied, turned and started to flare out with his back legs, thrusting them back with awesome power and intensity. On the fourth kick, he found Erin's head. She was dead immediately from that sure kick. Both Tommy Lee and Rickie knew the minute he connected as they looked at each other knowingly. It was like, Tommy Lee thought, a power hitter connecting with a baseball -you knew it from the sound - a home run.

To be on the safe side, he felt her pulse; there wasn't any. The bitch was dead. He continued to provoke Cassie while reaching through the gate and the floor of the stall and sitting her upright, but her head now rotated in a macabre fashion as her neck was broken. He left her that way knowing that in all likelihood her body would be stomped and kicked for a good while. Too bad about killing her, but what can you do, the retard threw a name, and Eddie Fox wouldn't like that.

He turned and saw Rickie across the aisle looking dazed and ashen. Tommy Lee had figured this could be the situation, a grief-stricken moron whom the cops would break in five minutes.

"Come on, let's get outta here," he snapped.

"But we did something real bad. Oh, no, this is bad." Rickie was whimpering as Tommy Lee led him from the barn to Rickie's pickup truck.

"I'll drive, Rickie. Yuh just sit there and have a few good swigs from that whiskey bottle. Settle down, it's gonna be OK for Christ's sake."

Tommy Lee drove over to his own truck and got a hose that he had kept in the bed of the truck along with some electrical tape. When he got back to Rickie's truck, Tommy Lee told him to drive out of the barn area. As Rickie moved over to the driver's seat, Tommy Lee jumped into the back of the pickup and placed a tarp over himself. Rickie drove through the guarded gate of the backstretch. The guard waved to him, but Rickie hardly noticed. His face was a blank.

When Tommy Lee was aware that they were out of the stable area, he knocked on the window of the cabin and motioned for Rickie to stop the truck. Tommy Lee then took over the driving while Rickie drank every drop from the whiskey bottle. He drove about one mile from the track. Rickie was in a serious drunk and fell asleep. Tommy Lee pulled off into a corn field and turned off the lights of the truck.

He removed the hose and tape from the back of the truck, pushed the hose into the exhaust pipe and taped it. He brought the other end to the cabin where he inserted it into the window. He then opened the door and sealed the window on the inside of the door, threw the tape into the cabin, closed the door and let the carbon monoxide find its way into the semiconscious body of Rickie. Rickie was dead fifteen minutes later. Tommy Lee then walked back to the track, jumped a fence that got him into the backstretch and was in his groom's room by 3:30a.m. All during this time he had kept his calfskin sulky driving gloves on. He now took them off, smiled to himself, and went into a deep sleep.

CHAPTER 2

Orville Tobin stood beside his daughter's casket and said to anyone who would listen that the horse might as well have kicked him in the head and in eight years thereafter, he lived out a life that stayed close to the margin between unhappiness and misery.

The police investigation had unanswered questions to it, but Detective Mark Goody of the East Moline Police Department had pretty much made up his mind before he called in the Illinois Criminal Investigation (ICI) unit. Erin Tobin's death was called in at 9:33 a.m. on Sunday, May 24, 1987. One of the grooms in the next aisle had come over to Erin's row to borrow a leg wrapping. He was surprised that she wasn't around. He saw her left foot just protruding from under the gate. Cassies Ruler stood there, his ears pinned as if looking for more intruders. The groom instantly got hold of her leg and then the other and pulled her out onto the floor of the barn. He started to scream at the top of his lungs. The backstretchers ran over, someone called 911, an ambulance and police car were routed to the scene. She was taken to the hospital, even though long dead. No one thought murder. Everyone thought Cassies Ruler, the consensus being that she made a mistake around him and he got her. Her face wasn't recognizable.

Her body had been taken to Illini Hospital, permission given by Private Connell who was on patrol for the East Moline Police Department.

It was only when the gas-filled and bloated body of Rickie was discovered at 11:15 a.m. that morning that the radio operator thought that Mark Goody should be called in. Goody had been on the force for three years, the son-in-law of the police chief. A year ago he had been promoted to a detective slot where he was joined by two others, the most able of which was in Montana on vacation white water rafting. Mark was on call. Two things troubled him: they were two track people, and the Coroner's Report stated that there was semen from two different men. But he dismissed the former as coincidence and the latter by believing that track backstretches were havens for drunks, lechers, druggies and the like. Mark had pretty much wallpapered the entire world with his assumptions, which were patterned in black and white.

His report stated that Rickie was a carbon monoxide suicide, his body registering a 3.28 in alcohol toxicity. Erin Tobin, on the other hand, was clearly the victim of a horse known for his viciousness and ferocity. Questions about the condition of her genitalia, rope burns on her wrists, and the oddity of two feet with opposite shoes were considered peripheral and irrelevant.

The ICI investigators, so pissed off at the trampling of the killing scene by over seventy-five backstretchers, the removal of the body, and whole state of incompetency, washed their hands of the case and went along with Goody's assessment. Lieutenant Gardner, an investigative administrator with the ICI, was bothered by the whole thing, but within days he was on to other matters and the case fell into the closed file drawer. After all, you can't bring charges against a horse or a suicide.

Orville Tobin was officially notified of the police decision in the matter seven days after the burial of his daughter, on June 2, 1987. Mark Goody didn't mention the sperm analysis or any of the complications. Orville Tobin let it go. What else could he do?

On June 3, he drove over to the Quad Cities Oval, loaded Cassies Ruler into a trailer and drove him back to his farm in Aledo. He went to the outskirts of his corn field and drove a ringed spike into the ground with a sledge hammer. He went back to the trailer, led Cassie out into the field and tethered him to the spike.

His two farmhands saw him doing all of this but were not about to say anything. They looked at each other in a knowing way and slowly nodded their heads in unison.

Orville came out of his house with a breached shotgun and walked toward Cassies Ruler. When he reached the horse, he put two slugs into the chambers of the gun and slapped it shut. Cassies' ears were pinned, as if anticipating trouble. Orville raised the shotgun and blasted the animal from a range of six feet. On his four knees and wobbly, Cassie was shot again. His death didn't please Orville, but he did feel a slight weight lift off his shoulders. The farmhands were told to bury the murdered horse.

No investigation of this incident ever occurred, even though word of it drifted back to the Quad Cities Oval and the East Moline Police Department. The sheriff of Henry County chose not to pursue the matter knowing that a conviction of animal cruelty would not prevail given the circumstances surrounding the matter.

Eight years hence, August 31, 1995, was a twin feature for Orville. He was having a heart attack on his seventieth birthday, as he was gripped by a piercing pain in the chest that went on for about thirty seconds. He reacted to it, as he had too many things in the past eight years, with indifference. If it was time to go, it was time to go. When the pain stopped and he regained a calmness, he felt disappointment.

His continuing grief over Erin's loss permeated everything that he did. When he looked over his corn field, he could still see the bare outline of track that was there and then planted over after her death. Even worse, he could still visualize his daughter in the sulky methodically jogging the pacers through her adolescence. Even though he cut himself loose from any association with harness racing, having sold off Erin's stable and all of her equipment along with all related materials in his own barns, he was still haunted by it all. He found no route that enabled an escape from his torment.

Physically strong, he weakened; a hearty eater, he ate little; sexually active, he became celibate; socially involved, he became a loner; religiously focused, he became agnostic; optimistic, he became dour. Thus he saw the heart attack as a welcome finale to what was a universally bad piece of life.

On this very same August 31, 1995, he received a letter that entirely altered his viewpoint. He had something to live for - a mission.

He trudged along the gravel road to pick up his mail.

He could taste the dryness of late August in his mouth; the constant swallowing of parched grains of soil that hung in the hot air. It was 1:00 p.m. and already it was 92 degrees Fahrenheit. He had just listened to the WGN Farm Report out of Chicago. The Commodities Exchange brokers were having a great summer driving up the corn and soy futures, everyone seeming to have his own personal weather forecast. It was getting so bad now that the fools would bet a fortune on the possibility of thunderstorms in southeastern Iowa. The information revolution was just another way of screwing your neighbor, he ruminated.

Beside two catalogs and a gas and electric bill was a business envelope, no return address, made out to Orville Tobin, RR #3, Aledo, Illinois. There was no zip code on the letter, and it was postmarked out of Chicago-August 26, 1995. He felt on alert the minute he saw it because it was extremely unusual for him to get a personal communication like this, except for a few birthday cards from his ill-wishing relations. Maybe it was ESP. The walk back to his house was more brisk and purposeful than normal.

He sat at his kitchen table and opened the envelope. Inside was a single piece of lined paper, 8 1/2 inches by 11 inches, from a legal pad. He opened it and read the printed note, which was undated and untitled:

> *Your girl was murdered.*
> *If you want a name it will cost.*
> *Tie a blue piece of material to the*
> *bottom of your mailbox post if interested.*
> *If you're not- just remember*
> *I'm only coming this way once.*

He read the letter at least twenty times. He thought about cops, extortion, himself, and especially Erin. He could let it go and wait out the son of a bitch, whom he figured would come back many times over until convinced that he wasn't buying. But he thought of the heart attack and knew that at his demise, any interest in Erin's death would be nil. Financially, he had comparatively great wealth and concluded that between giving money to his sordid relatives or exploring Erin's death with an extortionist or perhaps even the murderer himself, the latter was the best choice. For the first time in eight years he felt a sense of excitement.

He went into a closet off the hallway to his house and removed a blue denim shirt that had hung there unused for years. With scissors, he cut a four-inch wide swatch of material, starting with the bottom flap and going all the way through to the collar. He took the cutting and immediately went to the road where he knotted the material to the base of the mailbox post. His wait began at 2:00 p.m. that day. There would be no cops in the grim game that he would play with this vulture; at least until he sensed what was at stake.

The call came on September 3 at 8:30 p.m. Tobin picked up the receiver after the third ring. "Yes?"

"Is this Orville Tobin?"

"Yup."

"You got my letter the other day about your daughter. I'm not in this for charity. I need bucks and I'll give you information about the murderer."

"I understand ... keep talking."

"If I sense cops or PIs or anything like that ... I'll cut out and that's it. Do you understand?"

"Yes, I do."

"I will only call you from public phones, always different, and by the time you try a trace ... I'll be done. If I see a cop around, I'll know that you screwed me. Got it?"

"Yup." Orville was trying to maintain his calm.

"I'm going to give you this information in three steps. It's going to cost you $100,000 total- $20,000 for the piece that establishes me as knowledgeable, $30,000 for filling in a lot of details, $50,000 for the name of the murderer. I won't dicker with you, and I know that you have the bucks. Yes or no?"

Orville knew all about trading, bluffing, and bidding. He figured that he could knock the price down, but there always was the risk of withdrawal and with it his last best chance to discover the truth about Erin's death. He also calculated that the caller's third step might become more expensive, but in personal fortune, he had twenty times what he was asking for and came down on the side of the gamble.

"I'm still listening, mister. You haven't lost me."

"I want the $20,000 in tens and twenties - old bills. Across from the backstretch gate to the Quad Cities Oval is a feed building. Walk around the building and you'll be facing Interstate 88. Behind you is the back side of the building. It has a sign called Kent Feed. Put the money right next to the building under the 'K' of Kent. Do it on the night of September 5 at 9:30p.m. Be as discreet as you can and then leave. When I get the money, I'll call you. Questions?"

"Nope. I'll do it. But let me tell you one thing I have a bad heart and could go at anytime. So don't extend this game too long, mister." The caller clanged down the phone.

Getting the money in small bills was a little harder than Orville expected, but he got it and packaged it in an athletic bag that he bought in the Aledo Wal Mart.

On September 5, he drove to the Quad Cities Oval Betting Parlor. It was no longer a live harness track, having been shut down after a shortened season in August of 1993. The owner, a Chicago millionaire, stated that the river boats that docked on the Mississippi River on both the Illinois and Iowa sides of the river were simply too much competition for the entertainment dollar. That this same owner had relentlessly mismanaged the track so as to achieve the goal of shutting it down was the other side of the coin. There was more to be made in betting parlors than in running a labor-intensive "live" track.

Orville knew exactly where to go. He drove up the side road to the backstretch entry gate, which was now under lock and key, there no longer being any horses or backstretchers. The feed building across from the gate was barely discernible in the darkened area. He took the bag and walked behind the building and looked over at Interstate 88, which was about 500 feet across a flat field. He turned and saw the sign Kent Feed and placed the money under the "K" and then went back to his car figuring that he was being watched from somewhere. He drove back home, pretty sure that he'd get a call. His statement about the bad heart was probably well-taken by the extortionist.

The call came the next night at about 9:00p.m.

"Yes?"

"I got the money."

"Good - now I believe it's time for you to establish yourself as knowledgeable."

"Did you ever read the police report?"

"No."

"You should sometime. Your daughter was beaten pretty badly by two men, then she was raped. A supposed suicide that was not associated with your case file - should have been. He was one of the rapists. He was murdered, too, after they had done your daughter. There's more about this. I'll call you soon. You might as well start to work on the next installment- 30 thou, same kind of bills- same kind of deal. Questions?"

"Twenty thousand dollars is a lot of money for what you just gave to me."

There was a small gutteral laugh. "Take it or leave it- it's a seller's market. Bye."

Orville went to his rocker and thought through what he just had been told. He decided to drive to the East Moline Police Department the next morning and look over the police report. After that he could decide about the next $30,000.

The East Moline Police Department is located in a dubious downtown. A breakaway from Moline, Illinois, East Moline's top population was 20,000 in the mid-seventies when the farm manufacturers: John Deere, International Harvester (IH), and Farmall drove the economy of the Quad City region. By the time the farm economy had started its turnaround from a devastating depression through the late seventies and into the eighties, there had been considerable downsizing. East Moline had lost some plants and had picked up an ugly and violent slum through these processes.

"I'd like to speak to a detective please."

The uniformed woman at the desk asked him to sign in

and told him to wait. After twenty minutes, a plainclothes man came to him and extended his hand.

"My name is Detective Mark Goody. I believe we met some years ago when your daughter was killed by that wild horse, Mr. Tobin."

Orville remembered him. He had gained considerable weight over the years.

"I'd like to see my daughter's file, if you please," Tobin said.

"I think that could be arranged, sir, but would you mind answering a few questions?"

"No, go ahead."

"Why do you want to see this file? The accident occurred a good eight or nine years ago."

"I have a bad heart and I just want to put a few things into perspective. I have a few doubts."

"What doubts would those be, sir?"

"Well, Detective Goody, I just can't believe that Erin could be fooled by a horse. She was just too good around them. So, I have this lingering doubt about what happened. I have a bad heart and I guess I'm trying to die in peace."

Goody's eyes squinted slightly. Orville figured that he was trying to remember the file and whether or not there were problems in it. After a few seconds, Goody said, "Sir, we don't advise parents to look at these files because sometimes things are said and comments are made that are a bit raw, and sometimes just downright lies."

"I can handle all that crap. If it comes to be that I can't, I'll let you know."

"OK. Can you come back in about an hour? I'll have it ready for you."

"I'll be here."

Orville went across the street to a diner; Goody went to the basement of the East Moline Police Department and dug out the file on Erin Tobin. Goody rifled the file and removed almost 75 percent of the materials, especially those focusing on the background data that suggested that Erin was a loose woman and the nasty exchange of communications between the East Moline Police Department and the Illinois Criminal Investigation Unit. What remained were ten pages of material, including a summary statement of the pathologist's report, but absent the full analysis. He hoped that this would satisfy this rather pathetic old man.

When Tobin came back, he was given the file and told that he could not remove any of the contents, nor could he photocopy. The uniform told Orville that Mark Goody had to leave for an investigation and wouldn't be back until late that day. If he had questions, he could call.

The file was in a lawyer's folder that had a stretch canvas as binding. The minute Orville looked at the canvas, he knew that the file had been thinned out considerably. When the uniform was busy, he took out a ball point pen and put a small dot in an identical spot on the bottom left back of each of the ten pages. Mark Goody apparently took him for a fool and was unlikely to see what he did.

What he read was no great surprise. The pathologist observed that she had been kicked during the course of the night and morning some twenty-two distinct times, three of those times had been to the head, all three of them enough to be fatal in themselves. Besides that, she had been kicked in the chest area on four occasions and had sustained massive internal injury to almost all of her internal organs.

An analysis of the vaginal content showed that she had had intercourse and further analysis had indicated that two different men had been with her. He observed that the vaginal area had been bleeding and that the sexual contacts appeared to have had a "somewhat aggressive" component. But the clear and obvious cause of death was due to the horse named Cassies Ruler "whose bloodstained feet and shoes showed a clear match to the decedent."

Orville Tobin was not surprised that Erin had sex. She was brought up to be herself and to accept her urges as natural. The two-men aspect, though, did not fit his sense of her, nor did the aggressiveness part. She was not the type of person to let someone brutalize her. On the other hand, parents were the last to know sometimes.

But now the caller's words bit at him- she was raped by two men and she'd been beaten. How could the caller know about this? It was never reported in any way like this in any of the public media. What had been reported is that she had been kicked by the horse and had died. To Orville, what the caller had said squared with the pathologist's report. Her being raped also squared with the report.

Other information in the folder went through times, action taken, and seemed to suggest that the ICI was being heavy-handed in the matter of the investigation.

Of course, this was all from the viewpoint of Mark Goody. No state reports were in the folder, and that struck Orville as odd. A brief background check on Erin reported her to be somewhat promiscuous and a regular pot smoker.

No sources were identified for these conclusions, much to the chagrin of Orville. Were they also missing?

Track backstretchers were notorious for their gossip and backstabbing. Most of the people there had never graduated from high school; near poverty hovered at tracks as pay was low, and they pretty regularly bet their lives away on backstretch talk about horses who were "sure things." No one could survive an existence in the backstretch without making adversaries and creating huge pockets of rumors and lies. It simply was the way it was. That a strong and beautiful woman like Erin, trying to make it in a man's world so cozy with jealousy, treachery, and betrayal, couldn't go unscathed even in death didn't surprise Orville.

He reached the conclusion that the report given to him was not only incomplete, but that it was a bad piece of investigating and that rather than laying to rest his new-found source's opinions, he now renewed his resolve to continue to play the game out. He returned the file to the uniform.

Later that day he called Detective Goody. "Detective, I looked through what you gave me, but it seems to be a rather thin file. Are you sure there's nothing else?"

"No, Mr. Tobin, that's it. We get rid of a lot of material when we close the file, and when we didn't see any criminal stuff, we just usually use summaries and the like. To put your mind to rest, I'm quite sure it was just a terrible accident. By the way, the Illinois Criminal Investigation Unit also signed off on the case, and they're world famous. Sorry for your loss, Mr. Tobin, but this is the best I can do. And by the way, don't believe most of that crap they said about your daughter. People in that world are pretty nasty as a rule."

CHAPTER 3

The white bastard - Scorpio - regularly strutted over on his sleeping body at 6:30a.m. He had just heard the paper girl drop the Quad City Times on the doorstep and with a low guttural growl had sent her back to where she came from. In itself, that scene would not usually have awakened Bertrand McAbee, who at best was only semi-aware of the daily battle between these two adversaries. It's what followed that brought him to consciousness as the 100-pound white German Shepherd beelined to his bed, leaped up - mostly to an unoccupied section of the bed - and began his strut around the mattress. Scorpio was conditioned by the paper girl to want to go on his run, and he, in turn, conditioned his alleged master to comply. It wasn't particularly funny at 6:30a.m., but McAbee had learned to laugh about it as the day went on.

He got up, tossed some cold water in his face, dressed, and poured himself an eight-ounce glass of orange juice and headed out the door for a five-mile run. He pretty much stayed in a routine of three - five — seven - rest - three - five - seven - rest. Scorpio loped along beside him as the two found country routes within a half-mile of home. And except for Scorpio making his occasional territorial claim, they kept a pretty good pace of between nine and eleven minutes a mile. When he got back, he filled Scorpio's water bowl, put some food out for him, and then proceeded to get himself ready for the day while he listened to WVIK out of Augustana College in Rock Island, Illinois, which was the public radio station for the Quad Cities (encompassing the main communities of Davenport and Bettendorf, Iowa and Rock Island and Moline, Illinois). The IRA had just exploded a bomb in London, Israel had just pounded a Hezbollah headquarters, and a team of investigators had just come upon a massive grave site somewhere in Bosnia. He missed all of the details while in the shower and felt none the worse for it when he finished and heard about the re-emergence of the buffalo in the western United States.

After two cups of coffee and a toasted bagel with Smucker's low-sugar strawberry jam and a quick perusal of The Chicago Tribune and The Quad City Times, he brought Scorpio out to the backyard and put him in his run. He had to walk into the run with Scorpio as if to reassure the dog that he would be back. His neighbor, Gloria, would keep an eye on Scorpio throughout the day, and if McAbee got caught up in anything, she'd see to it that Scorpio received fresh water and some food. As he backed out of the driveway, he saw Scorpio staring at him with those intense black eyes, and he'd hear the slightest of whimpers from this estimable beast. Virtually every day this scene reenacted itself, and everyday McAbee's heart caught itself from falling.

Beth, his estranged wife of thirteen years, had just left him nearly six months previous to pursue other interests. He conjectured that among these other interests was some guy whom she met on a bike ride in Colorado. Beth had become a fanatic about cycling when she was diagnosed as a diabetic ten years ago. Between her law practice and her biking, she didn't have time for the relationship that had a fifteen-year age difference to begin with. All the stars were aligned for the collapse, which was evident to everyone except McAbee himself. He had the half-paid-for Condo, the dog, and a son by another marriage. At fifty-six years of age, he felt much more insecure than he had conjectured he would be when he married Beth, who would turn forty-one in another month.

He crossed from Bettendorf into Davenport, on Kimberly Road, which was also known as Highway 6. His office was in downtown Davenport and provided a marvelous view of the Mississippi River, and on the opposite bank, Rock Island, Illinois. He was the founder of the ACJ Private Investigation Agency. Few knew what ACJ meant, and when asked, McAbee would be oblique in his response. In fact, it meant Anthony - Christopher - Jude and was based on the lives of these three saints who may or may not have existed, and if they had, whatever was said about them was probably about as reliable as a Bill Clinton campaign promise. Ostensibly, however, Anthony was the patron saint for finding lost objects, Christopher the patron saint for safety, and Jude the patron saint for lost causes. Most of McAbee's work never escaped the aegis of this powerful trinity of saints.

It was twelve years ago that McAbee left academia. He had been a professor of classics and philosophy at St. Anselm College in Davenport, Iowa. His speciality was anything Greek or Latin; his appointment in the Philosophy

Department was only for purposes of his teaching Ancient Philosophy. When the College decided to play down its liberal education heritage and direct its attention to the consumer, which meant that no student in his right mind would take Latin, Greek, or ancient philosophy, McAbee was promoted to Academic Dean. When he found out the eventually fired President of the College had lured foreign students with open admissions acceptances to any of them wanting one, had supported an extensive package of harassing activities against a protesting female faculty member, and was engaged in petty thievery from the dwindling College resources, he decided to leave academia for a while. As it turned out, he never looked back.

"Doc, good morning." Pat Trump had been his secretary and assistant for all twelve years. She was about five foot three, thin as a rail, a chain-smoking redhead, and about as loyal as people come.

"Hello, Pat, what's up?"

"A few calls, one from your brother who wants to know, quote, "When the hell does he ever work?" and an urgent one from a Moline attorney's office- Jim Van Spies. There are some letters on your desk to sign. Don't forget you have a racquetball game with Lou Kodowsky at noon at the Y."

"Thanks, Pat. How was your weekend?"

"Yeah, OK. I met Ray in Indianapolis on Friday night. We spent the weekend there."

This was hard on Pat and scared the hell out of McAbee. Six months ago, Ray had been transferred to Cincinnati by his company, and Pat and he had been doing things like going halfway to meet in Indianapolis. He knew that this couldn't last and kept waiting for her to proclaim the end of her job with ACJ. The thought of getting a replacement for this multi-talented woman sent him into an instant state of panic.

"Aren't you tired of all that driving?"

"Nah, it's OK. I have some good tapes, and it's only about four and a half hours."

He called Van Spies. He had done two minor pieces of work for him three or four years ago, missing persons to the best of his memory. McAbee didn't remember turning up anything for him.

"Bertrand, thanks for returning my call. I have a most unusual situation with a client, and you happen to be right in the middle of it if you'd care to hear about it. Is there any way I could get you to my office this afternoon at three? I'll warn you right now, you're going to be presented with a proposition that is potentially quite lucrative."

"Jim, what's the big mystery?"

"That's for my client to tell. How about it?" McAbee took River Road on Highway 61 (Davenport and Bettendorf loved renaming their highways) and Interstate 74 and its bridge, which spanned the Mississippi and brought him into downtown Moline. He was in Van Spies's office at 3:00 p.m sharp.

He was introduced to a man named Orville Tobin who was a tall and distinguished looking man of about seventy-five years of age. He had a full head of white hair and a pair of unflinching and piercing blue eyes. He was nervous and intense, a man in a hurry.

Tobin said, "You probably are wondering why I asked Jim to call this meeting with you?"

"Very much so."

"Let me explain. My family, which now means only me, has been in Aledo, Illinois, for over 110 years. When I die, that heritage is gone. At any rate, I go back a long way with a lot of people in that area," his right hand had a slight shake to it as he gazed at McAbee unrelentingly. "One of them is my neighbor, Hal Ledbetter. One of Hal's sons became an FBI agent, Danny. I got hold of him yesterday and talked with him for a bit. I believe the two of you know each other."

"Dan Ledbetter? I sure do. Chicago office-FBI. A very good person, Mr. Tobin."

"Well, he shares that opinion about you. He said there is you and then a whole bunch of others in the second tier. I'm buying what he says. Will you hear my story?"

"That's why I'm here. Please."

Tobin took out a pad and recounted the story of Erin, complete with his dealings with the caller and the East Moline Police Department.

McAbee watched Tobin ride his roller coaster emotions. He would be a bit manic, especially when he dealt with the caller and the information that had come his way, but he would be depressed when he spoke of the East Moline Police Department. McAbee saw a man who was cheated out of his only true love - Erin. He found it ironic that Tobin was happier with the murder rape scenario than with a horse getting the best of a promiscuous daughter. McAbee put it down to a judgment on Tobin's part concerning a matter of free choice and how that related to his daughter's rape and murder being involuntary, whereas a horse getting the best of you had a ring of irresponsibility.

When Tobin was done, McAbee said, "It's very hard to go back on cases such as this. The police have an inherent interest in keeping the file closed, since the whole thing suggests incompetency and at the least, superficiality, on their part. But the caller is interesting to me. Without him you wouldn't have had any change in your outlook. Did you tell all of this to Agent Ledbetter?"

"No, nothing. I just asked him for a name."

"The reason I ask is that an official agency can frequently do a better job at this stuff than I can. They can get to the files, they can access officials, and so on. For me, that comes hard. I have to use leverage, favors, friendships, and sometimes downright bribes."

"Money is not an object here, and official agencies are bullshit, pardon my expression, since it's because of them that I'm here now. Look, I get good feelings about you, sir. I'm desperate. I think that my heart is going to give out anytime. I'm worth about two and a half million, and I have a few relatives who are pretty much going to get everything. I can't stand the bastards, but our family tradition says that it stays in the family. So OK, I'm willing to do that, but what I do before I die is my business totally. I do intend to pay that caller his $100,000 - I already have the next installment- $30,000- ready to go. I've lived a terrible life since Erin's death, and if there's any way I can right the scales- I'll pay."

Tobin's intensity and sincerity impressed McAbee, but he put a marker next to his analysis of the man's mental stability.

Tobin continued, "If you would take the case, I am prepared to pay you $1,500 a day plus any expenses - including bribes - and if you can get an arrest, conviction, or death for the murderer of Erin, I will give you $200,000 as a bonus. I've already instructed Jim, here, to rewrite my will to reflect this arrangement, since, as I say, I don't know how much longer I have. What do you say, sir?"

"I'll tell you what I'll do and then tell me if you still want me. First off, I want control of the case, and that includes checking with me on how you handle the caller."

"Hold on, Bertrand- I intend to see him through. I'm not going to tinker with that."

"I don't want you to, but I want to be in on what you do. You'll just have to have absolute trust in me, Orville. If you want to fire me, fine, but until you do, I'm in charge."

"This is hard on me. I don't really see any good reason to trust people, something personal; that's part of what I've become over these last years." He shook his head, lowered his eyes, and stared off to his right. Everything became quiet in the office.

If he gave him the wrong answer, McAbee was prepared to get up, shake his hand, and leave the office. He had learned many things in this game of investigation, and the question of his control was an inviolate rule for him, even to the point of losing some lucrative contracts.

Tobin finally spoke, "It's that important to you, but so is my concern to keep my caller on the air. If you intend to break that connection, I'll have to say no to you."

"No, I don't intend to break that connection unless he decides to take you on a long ride through still another series of calls or that the rules that have been set up - are getting violated and I can't live with what's happening. It's your money, Orville, and I don't have any intention to get in the way of how you spend it. But if I think the objective of finding the murderer, if in fact that's the case, is

35

being hindered by judgment calls that are affected by your personal feelings, we have a problem. You are, after all, very emotional about this issue, and it's not all that hard to make mistakes when emotions are flying high."

"Okay, I think we understand each other. Now what?"

"If the caller connects again- do what he asks. We need all of the information that we can get. Do you have a tape recorder that is set up to record calls."

"No."

"I'll have someone at your house first thing tomorrow. We'll call first. I'll see to it that they're driving a pickup and it fits the local scenery. You'll just have to push two buttons before you pick up, and it can't be intercepted by the caller. So, let's start there. If he calls just do what he says -his big score will be on his third call. I won't endanger anything by a surveillance. I will check out the drop tomorrow. Here's my office number and my home number to call, if necessary."

When McAbee left, Tobin stayed with Van Spies in order to continue to make changes in his will.

"I like him. He seems to be honest, although I don't particularly like PIs and the stuff they get into. But I want him treated fairly, and if in your judgment, he has pulled this matter to completion, give him the money," Tobin said.

"Well, Orville, he's as honest as people come. His reputation is flawless, and he gets results. Don't underestimate him," Van Spies said.

McAbee drove across town reflecting on the things he had heard. He wasn't very optimistic about the success of reopening the case. It had such tremendous age. Files were gone, memories tarnished, people dead, and except for Orville, no one had any interest in reopening this case. The key to the matter was the caller, but he hesitated to be active in pursuing the man lest he blow the only possible lead around. He decided to give it a week and then make judgments about feasibility.

Tobin arrived back in Aledo at 6:30p.m. He was about to open his refrigerator when the phone rang. He felt that it would be the caller.

"Yes?"

"Did you collect the next installment, Tobin?"

"I have it right here."

"Same time, same place - tonight. And again, I'm looking- any funny business and the deal is cooked. You understand me?"

"Yes, I do. I'm ready for part two."

Tobin pondered awhile after the disconnect. Is it possible that he was followed to Van Spies's office and that McAbee was noticed? Is it possible that the phone is wired and that the caller knows that his conversation with Van Spies involved the hiring of McAbee and thus that he was in violation of the agreement? That he knew of the call to the FBI? He decided that it was all unlikely and called McAbee's office. He wasn't there. Tobin then called McAbee's home and found him.

"Bertrand, you won't believe this. He just called fifteen minutes ago. He wants me to put the money out tonight at 9:30 again."

"And you intend to?"

"Of course. I just wanted you to know that I'm going

there - and that I should have some information maybe by tomorrow night. He waited a day to call me the last time."

"Well, Orville, be careful. Just get out, put the money there, and drive away. You know the game."

"Yes, I do. I'm going to leave now and go to the Wal-Mart in Aledo to pick up an athletic bag. Funny, the last time I just bought one; I think tonight I'll buy two. I can't believe he won't go for the third. Don't you think?"

"I agree with you. That's the big score. The problem is he may try to draw it out to make more money because you've been so cooperative. But we'll deal with that when the time comes. By the way, keep the tags from the bag and jot down the color, just for the hell of it. Good luck, Orville."

McAbee called Augusta Satin at 10:00 p.m. that night. He told her to call Tobin in the morning and then be at his place by 9:00 a.m. at the latest with a tape recorder and mouthpiece microphone for the purpose of taping the caller.

"Oh, and don't go out there dressed professionally and get your hands on an old pickup truck. Somebody might be watching. You still have that recorder from the Tuttle business?"

"It's right here."

"Be as inconspicuous as possible, Gus."

"Right. We black, female professionals are always floating around back county roads in dirty pickup trucks. Want me to chew some tobacco, too?"

Augusta Satin came into McAbee's life some five years previous. She had quit the Rock Island Police Department because one of her three children had developed cancer. She was trying to get her ex-husband to pay child support, but he skipped across state lines. He was a black M.D. and a first-class scoundrel who didn't give a damn about his kids and who had acquired a special hatred for Augusta. She had hired McAbee, and he had succeeded in getting information that at last compromised him enough to get him to cooperate- even though he was continually late with his support payments. The unlikely duo had hit it off and she became a private contractor for McAbee. Her cancer plagued daughter had died two years ago. McAbee relished her acerbic sense of humor.

The next morning Augusta called Orville Tobin. She knew that her accent was picked up by whites as being black and she assumed that some old farmer like Orville Tobin might flip out. She enjoyed watching whites make believe that they didn't notice.

"Yes?" Tobin had growled on the third ring.

"Mr. Tobin, the name is Augusta Satin. Would it be OK for me to get to your place about 9:00a.m.? I believe that Bertrand has talked with you."

After a few seconds delay, "Oh, yes; sure, OK. I'll be here."

"See you." She hung up and drove across town to the west end of Rock Island, which was about 90 percent black and 10 percent white, the white being the old Belgians who had never gotten out of this section of town, mostly for reasons of poverty. She had arranged to borrow Henry Sidon's 1981 Chevy pickup. She wore a pair of jeans, an old sweatshirt, and an old pair of western boots when she drove into his driveway. He came out and when she got out of her 1995 Honda Civic, he smiled.

"My, oh my, aren't we looking countryish today. Would you like to borrow a Reba tape?"

"Don't be so funny smartass. I'm on a job. Don't need any crap from you. Where's the truck and where are the keys?"

"You want a cup of coffee or anything?" Henry Sidon was an old-time friend of her deceased father. He was a good ally and they had traded favors for years.

"No coffee, no nothing. I gotta go to some farm in Aledo. I don't think there's a black in that whole county," she said.

"Probably a few - six feet down. But, yeah, Henry County ain't no black man's Mecca."

"Henry, I'll try to get this back by early afternoon. If you need my car, here are the keys. But don't you be going to Chicago or anything."

He laughed.

Augusta took the Rock Island Bypass and hit fifty miles per hour and backed off on the accelerator. She felt like the truck was going to come apart from the rattling and shaking. McAbee asked her to teach Tobin how to use the device comfortably, and also to do some checking around for a possible tap.

The directions were good and she drove into Orville's driveway at 8:55a.m. She went up to his door, knocked and he came out. He said, "You're from Bertrand?"

"Yes, sir, I am."

After a slight hesitation, he said, "Why don't you come in." They shook hands.

Augusta figured that she was the first sister to ever get inside this old house. She removed the recorder from her bag and said, "Mr. Tobin, what phone do you use most regularly?"

"This one here in the kitchen."

She showed him the suction cup and after wetting it, placed it on the ear part of the mouthpiece and plugged in the other end to the recorder. She familiarized him with the play/record switches and told him that just before he picks up the phone to press both buttons simultaneously.

"If it's OK by you, I'm going to call you with my cell phone. Let's just do a dry run."

His phone rang; he did it right. They talked about the weather for about thirty seconds. They rewound the tape and they listened. The conversation was clear. She gave him extra tapes and her phone number. She investigated the phone and the wiring into the house, with nothing suggestive showing itself, and then she left. Orville Tobin seemed bemused perhaps by the wickedness of having a black in his house. He wasn't hostile so much as awkward. Whatever it was, Augusta Satin wasn't surprised, most whites were just plain goofy in these kinds of circumstances.

CHAPTER 4

Tobin fished the tape out of his front pants pocket and handed it to McAbee. In the one foot of empty space between their hands the slight tremor detected by McAbee two days ago had now become a serious rumble. McAbee placed the tape in his recorder and pressed play.

"Yes?"

"It's me, Tobin. So far you're doing fine. Keep it up. Here are some details, old man. He wasn't supposed to hurt her or even touch her. Also, the supposed suicide wasn't part of this; in fact that guy Rickie- had no business in on this. The murderer made him part of it for some reason. The guy was asked to get your daughter straight on some betting schemes and also to let her know that good things were meant for her. When I got wind of what he did, I was upset. The guy's a psycho and I'm taking a chance even talking with you. He killed two people in one night, and there's no doubt in my mind that he'd hit again. Be ready soon. Bye." There was a click.

"Hey, mister ..." the conversation was over.

McAbee rewound the tape and played it two more

times. He looked at Tobin and said, "Well, Orville, was it worth $30,000?"

"If it's helpful, sure. What's your impression?"

"The caller's believability has gone up in my mind. He's trying to exonerate either himself or someone he knows who more than likely didn't order a killing -just some intimidation. He asked the wrong guy and bang- two murders. I think that he's very worried that you'll set a trap for him and that he might be uncovered, and just in case, he wants to make it clear that he wasn't involved. But the fact is that he's in felony territory."

Tobin narrowed his eyes and looked at McAbee, "You seem to be saying that there might be something here after all."

"I had the suicide matter looked into. There was, in fact, a suicide that night. A backstretch guy named Rickie Crocker. It took place a mile or so from the track in a farm field. Carbon monoxide and massive alcohol count. I got that from a friend, but I haven't seen the full report yet. So, your guy has his facts fitting together. I surveyed the drop area yesterday. It wouldn't be that hard to get surveillance out there with infras and so on. We could probably get a license number and some pictures with minimal risk. I'd recommend it, because he just may take your $50,000 and quit. He has no incentive to give you the name. We could be more direct, of course, and bust him at the site."

"What if it's not him? What if it's a friend who's picking up the money?"

"That's the rub, Orville. Just how active a response do you want, if any? There's a lot of forestation and nooks and crannies in that area. It's good concealment for him, and it's good concealment for us. Think it over, but we've got to be prepared to move quickly. Do you have the $50,000?"

"Yes."

Eddie Fox had just showered and shaved and was looking out the kitchen window of his third-floor, walk up apartment in Forest Park, a near-west suburb of Chicago. He was ricocheting back and forth on what to do next. The $50,000 that he had finessed out of Tobin had finally gotten him out from under his gambling debts. No more threats from those Sicilian bastards! The money was so easy, and Tobin so compliant. Fifty thou more could really help him get his feet back on the ground, but what if he could get $100,000 more from him? Was the old man in touch with the cops? PIs? Was he taping, tapping? Maybe it was the time to cut out while he was ahead.

He could still remember the incident eight years ago. He had gotten to the clubhouse at the Quad Cities Oval at about 10:00 a.m. There was a popular Sunday brunch menu that was served beginning at 11:00 a.m. preceding the race card that started at 1:00 p.m., and he was on duty that day. When he had gotten upstairs to the clubhouse, three of the help were looking out the massive windows which overlooked the track and the backstretch beyond. They were pointing and he followed their arms. There was a police car and an ambulance in the backstretch near one of the many barns. Their lights were flashing.

"What's going on?" he barked at the three employees.

"Don't know, sir, all those lights just came tearing into there about ten minutes ago."

"Well, let's get back to work." He gave a soft tap on the

ass to the cute server who had just started working there about two weeks ago.

He went to his office and called the security gate.

"This is Fox. What the hell's going on back there?" he demanded.

"There's been an accident, sir."

"Great! That's a really impressive report. Where's Carter?"

"He's over there with the ambulance."

"Go get him and have him call me right away!" He hung up.

Chief of Security Dave Carter called Fox about ten minutes later.

"Mr. Fox, Dave Carter."

"What the hell's going on?"

"We have a death." As if on cue, Fox could hear the staccato bursts of the ambulance leaving the Quad Cities Oval backstretch.

"What? What? What do you mean, a death?" To this point, Fox had never connected his chat with Tommy Lee and the ambulance pulling away with a corpse. And it was precisely on this time evaluation that he felt that he was innocent in the matter.

"Erin Tobin, sir. She's dead. Seems like Cassies Ruler got her in the head."

"Dead? What the fuck do you mean dead?" Fox screamed at him.

"Dead -like -a broken neck, dead, sir. I don't know how else to say it to you, sir. The medic pronounced her dead the minute he got here. Said she's been dead for hours. The horse probably got her last night after the race he was in. Cassies Ruler was in that last race last night."

He took another cup of coffee from his Mr. Coffee machine. Even at this point, he didn't connect Tommy Lee, as if to underscore his innocence still further.

And then at about 2:00 p.m. more news came across the track. Rickie Crocker, the dimwit, had suicided! He heard that piece of news from Carter just as the third race ended. He was instantly worried about the bad press associated with the two deaths. They had underwent a massive drug bust on the backstretch last year and didn't need the bad rap. He was trying to conjure up sympathetic headlines: "Track people cope with untimely deaths." "Two lights go out at the Quad Cities Oval." "Oval personnel dismayed and shocked." "Religious rites performed at Quad Cities Oval." He could live with any of these. The trick was, position yourself as a victim and people back off.

When the tenth race ended the Sunday card at 4:30 p.m., he sat at his desk to do a run on the attendance and betting handle. Then and only then did he smell something, and that came when Tommy Lee walked through his door - unannounced and without knocking. The burly bastard had a smile on his rotten face. "I need a thousand bucks! I gotta get out of here."

"So, get out of here! A thousand bucks? You're dreaming!"

Tommy Lee got up and bolted the door and turned around and faced Fox: "Listen - I did yuh bidding with that blonde bitch. Don't forget that, Fox. I even loosened her up for yuh by screwing her; in fact, I even let the retardate have a shot at her. But the retardate threw yuh name to her, so I had to kill her and him to protect yuh!"

Fox recalled how he felt. His stomach tightened, he

began to sweat, and he felt faint. He was utterly shocked with disbelief.

"What the hell are you telling me?" he said haltingly.

"Hey, don't worry. They were both clean kills. But it doesn't hurt to clear the scene for a while. I'll head south and catch on somewhere."

"Who the hell told you anything about murdering someone, and how did Rickie get into this? I told you to tell her nicely to cooperate and that I liked her - what does that have to do with murder for Christ's sake?" Eddie Fox was being enveloped by the enormity of the crime, if in fact Tommy Lee was telling the truth.

"Hey, man, she wasn't buying. She had a chip on her shoulder. Most broads crack when yuh belt them - but not her- she got worse. Rickie, I just felt sorry for; it was a mistake. It's OK. Just give me a thou and I'll be gone by tonight. These aren't firsts for me." That semi-insane stare caused Fox to shudder. He had no idea that his carefully pitched comment in the bar to this seemingly friendly backstretcher who claimed to have a good relationship with Erin Tobin could go this way. He gave him a thousand dollars and for eight years that was the last he saw of Tommy Lee until three weeks ago. Fox didn't know if Tommy Lee saw him, but the vision of that weirdo, along with a very explicit threat by the two Sicilians, had set him on his course. He mulled on how these two extraordinary situations could yield a third that could neutralize the first two - he could pay his debts and get Tommy Lee the hell out of Chicago.

After McAbee concluded his meeting with Tobin, he decided by to go full throttle for a few days. Tobin didn't blink an eye at the potential expense. He set up a series of meetings with his contingent of freelancers.

Pat came to his door and said, "Are you ready for Barry?"

McAbee nodded.

Physically Barry Fisk was one of the strangest men McAbee had ever encountered. About five foot, two inches, he had a hunchback that caused him to pitch his right shoulder about ten degrees so that he was always looking at someone aslant, his head was thrust to the right and pointed upwards on top of a quite shortened neck. He seemed to be always calculating. His was not a pleasant visage - pointy eyes and ears with razor-thin lips, and a tiny chin. In contrast, his nose, normal by usual standards, was large for his face. His personality wasn't compensatory.

He had a doctorate from Yale, specializing in American History, his dissertation dealing with the Lewis and Clark expedition and its relationship to subsequent American espionage. His flinty brilliance, however, could not overcome the personalized, mean spirited bigotry he encountered in the classroom. He was driven from the teaching ranks at Western Illinois University in Macomb, Illinois, within a year and a half by students who used his physical traits as the burning acid to destroy the man's unpleasant personality and meticulous scholarly standards. He chose not to persist in teaching and became instead a researcher and author on nineteenth-century America. That choice alone would have earned him poverty. His freelancing skills, however, did not go unnoticed or unrewarded.

McAbee had made his acquaintance six years previous during a trial where Fisk was testifying on behalf of a local naturalist group which was trying to stop an encroachment by a large motel chain into a bald eagle sanctuary area.

"Barry- have a job for you if you're interested."

"Let's hear about it," Fisk said in his most belligerent manner.

"Are you in a bad mood, Barry?"

"I don't see whether that's here nor there."

With Barry, relationship perceptions were of no relevance. He was pure task. Barry could run people through to get the job done and was independent enough to tell anyone, God included, to go straight to hell. For reasons in the shadows of McAbee's personality, he couldn't resist an occasional tweek at Barry, and every once in a while he wondered whether Barry didn't get some pleasure out of the whole thing.

McAbee had worked up a one-page summary of the investigation and handed it to Fisk who pored over it for a few minutes. There was no rushing Barry who, in his tum, would not miss a nuance in any written material. What McAbee needed from Fisk was typed on the bottom of the sheet.

"This might take awhile. I don't know what records they have out at that track. Most of those guys are transients, too."

"I know, Barry. It's a tough situation. But money's not an issue. I need a list of everybody who was within those track confines from opening day of 1987 to the murder and then, especially, did they keep records of the comings and goings of these same characters? Then run them down until we can make some isolations."

"This Rickie guy -you want everything on him and Erin Tobin?"

"Just stay to the print, Barry. I'll be running some verbals through other sources."

"Yes, yes. I know what you think of my interpersonal skills." That sarcastic comment drew the closest thing that McAbee ever saw to a smile from Fisk.

"Oh, and Barry- I need this ASAP."

"Really, and what else is new with the ACJ Agency?" He got up and without so much as a goodbye -left. McAbee concluded that he took the job and that he'd move on it quickly, since there wasn't a "no" anywhere in the conversation. If anything could be turned up in the direction of written documents and records, Fisk could get it done. Three years ago, because of Fisk's extraordinary work, McAbee had captured a $75,000 bonus on a job for a national trucking company which had a regional depot in the Quad Cities. He used $15,000 to get Fisk a state-of-the-art computer system for his home. That time, and that time only, McAbee heard "Thanks" from Fisk. McAbee figured that he had brought Fisk up to a new level on the researcher Richter scale. God help those on the oppositional side of Fisk's modem.

McAbee's final appointment for the day was with Jack Scholz. Scholz didn't come cheap, but his work was flawless. His politics and vision of what a democracy should be caused McAbee to never want to ask him a favor. For this reason, McAbee kept him well paid for his occasional services, but also kept his meetings with him as clandestine as possible. Jack Scholz lived for conspiracy, cloak and dagger, and anything that even hinted of danger. Due to this, McAbee always added a stroke of the mysterious to their meetings.

About two blocks west of the giant Oscar Mayer plant

on Rockingham Road in Davenport, McAbee waited in a back room at Sophie's Loose Garter Club. Sophie knew the underside of the sometimes pretentious and righteous Davenport. She was somewhere in her late sixties, frumpy, orange-haired, and she spoke with a slight Russian accent.

"Doctor McAbee, who are you waiting for? A blonde, a brunette?" she laughed as she sat across from him. Her club had strippers, but they didn't come in until 3:00 p.m. when a big shift change was coming due at Oscar Mayer. That she was fronting a prostitution business was known by all who wanted to know, but the understanding between her and the police was based on subtlety and no trouble. A long-forgotten friend of hers had once attended McAbee's Ancient Philosophy class. She held college profs in some kind of awe. She was a wary ally of McAbee, and their relationship was closely monitored by both on a favor-for-favor basis.

"I'm meeting a blonde man, Sophie. I've had enough of you beautiful women, and I thought I'd go for a man," McAbee joked.

She smiled, but then looked at McAbee suspiciously. "Oh, no, you're not meeting that psycho who thinks he's Arnold Schwarzenegger? He really scares me; not too many do, but he does."

"It's OK, Sophie, I'm just going to chat with him. It has nothing to do with you. He likes backdrops like this."

"Backdrops you say, but I think guillotines and head drops when I see him. He's the type," she lowered her head and moved to within a few inches of McAbee's ear, "who snaps and walks into a place like this and blasts us all to hell!"

"Well, you have the part on going to hell right, Sophie, but you'll be OK as long as you don't look wrong at him."

There was a rap on the door. Sophie looked up and said, "I go."

"Don't frisk him, Sophie, you couldn't lift all the steel that he carries."

"HA, HA!"

She opened the door, looked at Scholz and pointed toward McAbee who was now standing at attention as it were. There was no doubt as to who perceived where the hierarchy began and ended between these two. McAbee didn't give a damn about the protocol and accommodated Scholz wherever possible.

Jack scholz was probably a retired United States Marine Corps Captain. He was sixty-three years of age and everything about him was taut, his back and his neck were the giveaways along with his crew haircut. His only concession to age was a pair of steel-rimmed glasses which had the effect of making him even more rigid and remote. His manner of speech was clipped, precise, and terse.

"Places like this, McAbee, give me nausea. These filthy holes should be burnt down along with the rubbage that supports them!"

"I know, I know how you feel, Jack, but they give us solid cover. I also think it's good for some of the locals to see the angel of death once in awhile," McAbee said ironically and unsmilingly. Scholz, unlike Barry Fisk, wasn't someone you could tweek. McAbee was sure, however, if the right right-wingers were constitutionally elected and Scholz was ordered to torch the place and shoot the fleeing patrons, the job would be done and done efficiently and ably.

Scholz saw America as ruined by liberals, gays, blacks, Jews, environmentalists, Hollywood, universities, and so on. It was because of McAbee's ability to listen that Scholz trusted him. McAbee made it a rule to never argue with him nor to display to him any brand of political sympathy. All jobs that McAbee used him for were pitched in a way that brought up the forces of good versus the forces of evil. McAbee knew the type he was dealing with - a Manichean, a St. Augustine who although converted from this sect, never left it- Scholz was a Manichean nationalist as opposed to a Manichean Christian. That Scholz and Augustine were cut from the same rock was an a priori principle for McAbee.

When McAbee had visited the drop scene, he had taken forty-eight pictures of the area with varying lenses from the inside of a one-way glass in a van driven around the area by Pat Trump. He carefully explained the situation to Scholz, who was equipped with the latest night vision scopes and cameras. Where Scholz managed to get this equipment from was not McAbee's concern, but he was sure that Scholz, in the name of patriotism, America, and justice, stole and bribed his way to some of these materials.

"So, what exactly do you want from me? A bust? Pictures?"

"Pictures and especially the vehicle and license number, and, of course, of the guy."

"If I have this right - this is extortion. Why don't you just let me get him, take him out into the field and get the info from him, and also recover the bucks! Why play footsy with this criminal?"

"Now, Jack, not this time. I promised my client that I would not endanger what he had by way of a contact. But

I want to know who he is just in case he cops out. Then, maybe we'll have a go at him in your style."

"You got it- just say the word. But I guarantee, I could break him in probably twenty minutes."

"I know, Jack. I'll also want some kind of tail on the guy if you can do it with a honing device. Nothing up close."

"This is getting expensive. It's a six-man job. I have to scope it out, get my men, and maybe I can practice tonight."

"How much?"

"Five thousand a night!"

"OK, Jack, you're on. Usual channel of communication, and let's be especially indirect."

"Goes without saying."

When Scholz left, Sophie came into the room. She said, "My God, Doctor McAbee, why do you bring him in here? Every one of my customers thinks that he's a Fed. The Mexicans get nervous about green cards, my girls get nervous about their venereal disease, my bartender gets nervous about underage drinking, and I get nervous about tax evasion. Maybe next time you could get him to come in drag!"

McAbee called Orville and told him not to do anything tonight or tomorrow night, given the setup necessities that Scholz was under. Tell the guy you only had $15,000, in two days you'd have it all.

The play was starting and McAbee felt that it would be one of many acts. When he got home, Scorpio jumped up and down on the gate of his run. It never failed, this thing about dogs, they just took you for who you were and gave you everything that they had. He opened the gate and brought him into the house. It was hot. They both appreciated the air conditioning.

CHAPTER 5

Tommy Lee remembered living in Cazenovia, New York, for four years between his twelfth and fifteenth years. His father had finally held down a job as an auto mechanic and had brought the closest thing to stability for his mother and Tommy Lee that either had known since Tommy Lee's birth.

It was during those years that Tommy Lee had been introduced to harness racing in Vernon, New York, at Vernon Downs Race Track. By the age of fifteen, he was accomplished enough to be trusted as a groom whose job it was to take care of pacers for a licensed trainer.

He quit school on his sixteenth birthday and left New York on the same day. He hadn't been in touch with his mother or father since, nor did he know whether or not they were even alive. He just didn't care.

His escape from home found him in a fellow groom's car heading to Pompano Park Harness Track in Florida. It was at Pompano, during the late fall through spring meet, and Northfield Harness Track, on the outskirts of Cleveland for the rest of the year, that Tommy Lee came to his maturity, complete with a self image and a philosophy of life that was without contradiction.

He was six-feet tall and about 250 pounds. His black hair always had a gloss to it due to his excessive scalp oiliness. His face correlated well with his head and muscular body, which he honed to muscle through a religious weight-lifting program. His square face was anchored to his torso by an unusually short neck. His lidded brown eyes, sullen expression, and protruding lips attracted women to him, for which at first he was grateful, but as he aged, he resented. He didn't like being used, and he felt that some women did just that. As if to offset this, he became more and more violent in his sexual relationships, and to his amazement, he found that some women would come back for more accelerated forms of viciousness.

By his twentieth year, sex and violence became associated for him. He was a sadist who sexually couldn't deal well with women except through violence. As he would tell his fellow grooms: "You might have to sweet talk the bitches, but once you get em, rip em up, useless cows."

He had his share of fights with brothers, fathers, boyfriends, and whoever would come to the rescue of some whore, and he was never bested. He was arrested in Florida on two occasions for severely beating male antagonists, but the charges fell through as they did once in Cleveland as well.

His closest call with a felony conviction came when two spring-break co-eds pressed violent rape charges against him in Ft. Lauderdale. He was arrested and booked. He made bail because of a friendly trainer. The two girls had returned to their campus, pending trial, at Harcrest College in Davenport, Iowa. He had heard about a harness track in that region and hired on as a groom at the Quad Cities Oval in East Moline, Illinois. But his real purpose was to stalk the two girls and frighten them into withdrawing the charges. He was gone from Florida for three weeks.

He noticed that they would walk around the perimeter of the small campus at about 10:00 p.m. each night. When he saw the pattern, he saw his chance. He parked a borrowed van next to the sidewalk where the girls walked, opened the back door, and pretended to be removing an object from the back of the van. As the girls passed the van, in two short steps he was directly in front of them, whereupon he hit both of them, almost simultaneously, with a repetitive right and left cross that knocked both of them unconscious. They were in the van, tied, taped, and under a carpet in a few brief minutes. He drove them to downtown Davenport where he parked on the levee overlooking the Mississippi River.

When they came to, the terror on their faces sexually aroused him. As in Ft. Lauderdale, he raped them both again brutally. Afterwards, he sat them up against the side wall of the van, looked at them, and said, "Now listen to me. Yuh're both going to be dead within the next hour, after I have another go at yuh." They both whimpered through the electrical tape. It was clear from their terrified eyes that they fully believed what he was saying. He took out a knife and started to hone it against a stone knowing full well the effect that this was having on his two victims. Then, as if as an afterthought, he looked at the two of them and said, "But if yuh'd promise to forget Lauderdale, maybe I'll let yuh go. I'll never bother with yuh again. You're both ugly little bitches anyway. But if yuh cut a deal with me," he was stabbing the now-sharpened knife into the air, "and break it, I will come back and cut up both of yuh into little pieces, even if it takes me ten years. I'm that kinda guy, girls."

They both shook their heads, their lives, given these stark terms, the more important.

"I don't think yuh believe me," he snarled, and he slapped both of them knocking them to the floor of the van. He then brought the knife to the throat of the one who seemed to be the bolder and ripped off the tape on her mouth, "Well, bitch, what's the answer?"

Speaking hoarsely and haltingly, she said, "I promise, we'll call Lauderdale tomorrow morning and drop the charges. Just please let us go."

"And yuh?" He tore off the tape of co-ed two and from her he got a continuing up-and-down shake of the head along with the words: "Yes, yes, yes, yes, ...

With unusual restraint, he didn't touch the young women again. He drove them close to the Harcrest campus and went back and cut the ropes that bound them. As he was about to throw open the doors of the van, he looked back in and said, "Don't forget, if anything comes from yuh ... I will get yuh and slice yuh to shreds."

When Tommy Lee got back to Pompano, he was informed by Detective Marcus Wells that the charges were dropped.

"You wouldn't know why, now would you?" the black, streetwise detective asked.

"Because I didn't rape them, that's why!" Tommy Lee looked him in the eye.

"Well listen, man, I got your number and one of these days I'm going to get your ass into jail. You're lucky this wasn't a sister, fucker."

That night Tommy Lee went to South Beach in Miami where he beat up and raped a black prostitute. Before he went to sleep that night, he said, "No fucking nigger's gonna talk to me that way!"

Thus, at the advent of 20, Tommy Lee was well advanced for his age. His swarthy handsomeness was akin to a flame that drew moths. He continued to stay on the fringes of police departments, but he also began to trust in his luck, which at times was abundant, since in seizing opportunities, he was prepared to expose himself to high risk as in his intimidation of the two co eds. He began to believe that he really couldn't be tricked by stupid cops and the whole feckless system of laws that so wondrously protected his rights.

His first murder, when he was given the right to imbibe alcohol, had nothing to do with his association of sex with violence. His unmitigated brute strength brought him an offer from a crooked trainer by the name of Axel Jurgens. Jurgens had sold a pacer to another trainer for $30,000. Two things happened to create the issue that would bring in Tommy Lee. Axel Jurgens immediately went around the backstretch of Pompano announcing that he had unloaded a horse with a broken pastern onto Hugh McBrien, a fellow trainer. Hugh McBrien had bought the pacer for his grandson and in doing so had used a goodly part of his savings. Upon hearing of Jurgens' boasts, McBrien had the horse x rayed, and sure enough, it had a broken pastern, which, even if it healed, had immediately diminished its present value to $8,000, at best. McBrien told Jurgens, in no uncertain terms, that he was about to be sued.

Jurgens told the story to Tommy Lee with the hope that the wild-looking stud would beat some sense into McBrien, who was taken fair and square in the eyes of Jurgens, and unsurprisingly, Tommy Lee. As agreed to, when Jurgens was in Georgia picking up two yearlings, Tommy Lee came up to the sixty-one-year-old McBrien in his barn on the track and caught him with a right cross just as McBrien was about to say hello. McBrien fell like a rock. His head smashed against a two-by-four. Much to Tommy Lee's surprise, McBrien was dead, then and there- that simple. Undetected, he went back to his 9-by-9 foot room in the backstretch. He was both surprised and proud. Jurgens gave him a thousand dollars and never spoke with him again. Jurgens, for all of his bluster, was not in the same league as Tommy Lee. It wasn't long before Jurgens took his stable to Michigan, as far away from Tommy Lee as he could get.

It was somewhere in that twenty-first year that Tommy Lee created the trinity that would wreck so many lives: sex - violence - death. He had passed through and connected the three cloths like a quick sewing needle in the hands of an expert seamstress. He saw different levels of happiness as in Dante's heaven and the apex was his fantasies of victim murder. His second murder would bring clarity to him as he had never had before, his deliverance would be at the price of the unfortunate women who would unsuspectingly wander into his life. When his calculations of getting away with it turned positive, his missile locked on, as it were. The handicapping skills of the race track had become the same skills that predicted murder.

He was supposed to pick up a horse in rural Broward County and transport the filly back to Pompano Race Track. It was early April and the heat and humidity made the drive uncomfortable. He was trying for forty-five minutes, without success, to get the filly into the trailer as she kept backing off and eventually started to kick with her hind feet. He got a driver's whip out of the Ford 250, while pulling on the tether, he started to beat the horse on its long neck, drawing blood with each blow. Still to no avail, he tied her to the end of the trailer and went to get help from the farmer whose horse it was.

When the farmer came over to the trailer and saw the streaks of blood flowing down the filly's neck, he looked at Tommy Lee and said, "What the hell is wrong with you, dumb asshole! Do you think this is a meat packing plant?"

"The bitch was trying to kill me. She needs to know who the boss is. What the hell do you think it's like on the track?" Already Tommy Lee was weighing the possibility of beating up this dumb farmer when he saw two women coming from the farmhouse. One was probably the farmer's wife and the other the daughter. Tommy Lee catalogued them as bitch one and bitch two.

"What's wrong, Harry?" the wife asked.

Before he could answer, the girl started to yell and cry, "Oh, what happened to Mae? Mae - look at her, oh poor Mae." She started to hug the filly, but all the time becoming more and more hysterical.

Tommy Lee, whip in hand, blood splattered on his T-shirt, couldn't understand the emotion in the scene. It was as though he was color blind and was unable to identify the numbers imbedded in the color blindness test.

The farmer took the filly and said, "Get the fuck off my property. I'm calling up Wayne and telling him what kind of employee he has. Now get outta here!"

Tommy Lee felt the blood rushing to his head. His body

tightened in anger. He knew that in thirty seconds he could kill all of them. But he knew the odds and calculated that he wouldn't be able to beat the cops on this one.

He went to the trailer gate and locked it in place, got in the Ford, and sped from the farm, blowing up dirt and rocks, and resisting the fierce urge to go back and kill every one of them.

Within two miles of the farm, on a two-lane stretch of fairly desolate rural road, he drove past a Volkswagen bug whose back hatch was open. He saw a woman in the front seat just sitting there with her head slightly down toward her chest. He put his brakes on and started to back up toward the Volkswagen. When he got within fifteen feet of it, he turned off his truck ignition and walked back toward the disabled car. As he was traversing this short distance, a woman of about twenty-five stepped out of the driver's seat and stood by her door.

She was a smallish, short-haired brunette, and quite attractive.

He said, "What's the problem, ma'am?"

She hesitated before speaking and then finally said, "It's my belt. It broke. I always have trouble with this car when I'm going to a meeting."

"Would yuh like me to take a look at it?"

"Sure, but I know what it is- this isn't the first time."

He went back. The fan belt was shredded. She was going nowhere. He handicapped her to be at a great disadvantage, especially with there being no traffic on the road. He decided to make his move.

"I'm going into Pompano Beach. I'm not that familiar with this area, but if yuh want, I'll call a gas station for yuh."

He was so proud of his subtlety, his objective being to get her into his 250.

She again hesitated.

"If yuh want," he continued, "I'll give yuh a lift to a gas station. But that's up to yuh. Either way, I gotta go, ma'am. I'm on a run here."

Finally she made the decision: "Let me lock it up and I'll come with you."

He looked around, pleased that still no vehicle was in sight. He liked her engaging smile and energetic attitude. She was peppy and cheerful as she got into the cab of the Ford.

Suzy Wade was impressed by Tommy Lee. She had deliberated about getting into the truck with him, but he presented himself in such a laid-back and helpful manner, and after all, it was broad daylight, and he had to be a working man since he was hauling a horse trailer. Your typical rapist doesn't run around with a horse trailer. And he sure was handsome -just a touch of Elvis in him.

The truck came to a halt at the end of Tuttle Road, which came out onto Sample Road two miles west of the Florida Turnpike. She knew there were gas stations a mile east of where they were. Just as she was feeling good about her decision, he put his hand on her knee. "Crap," she thought to herself. She took his hand and put it back into his lap and said, "Look - I'm not interested- there's a station a mile from here- I'll get out there." She smiled in her warmest and gentlest way so as to avoid any confrontation.

"Sorry, sorry," he said soothingly. When he braked at a four-way stop, Suzy Wade had her last best chance at life.

Fleetingly, she thought about jumping out, but his response was without rancor. Her internal sensors just didn't catch the danger. As he accelerated out of the stop, he looked across at her, she smiled again and looked out the side window. When she started to turn to face forward, she saw out of her peripheral vision his fist lurching out at her.

When she awoke, she was lying in the horse trailer. She had a terrible headache and her jaw and teeth throbbed with pain. Her greatest fears had been realized. He was sitting against the side of the trailer. The light was dim because he had left open only one two-by-two window in the horse trailer. He ran his giant hand through her hair. She turned her head in revulsion. When she tried to speak, she knew that her mouth was taped. He slapped her resoundingly and snarled at her: "Don't pull that on me, yuh bitch!" When she tried to raise her hands, she realized that they were taped to her sides. She also realized that she was naked.

Sheer terror began to possess her generous and kind personality as he unzipped his jeans and began to spread her resisting legs. Another slap to the face and then another brought her to such distraction and pain that his rape of her was a minor part of the cacophony of pain she was experiencing. When he was done, he hit her with another right cross to the jaw. The last thing Suzy Wade ever saw was the gold chain dangling from his neck as he came forward in the delivery of the punch.

He strangled her to death. His best punch didn't kill her and it didn't matter to him how the bitch died. The thing was that she was dead and he wouldn't have to worry about her testifying. It was him against the cops. He liked those odds. He also never felt better in his whole life; it was as though the weight of the world was lifted from him. He was joyous. He drove down a small lane and stuffed the body under a culvert in a ditch.

When he got back to Pompano, Wayne was waiting for him. He went up directly to Tommy Lee and handed him $230 and said, "You're fired!" Tommy Lee was on a Greyhound bus that night headed for Syracuse and ultimately, Vernon Downs. He saw himself as a professional drifter. He was a man outside of the system. He could operate from his own set of rules and let them take him where they would. The murder of Suzy Wade was the day Tommy Lee created his persona. He was afraid of nothing and no one. If the odds were in his favor, he would back away from nothing if it was to his profit.

Deputy Dal Goetz of the Broward County Sheriff's Department was on his fourth double Manhattan. His wife, Alice, just sat there watching him. He wouldn't talk when he got home; he just went to the liquor cabinet, took out a bottle of Jim Beam, a bottle of Noilly Prat sweet vermouth, and a small bottle of maraschino cherries.

"Dal, what's wrong?"

"Forget it, Alice. Just leave me alone for a while."

With that warning/plea, she let him go into the recesses of a beginning drunk. In her bedroom, she called Stu Kelly, Dal's partner. He answered on the first ring. He also seemed very tight.

"Stu, Alice Goetz."

"Is Dal OK?"

"I don't know. He's about to drain a fifth of Jim Beam. What the hell happened out there today?"

"Listen, I don't want to go into it either. I'll just tell you this. We had a body called in and we were first on the scene, a young woman all bloated, rotting, stinking, fly and worm infested. Her face had been a punching bag for some bastard. She was taped. It was dreadful. We worked around it for about four hours. The smell is in my clothes and nostrils. My advice? Let him drink the fifth! Bye."

Alice Goetz put on the 6:00 p.m. news. It was the lead story. The woman, Susan Wade, had been missing for six days. Her car, a VW Beetle, had been impounded five days ago and the police had been investigating her disappearance. Her body was discovered by a bicyclist who called in the sighting. A full investigation was under way, but police were discouraged by the amount of time that stood between the disappearance and discovery of the body. Anyone with information should call the Broward County Sheriffs Department.

CHAPTER 6

McAbee sat across from Jim Panayotounis who had been the principal owner of the Quad Cities Oval before it had been bought by Chicago interests. From information he had received from an attorney friend familiar with the sale, great pressure had been exerted on Panayotounis. The attorney didn't know how rough it had gotten before Panayotounis gave in and sold.

Panayotounis, in his late sixties, had an extremely long and narrow face. His thick glasses and skin with enough wrinkles for two men his age, gave him a look of weary wisdom. McAbee had an inherent distrust of track people. Nothing about Panayotounis, at first glance, was giving him any reason to change.

Panayotounis fixed him with his gaze and said, "I'm doing this as a favor. Everything I say is off the record, is that understood?"

"Absolutely," McAbee said as he gazed at the man's office. Panayotounis was President of Panayotounis Press in Rock Island. The presses could be heard all too distinctly and pervasively for McAbee's tastes, and he wondered if Panayotounis had to listen to this racket all day long. His office was totally disorganized and left the impression that Panayotounis had to have someone who knew where everything was. He was the entrepreneur in terrible need of an organizer.

"So what do you want to know?" he asked sharply as he fixed his magnified gaze on McAbee.

"How crooked is harness racing?"

Panayotounis leaned back in his chair and laughed. "A man who comes right to the point." He took out a Camel and lit it up. Most of his wrinkles were thus explained. "I'll tell you- no more than any other business that I've been in. It's just that in harness racing the emotions, the craftiness, the jealousies," he searched for the words, "are so ... so graphic and clean cut."

McAbee thought that Panayotounis' answer would refer to betting and bettors when it rather spoke to the principals in the industry. "They're always trying to screw each other, always trying to get the edge. It's pretty rampant free enterprise stuff - don't you kid yourself. The bettors come out there and they assume there's some fix in all the time. In my judgment, it's relatively rare." He flicked the ashes off of his cigarette and looked off into some far-off comer of his disarranged office. "Let me give you an example. You get some trainer who's bringing back an injured horse. Let's say the horse has been off for five months with some problem - you know they seem to have as many problems as a football player could have. So, he trains him down to a racing time and then qualifies him." He looked at McAbee and apparently remembered that McAbee had said on the telephone that he was a neophyte, so he explained, "By qualifying, I mean if a horse has been off for more than two months – it depends on the track - he has to show up in a trial run, a non-betting race, and meet some prescribed time before he can enter a pursed race. Those are usually held on mornings once a week. So back to my story, this trainer's horse has been off for five months and he puts him in a qualifier and let's say he qualifies, he meets the required minimum time, and let's say the time he has to meet is two minutes and three seconds, and he hits the three-quarter pole at I :30 and suddenly the trainer feels the horse take hold, he wants to race his guts out, but the trainer wants to conceal it, so he'll hold the horse back so that even though he finishes in a competitive time, no one, he hopes, really knows that his horse had a two- or three- or even four-second faster race in him. Of course, there's always someone out there who sees that he's got a giant hold on the reins and that person may or may not be an adversary. OK, let me go on. The qualifier shows up on the racing program and the horse looks flat - he made it in 2:02:4, that's two minutes and two seconds and four-fifths of a second, and the horses in the race that he's in entered into are averaging 2;00. He's been off for five months- so does anyone bet him? No! Let's say he goes off at 15-1, no respect from anyone. But the trainer knows what he's got, so he bets him across the board, let's say, $100 across, and let's say he wheels him in an exacta with four horses that he thinks will come in second for let's say $80, $20 for his horse with each of the four, four times at $20 a shot. An exacta means you have to pick the perfect order of the first two horses. So he's exposed $380 on his bet, plus he has the purse. If he wins, he gets half the purse, so let's say the purse is $2,000. If he wins the race he gets $1,000 from the purse, at 15-1, he'll get back about $32 for the win for every $2 bet, that's $1,600, and for the hell of it, I'll guess that he'll get ten bucks for his placing - uh - second, and five bucks for his showing third, so that's another 750 bucks. And then, let's say he's really lucky and hits the exacta for $75, which he has ten times- that's another $750. No taxes on his bets -$3,100. Nice return on his investment, plus he has the thou in the purse from the race- $4,100 in all. Here's my question- Is he a crook?" His gaze fell on McAbee as he gave off a sour laugh.

"What does the United States Trotting Association say? Is there some ethic?" McAbee didn't want to say the wrong thing and turn off the spigot.

"Ha! - good answer. What they say is race to win and be fair. In my book? He's not a crook. Is it any different in the NBA when they hold back a player and say he's hurt when he's not?"

"Yes, but they're not race tracks. The game can't be played for the purpose of gambling even though I know there's much gambling."

"Look, in my book there's no difference. Information is the one thing that gives you an edge. That's true in any business anywhere. The problem with you, McAbee, is that you're not a gambler. So this all seems like double talk to you. But it ain't. The thing that keeps sports so alive in this country is just that - gambling. If you put a $100 bill on the Bears, that game will come alive for you a lot faster than if you have nothing on it."

"Are you saying, that beneath the harness industry is a whole other dimension of insider knowledge and if you don't have it, you're at a big disadvantage?"

"Yes, but that's everywhere. That's true with

thoroughbreds, baseball teams, fighters, and, yes, businesses. If I know that my competitor is a drunk, or a diabetic, or whatever, I have an edge. If I know that some new contract is being let before he does, I have an advantage. It never ends. At tracks, about 20 percent is taken right off the top by the state, for purses, for the track owners, for breeders, and whoever else has their mitt in the pool. So about 80 percent goes back to bettors. That's a big peel off the roll. That's why handicapping is so important. You see the old-timers out at the track poring over the program and hoping that they see something that erases that 20 percent deficit that they bet into. Good for them- they're wise." His telephone rang. It was some run problem on his presses. He resolved it expeditiously. McAbee realized that the man, no matter how opinionated, was no fool. It was hard for McAbee to associate the concept of opinionated and smart, but in this instance, it was easily there.

"OK, as I was saying," he lit up another Camel, the old unfiltered kind that killed off generations of smokers, "backstretchers have some inside knowledge and thus they can get an edge, but only if they can lay off betting on races about which they know nothing. Most of them can't because they're always looking for the big inning- the trifecta that'll pay out $2,000 or whatever. So they keep betting and bingo, they're broke. We had a kitchen in the backstretch that had a betting window for the backstretchers. We used to have this priest who'd come over to work among them once in awhile. He came to me and pleaded with me to remove the betting window. You know a lot of those characters have kids, they're divorced and they haven't paid a child support payment in years. They spend it gambling, on booze and on babes. So OK, where was I? Oh yeah- so I close down the betting in the backstretch kitchen. Well you woulda thought that I had killed their first born! When I told them about the priest - they almost strung up the son of a bitch." He laughed so hard that he started to cough deep from the pits of his lungs. The laughter and coughing went on for about two minutes.

McAbee found his story amusing but noted that it was tinged with disrespect and had a brutally judgmental ring to it.

"So let me tell another side to this so that you'll see how complex the damn thing gets to be. A trainer has a sharp horse who's been winning, but he notices on the morning of the race that the horse's lungs are full of crap. The fucker is coughing his lungs out and he knows that when this happens the horse is useless. There's no way the horse is going to finish in the top three. But he sees that during the betting his horse is bet down to even money. If his horse doesn't show up in the top three, the payoffs are going to be big, especially on the gimmick races - exactas, trifectas, pick threes and the rest of that crap. That trainer has a real edge. Is he a crook? He bets against his horse?"

"Wasn't this part of Pete Rose's problem?"

"Yeah, but that's baseball," he said tersely and with a sure finality.

"What about race fixing, you know, between drivers or trainers. That seems to be a pretty regular rap on harness racing?"

Panayotounis pursed his lips, "Yeah, I know all about it. All I can say is that I tried to stop it, but it's so deep down it's impossible to totally root it out. Some of these drivers go way back- it's a fraternity- and let's face it, I'm an outsider. But I did make the effort. Every once in a while a race was so fixed it made my blood boil. We'd suspend and fine the bastards, but it's a judgment call. They'd say the horse didn't feel right as they stiffed the son of a bitch in the stretch. And who's to say? There was some crap going on, but they were smart enough to keep most of the races honest and competitive."

"But what about the Norman Rockwell types? How did they fit in?" McAbee asked.

"They'd do the best they could. I'd see it once in a while. The good guy's horse would be sat on, someone would come up on his outside and just stay there so that he couldn't get his horse off the rail. He'd be paralyzed as it were. 'Nowhere to go' the announcer would say. In some cases that was just the situation, but in others it was done on purpose. But here's the thing the adage- I never want to forget: 'It's horses- and anything can happen'- and believe me, it does."

"OK, so everyone's trying to get an edge," McAbee said, "I can see that. An insider's knowledge is an obvious factor in the sport. Emotions, envy and so on, run high on the backstretch. What about crime?"

Panayotounis leaned forward and said earnestly, "It's amazing. There's very little of it. People leave thousands of dollars of equipment in their unlocked barns, horses - some of them very valuable, are left standing in their barns looking out their gates - but hardly anything happens. There's a code there, believe me."

"That's theft-related. What about drugs and violence?"

"Oh- drugs- that's different. For most of them, it's booze, so no problem with the law. But there's a percentage into grass and coke and whatever. Look," he sharpened his look still further, "I have a 20-60-20 rule at the track, and oh, by the way, the ratios don't differ for non-track people either, in my book," he laughed and just missed igniting a coughing spell. "I figure 60 percent of them are neutral. They're neither good nor bad, but they do both depending on their mood, the opportunity, how they feel about you, how broke they are, you name it, and it's a part of the calculation. They're unpredictable. They'll do something outstandingly good today, then turn around the next day and be bottom feeders eating their young. OK, so that's 60 percent; the 20 percent are right out of Norman Rockwell's America, as you put it. They're scrupulously honest. They see the whole thing as a sport and a way to make an honest living. Satan himself couldn't get them to do something unethical. Believe me, they exist on the backstretch, but they max out at 20 percent. Then there's the other 20 percent - pure psychopaths! We try to bust them and lock them out, we fingerprint, do background checks, you name it, but they crawl through the defenses. With them, it's big trouble. If they can get away with something - they will." He lit another Camel and puffed at it approvingly with a big release of a breathy, croaking sigh. "If your inquiry has anything to do with one of them, be careful. You're fishing in dangerous waters. Your only advantage is that they'll give each other up for a dime if they're broke or they need a drink."

McAbee finally felt that Panayotounis was prepared enough to have a go at the issue of Erin Tobin's death. "Jim, I'm here about an incident that happened eight years ago. You had sold the track a year before, but I assume that you kept some interest in it?"

"Yeah, they kept me on as a consultant. In fact, I stayed pretty close to it for another three years or so."

"So, you were around in 1987. Let me throw you a name and get your reaction- Cassies Ruler."

Panayotounis stared at the end of his cigarette, finally aware of McAbee's agenda. "A few things. A very fine pacer, but mean and vicious. Killed a beautiful young trainer. The story goes, and I have good reason to believe it, that her father shot him in a fit of rage." He stopped, but then hastened to add, "But it didn't occur on the track grounds. He was a farmer. Cassies Ruler - all horse but dangerous. So what?"

"I have a client who thinks that it may have been a murder. Let me go on- Erin Tobin."

"Ah, she was the trainer. She got her brains kicked out by Cassies Ruler. That's the story I have and I've never heard anyone question it. She was one of the good ones, the 20 percent who worked hard at being good. Good family, good girl. Big tragedy! I think you're on a wild goose chase if you're checking out a murder. The cops seemed to have covered it pretty well. That's another thing about tracks and backstretches - they're rumor mills. Gossip and loose talk are fully accepted. You have to have a bullshit-o-meter with you at all times. My point? I never heard a peep about a murder." He looked at his watch. McAbee noted that although he was derisive of the backstretch community, he was also somewhat protective of them. Jim Panayotounis didn't seem to appreciate talk of murder. McAbee pressed, "I heard that Erin Tobin was promiscuous."

Panayotounis fixed McAbee with his gaze, "Look, I just told you, anything that can be thought, will be said on the backstretch. Maybe she was, for all I know. But it's much more likely that most of those characters made passes at her and when she wouldn't even look at them, they started to call her a dyke, a whore, a whatever. She didn't seem to be the type of person who'd let someone take advantage of her. I remember her as a gritty babe." He looked at his watch again.

"Just bear with me, Jim. One more question. Rickie Crocker- do you remember him?"

"Yeah, I remember him, poor innocent bastard. He was as simple as 1-2-3. He killed himself ... who knows why. The only thing that surprised me about that, was that it was pretty complicated for a massively drunk and terribly retarded guy to pull it off successfully. That was probably the only time in his life that he managed to do something complicated, correctly." He started to laugh and teetered toward a coughing fit. Just when McAbee thought that a coughing/laughing episode was avoided, it began. It made McAbee wonder how much longer this man would last before emphysema or some such blood-sucking disease would get to him. When the fit was over, Panayotounis once again looked at his watch. It seemed as though he had a love/hate relation with the track. Although it was OK for him to disrespect it, for others, he was not so generous.

"Jim, I know that I'm taking your time. I'm just about done. Would you be good enough to give me two names of trainers, one an honest guy and one a so-so? Crooks need no interviews. I'd like to use your name. I think that if I could talk to a few of them, it would give me a better idea of what you mean."

Panayotounis had a Rolodex that looked as though it had been around for twenty years. It was sitting on top of what looked like a ledger. He started to run his fingers through it, reminding McAbee of some movie general who would rotate a globe searching out some future ambition.

"OK, here you go for- a saint - Ray Ashburn, DeWitt, Iowa," he wrote down the name and a phone number; "a middling, Tom Barley. He's not around here, but I know that you'll find him in Springfield, Illinois. He trains pacers out at the fair track down there, all year long." Panayotounis tore off a sheet of paper and handed it to McAbee while standing up. "Goodluck, McAbee," he shook McAbee's hand and picked up his telephone.

When he left, McAbee felt the noise and smoke had just leaped off of his shoulders. The relief was tangible and beyond words. He got into his black 1993 Ford Explorer Sport and drove back to his office in Davenport. He mulled over Panayotounis' words and advice. If, in fact, there had been a murder, it was definitional that he was dealing with that 20 percent psychopath piece of the equation.

Pat was pleased to see him. He instantly knew why. He had seven calls. Things had been hectic.

"What do I have to know here, Pat?"

"Well, your brother called again, pushier than ever. He again wants to know if you ever do any work or ever come into the office. I know that he's kidding, but sometimes I think that he's serious."

"Just humor him, Pat. What else?"

"Jack Scholz called. His usual mysterious self. He wants you to call ASAP. The other calls are self evident."

McAbee called Scholz, remembering they both agreed to be very indirect. It was no fun for Jack if everything was done above board, free of conspiracy and hidden agendas.

"Jack, this is Bertrand. You called."

"Yes. I did all that work on the grounds and the crew is ready to cut the grass. From here on in, we will be responsible for the grounds. I promise we'll get those weeds. It's a pretty easy field to take care of. Stay in touch." He hung up.

McAbee raised his eye brows in mild disbelief and shook his head. At $5,000 a night, he had an insurance policy against an out-and-out swindle of Orville Tobin by the extortionist. Now if only he would call. McAbee also inferred that Scholz liked the lay of the land and thought he could get the job done.

McAbee hesitated to call his brother Bill. Bill was the older brother who was instrumental in his career shift to detection. Bill was the owner and CEO of McAbee and Associates in New York City. Very few people had even heard of it, and if Bill had his way, it would stay just like that. It was, in fact, one of the most respected private investigation agencies in the world. Its list of clients went from the Vatican, the Bank of Switzerland and IBM to the government of Israel.

Bill was a dynamo who moved in circles that few would ever enter. However, he was also overbearing, mordant and excruciatingly demanding. He judged all of life on the basis of favors and had a way about him that left him never owing anyone a favor but rather having it that he was owed. And he had no hesitation about calling them in. By McAbee's last count, he owed Bill about ten times. He knew it was a terrible position to be in. Bill was in the catbird seat -with seemingly lifetime tenure and an indefatigable desire to keep it that way. He decided to put off the call until later.

CHAPTER 7

Eddie Fox went into the White Hen Convenience Store on Harlem Avenue in Oak Park, Illinois. He had debated with himself how to deal with the remainder of the fleece. A seasoned bettor, he opted for the safe bet. The remaining fifty thou could free him from the predicament that circled him. Whether or not he would even divulge the name to the old man was another story. Seeing Tommy Lee, however, at Sportsman's, had sent him reeling into the nearest bathroom, since Fox, like most bettors, was also highly superstitious and subject to the power of omens.

He dialed the number and was told by the operator to deposit two dollars for the first three minutes. Looking to make sure no one was around him, he fumbled through the generous change he had placed on a Coke 12-pack adjoining the phone. The operator said thank you. Fox's entire focus was now engaged.

"Yes?" Fox sensed in that reply that the old man knew who it was.

"OK, Tobin, you've been doing well and you're close to the prize. A screw-up now and you'll have wasted a lot of money and you'll die frustrated. So, I'm warning you, don't try anything. You'll get the answer when I'm sure that you didn't pull anything. Am I clear?"

"Yes."

"Tomorrow night-$50,000-smaller bills. Nine p.m. sharp, in-out, use the same kind of bag. Bye."

Fox hung up hurriedly; he didn't want to hear about heart conditions, the wanting of assurances and whatever else the tormented old bastard was dealing with. But Fox couldn't put aside his guilt. He knew that he had had a hand in Erin Tobin's death, no matter how unwittingly, and now he was seeking to profit from it. It was 8:00p.m. He had the night off. He headed for his favorite liquor store in next over suburb, River Forest.

Tobin phoned McAbee immediately and played the tape for him.

"So, I guess this is it, Bertrand. But what bothers me is the wait. I'm worried for my heart and the tension that's in all of this."

"I'm sure you are, Orville. But if you feel this is right, I guess you'll have to do it." Tobin was never quite sure of McAbee. He trusted him, primarily, because of what other people said about him. But he found McAbee to be indirect and subtle. It was as if whatever McAbee said could be interpreted in many different ways. He was a man who lived in a house with many doors, contrary to what Orville stood for, and yet, Orville saw him as his best chance.

"Is there anything I should know?"

"Orville, the best drop is made by people who don't know anything about the drop. Can we leave it there?" Tobin took this to mean that McAbee was up to something and if Tobin knew about it, he'd be upset. He decided to trust McAbee and let it go.

"Yup," he said warily.

"After the drop, why don't you just go home immediately and call me right away. It looks like we'll have to be patient with him. When people say you'll get the answer when they're sure you didn't pull anything, it bothers me. Of course, we still face the possibility that he may just disappear or decide to hit for more."

"Bertrand, in the long haul, when push comes to shove, I now know it's a murder. In my condition, what the hell's money!? So, I'll call you tomorrow night when I get home."

"Be careful, Orville. Just drop the money and get the hell out of there. OK?"

"Right."

Orville Tobin rewound the tape recorder and set it for the next call with a new tape. He went outside on his porch and sat in the swing he had put up so many years ago. The September air had a bit of a bite to it as he looked off into the dark and star-filled night. He thought of the past and his love for Thelma who died from breast cancer. The experience had sapped so much energy from him, he had felt as though he could never come back from it. Erin had saved him. A spirited and vigorous girl, she had been touched by the love of horses. Orville knew this love would dominate her choices of lifestyle and employment.

When he tried, he could bring up into his mind the sound of the pacers on the dirt track. He could see the flowing blonde hair of Erin urging them on to the imaginary finish line. He shook his head and looked down as if to break the thoughts that were breaking him. His sadness eventually flowed into anger as he crushed the Bud can in his still-powerful hand. He knew the end of the game was near, both with the caller and with life.

McAbee called Scholz's cellular at 9:15 p.m., immediately after Orville's call. Scholz sounded his usual clandestine self with a whispered: "Identity please."

"Jack- tomorrow night. Meeting tomorrow? Give me a time."

"One- at the whore's."

"See you." McAbee smiled and shook his head in mild surprise. Scholz saw Sophie as a whore while Sophie saw Scholz as the embodiment of Hitler. Not for the first time, did McAbee realize that they each would kill the other if social conditions allowed for it.

Scorpio came over to the rocker where McAbee sat. In his mouth was an old tennis ball, which he dropped into McAbee's lap. "Damn it, Scorpio!" He had yet to take off his newly dry-cleaned tan pants, which now had Scorpio's drool and spittle on the panel in front of the zipper. Scorpio's white head with black eyes and a black nose stared intently at him. He panted slightly as if to encourage McAbee to break out of his work face and play. This fierce-looking therapist was trying to get McAbee to leave behind his adult for a bit and become a kid. He succeeded. McAbee picked up the ball and feinted a few throws, making Scorpio lunge forward each time. But Scorpio had been through this and was not easily fooled. He kept his eyes pinned to the ball. As McAbee released it, he was off-tearing through living room, dining room and into the recreation room. The dog was fully prepared to allow McAbee's child full reign.

Scorpio's ears went up another notch when he heard the telephone ring, but they quickly receded as if knowing the child would once again be put aside.

"Hello."

"Bertrand, it's me- Beth." This need to clarify her identity was strange to McAbee. They had known each other for twenty years. They had been married for almost fourteen.

"Hi, Beth."

"I just want you to know that the ninety-day wait is up in another week. I'm working on the divorce settlement that we've talked about. I need your signature when I get it done. Are you going to be in town?"

It was going to be an amicable divorce. Amity meant, to McAbee, that two cretinous lawyers were not going to suck out chunks of whatever assets were there. It certainly didn't mean that he was at peace and feeling good about it. He had waived representation almost three months previous as Beth filed her petition for divorce. She was one of the few people whom McAbee ever met that he trusted completely. Even with the guy in Colorado included in the picture, he couldn't shake his trust in her.

"I'll be in town for sure. Just give me a call. I can come over then."

"OK."

"How's everything going, Beth?" He didn't like the tiny speck of hope that crept into his voice when she'd allow a semblance of a discussion.

"Couldn't be better, Bertrand," she said too adamantly for McAbee.

"No reason to talk?"

"About what?" she said with a touch of anger.

"Well, Beth, like we've been together more or less for 20 years. Does that count? It's hard for me to let that go so easily and noiselessly."

"Look! Bertrand! My mind is settled. If we talk, you'll try to work on me and I can't have it. I don't mean to hurt you, but at this juncture of my life, I want to put the past aside. You're a big part of that. So you have to go. I don't want complications."

"It seems like you have your lines memorized. A conversation would mean ad-libbing." He was being sarcastic.

"See, that's the point. I don't need the dialogue or the sarcasm. I don't owe you a damn thing. The score is even and the game is over. Got it? I'll be in touch." She hung up with emphasis.

McAbee was unable to get her to communicate once she had made up her mind. Never in too much of a hurry about most matters, in this she moved with great haste. She had refused any third-party mediation. She had despaired for all of the reasons that she could stack together, yet did not want to communicate. Whether it was her version of a midlife crisis or his landing in his mid-fifties or whatever- it was surely over at this point.

McAbee didn't at first realize that Scorpio was resting his head on his thigh. The canine therapist was suggesting McAbee needed the release that caring gave. When McAbee started to stroke his all-too shrewd German Shepherd some of the ache left him.

Scorpio walked away in seeming disgust when the telephone took McAbee out of his therapy session with the dog.

"Hello."

"Goddamnit! He lives! Have you stopped returning my calls? What's goin on out there, Big Bertrand!?" It was his brother Bill. He hadn't returned several calls and he knew that his unrelenting older brother would stay on him until he ran him down. Now, sure enough, it had happened.

"Bill, I'm tied up with a bunch of tough situations. I didn't want to call until I had something on that Graziano situation and we can't find anything yet." He was alluding to a check he was doing for his brother on a matter being investigated in New York, but had a tentacle in St. Louis. What he wasn't telling Bill was that he didn't really feel like dealing with his abrasive and attacking brother.

"Well, that's one of the things I wanted to tell you. We found out that it's a dead end. So you can call it off. How are you and Beth?"

"It's done. The divorce is probably a week away."

"Do you want me to call her?"

"Why? What's the use? Her mind's made up, Bill. And you know as well as I do that she has no great love for you."

"Bertrand, every day's a new day. I have short term memory deficiency. You have to tell me to go to hell every day - all over again. That's really what persistence is- a short-term memory deficiency!" He laughed.

"I agree that you have short-term memory deficiency," Bertrand teased him.

What always struck the younger brother, Bertrand, was that this abrasive brother was constantly in touch with some on the world's great leaders and statesmen. He figured Bill had to restrain his nature in those situations. Thus family members became his outlet when he needed to vent.

"So, what are you working on?"

"Primarily an extortion case where an old man is being wormed out of his money for information about the possible murder of his daughter."

"OK, what's your read on it?"

"There's probably something there about the murder, but I don't know if he'll ever get a name."

"Heavy, brother. By the way, are you doing anything about self-protection? You mention the word murder to me and I don't like it. You may be a good runner and a racquetball player, but murder is another story."

"Bill, what do you want from me? I have a gun and I know how to use it. What else do you want from me? I'm not going to become a professional judo expert or boxer," he said defensively.

"Goddamn college profs. I got you into this game because you needed a break from academia. But this game is ugly, Bertrand. You never know what's around the corner." Bill was getting on the soapbox.

"Bill- hold it. I appreciate your concern, but I am pretty careful. Just because you wear a bulletproof vest and sit in a bulletproof car doesn't mean that should translate to out here in the bucolic Midwest. You move at very different levels of exposure, don't you think?"

"Well- yes. Have it your way. But you never know what's around the corner or where some investigation will take you. Do you see my point?"

"Yes, I do, Bill. I really appreciate your concern. But I'll take care of myself and for God's sake, stay clear of Beth. She's not going to change. I know her too well."

"Do you still have that mutt? What's his name Aries?"

"It's Scorpio and he doesn't forget rotten brothers who put dried hot pepper on his dog food."

"And I don't forget mutts who try to bite you when you turn your back. He's not a real German Shepherd. They're noble dogs. That thing you have is a goddamned sneak. And then you tell me about the time he let your sister-in-law into the house and then decided to turn on her about ten minutes later. He's a psycho!" McAbee chuckled through these reminiscences of his brother. There was an element of truth to the stories.

"Well, Bill, he's a deep thinker. Sometimes after reflecting, he changes his mind and sees the truth, as in your case. Do you want anything else?"

"No, Bertrand. Stay in touch ... and Bertrand, watch your back."

"OK, Bill."

McAbee reflected upon the inevitability of fate. Older brothers were older brothers. Lives had been lost over the ages on the question of primacy, succession, jealousy and the rest. With Bill it wasn't like that. It was a question of protectiveness after all these years. As brothers, they were still battling stickball opponents in Inwood in upper Manhattan. Neither brother would, or perhaps could, let go of all that training and behavioral conditioning. Why their widowed mother insisted on the name William becoming Bill and the name Bertrand staying Bertrand was never answered to either's satisfaction.

McAbee was late, there was no getting around it and he felt guilty. It was 1:10 p.m. He hoped that by this time Scholz and Sophie hadn't gotten into it.

His racquetball game with Lou Kodowsky, an old

college peer at St. Anselm, was under control until they were challenged to doubles. Kodowsky was terribly big and wide. Between him and the two challengers, who were of like-builds, there was little room on the court for maneuvering. The last game had gotten to 14-12 in favor of McAbee and Kodowsky when the serve to Kodowsky was sent back toward the front wall with all the steam and power that Kodowsky could muster.

Unfortunately, the server moved position and turned to glimpse at the ball's direction. With no protective eyewear, he took the shot full force in the eye. By the time they had iced the eye and the man, whom McAbee only knew casually, was taken to the hospital, McAbee realized he would be late.

He hurried through the back door toward the meeting room, whose door was closed. Outside of it stood Sophie waiting to pounce on McAbee. There would be no kidding with her today. She was hot for a fight.

"Doctor McAbee," she looked at her watch and then back at him, "I want that you should know that that fascist bastard is in there. He reminds me of the devil in the old country. I have locked him inside. I will not have his mean and judging face in my bar. Do you hear?"

"Certainly, Sophie. What happened?"

"He accused me of lying. He said that you are never late. It was ... it was ... as if he wanted to search my bar for your dead body. The vulgar pig. When I told him to go straight to hell ... he called me a filthy whore ... that I should be drawn and quartered and fed to dogs and rats. Oh, ... oh, no ... let me say this straight ... he corrects himself and says that dogs are fussy ... rats are what I need! How dare he! And in my place of all things. I do not care if he comes and goes into the room like the sneaky skunk that he is, but I don't want him talking to me again. He's right out of gulags!"

"Sophie, it's my fault. I shouldn't have been late. There was an accident on the racquetball court, a bad eye injury. I couldn't leave. I'm most sorry, dear. Now let me take care of this. Please unlock the door."

"Well, this time, yes. But from now on, I will not have a word from him." With that she unlocked the door and left with her nose pointed slightly upward in either pride or to show that the smell of Scholz was too much for her. McAbee wasn't about to inquire.

Jack was sitting in the center of the room with a giant sneer on his face. McAbee assumed he had heard the entire conversation between him and Sophie. He stared at McAbee and said, "The whore's baying at the moon! I don't know how you got mixed up with vermin like her, Bertrand. But let's get to the agenda. I heard about the racquetball accident. That's a very unsafe sport. I would never play it," he said forcefully.

McAbee knew that he was serious, but reflected that this same man had played deadly war games all over the world.

"Jack, tonight's the night. My client delivers at 9:00p.m. He's in and out. I have no idea when the caller comes onto the scene. For all I know, he's watching all day long. This bothers me. This has to be seamless."

"Bertrand, I can't guarantee a job of this sort without the realization that there's always risk. But, I'm quite confident of success. Let me tell you what's going on. We practiced after 8:30p.m. It's pitch dark, that helps. The drop building is in clear view of the highway, which is south. West of the building is a flat field and within 750 feet is a grove of trees. This is a gift for us. North of the building is the gate, the old backstretch and a small secondary track that they used to use for jogging horses. This is a gift, too. Our biggest problem is east. East is a continuing flat field for about 1500 feet until it meets a winding road that leads to the track grandstand. The grandstand is a little less than a half mile away and is, in my judgment, irrelevant. But I don't like flat fields of that distance."

"Jack, on a scale of one to ten, how do you rate the lay of the land?" McAbee asked. He watched Scholz's eyes closely.

Unflinchingly, Scholz answered, "Oh, it's an eight in our favor. All last night we practiced in these confines. The men I'm using are all former Seals and Green Berets. This is their game. Unless the caller is like-trained, he's at a big disadvantage."

"My guess is that's highly unlikely."

"Well, here's the plan." He reached down into his folder and took out a sheet of paper that was eight and-a-half by fourteen. It was a thorough, hand-drawn map of the area in question. "I've upped the personnel to eight besides myself," he made sure to catch McAbee's eye before adding, "at no extra cost to you. Everyone will be equipped with handsets and night vision wear. I have three with night-scope videos and stills for pictures of the caller and his car license. The son of a bitch is covered, believe me. Wherever he comes from, we'll get him. I have a man in the grove fully equipped. You couldn't find him if you stood and looked for a good two hours. I have a man in the field immediately to the south of the building. He's underground and won't come up until I tell him to. But he's only 200 feet from the drop. You could walk over his position and not know he's there. I have another east of the winding road to the track. That's a fully grown com field. He's waiting for whatever. I have one across the road and I have two track stars with locators ready to plant them on this guy's car. The minute he gets out to make the grab, they'll have a locator under his car. Every one of my guys has a vehicle equipped with a locator device. I have two cars positioned at either end of the highway to start the honing process. As soon as he picks up and leaves the area, everyone gets in their car and joins in the surveillance until we get a read on his end point."

"But, what if he's watching that entire area all day long?"

"No problem. We set this up at night. By 8:30 we'll be in place- in the dark. You just don't realize how good these guys are. We could take out the nuclear station in Cordova- if we wanted to."

McAbee didn't disbelieve him. The Cordova Nuclear Station was situated about twenty miles north of the Quad Cities. McAbee said, "That's really reassuring, Jack."

Scholz looked at McAbee with curiosity. He was a literalist, not given to catching much irony.

"I'll be in constant touch with the men and with you. But, I will be circumspect, of course."

"I appreciate the detail, Jack. I can't think of anything else you could do, unless you might need more men.

"No! I'm at a limit right now, that's tops. Too many men and you end up with potential problems. We're at a good place. Have faith, Bertrand."

"OK, Jack. By the way, when you leave here, just walk out the back door."

"Bertrand, I heard the Jezebel! She talks louder than a drunken lumberjack." He got up and left. McAbee waited alone for a few minutes, then left. Sophie wasn't speaking to him any longer today, she was nowhere to be seen.

CHAPTER 8

Eddie Fox woke up at 9:30a.m. He felt like a plugged-up garbage disposal. When he got up, he vomited, mostly in the toilet bowl. He had consumed almost an entire fifth of Jim Beam. His phone rang off in the distance of his living room. He wasn't about to get it. Head positioned over the toilet, he heard his taped voice: "Hello, please leave a message."

"Paul Shutton here. Eddie? Try to come in tonight at 4:30. We're expecting a big crowd. Call me!"

It took great effort on his part, to yell out to the empty apartment, "Fuck you, Shutton." He vomited again, this time successfully hitting the toilet bowl. After another five minutes and one more minor toss-up, he hobbled to his refrigerator, poured himself a large glass of orange juice and took out a bottle of B-vitamin supplements. He downed the juice and the seven pills that would meet USP recommendations for the next week.

In a series of acts that tried his mettle, he proceeded to make some coffee, shave, shower and consume six aspirin. Fox knew he was in big trouble because this process was becoming a ritual. Six months previous he had gone to an AA meeting near the Maywood Harness Track and didn't like what he saw. In fact, he made a joke of it to some of his friends at the bar at Sportsman's, "A bunch of red-faced, pock marked, chain-smoking, coffee-swilling, first-name-only bastards!" They all laughed, even though Fox, as he looked at his fellow drinkers, conjectured that some of them weren't far off the stereotype he had just employed.

After five Winston Menthols and three cups of coffee, Fox was beginning to feel the outer regions of his limbs. He was getting connected. He mulled over the one problem that could spoil the biggest payday of his life-the call from Paul Shutton and his demand that he come to work by 4:30p.m. Fox knew that he had already pretty much exhausted any remaining good will he had with Shutton, but there was no way that he would miss being at the Quad Cities Oval tonight to pick up his $50,000. From his apartment, it was about a three-hour trip. He dialed Shutton at the track.

"Paul Shutton."

"Paul ... Eddie Fox ... got your message. I've been up all night, my brother had a heart attack. He's got a family, three kids. I gotta go there, but I promise I'll be back by tomorrow night."

"Hey, Eddie. You have some relative going down on you every goddamned month. Brother - what brother? I never heard you talk about a brother. Look! One more time and it's over. I can find another grandstand manager. Do you hear me?"

"Yes, sir," he said meekly as he looked up to the ceiling and bobbed the middle finger of his right hand into the air for a few stabs. He had heard what he wanted. The drunk's elixir, "one more time."

He turned his attention to the night and the pickup of

the $50,000. This was, at least as far as they knew, their last chance at him. He worried about some kind of sting operation. He intended to get to the area at about 5:00p.m., drive around, keep a surveillance vigil and, perhaps in between, go into the betting parlor at the Quad Cities Oval. It was at times like these that he wished he had army experience. He considered himself fair game for a sting. He'd be on guard.

Barry Fisk was waiting for McAbee. He had decided a long time ago that McAbee needed focus, like so many people with whom he dealt. McAbee, after all, was a man of the classics. Like so many of them, he had the attitude that there was no hurry, since all that was great had already been written and life and value could only be found in the far past and then, only when one was in the mood to do it. Fisk would think thoughts like these when he was frustrated. He would shake his head in disgust with himself for having these generalized ideas, which were often untrue. Then, he would spend the next bit of his time berating himself for having thought them. If his wait continued beyond that time, he would begin the cycle again. He knew what McAbee would ultimately see if the time was prolonged, was a nasty, supercilious, little man incapable of expressing gratitude for the computer system, the jobs and the extended hand of friendship that McAbee gave to him. It wasn't long before Fisk had generalized this to all of his relationships, descending self-hate and disgust upon himself like a black cloak over a casket. When he reached this level, he would unconsciously grasp his data as if reaching for a life jacket. This was his forte and his value.

"Barry!" McAbee said cheerfully.

"I have some data for you," Fisk said tersely.

"Great, just give me a chance to talk with Pat for a minute and I'll be right with you." Fisk distrusted what he perceived to be the overbearing graciousness of McAbee, on the one hand. Correspondingly he hated himself for being unable to react in any recognizably friendly way himself, on the other hand. What bothered him even more, was the telling fact that McAbee accepted him without any apparent reservations, thus triggering still more distrust.

He looked over at McAbee's secretary. Pat was the red-haired, wire-thin, efficiency bitch who had the power and smoothness to make Fisk pretty much speechless and docile. No matter what game he played, she played it better. McAbee and she were like a tandem wrestling team that could best you individually and, if the occasion rose, could devastate you as a pair. When up against odds like this, he'd clutch his work so tightly that his arms would be sore.

McAbee walked over to him and said, "Come into my office, Barry. I was wondering about what you had come up with."

"Comparatively speaking, I have a lot."

McAbee's office was a Spartan affair. A long mahogany desk with an unassuming in-out basket, two straight-back chairs in front of it, a leather chair behind it, all sitting atop an oriental rug with dark blue and maroon overtones. There was one long library shelf, free of any law tomes, anatomy books, detection books and other assorted nonsense. Instead, he saw books like Bullfinch's Mythology, The Complete Works of Plato, The Complete Works of Aristotle, Plotinus' *Enneads*, Marcus Aurelius' *Meditations* and what seemed like the entirety of both the green- and red-clad Loeb Collection of classical antiquity. His books ended with Francis Bacon. It was as though a wall was hit when Bacon died. Aptly enough, he was a man of the Renaissance and an archetypal founder of modem philosophy and science. To Fisk, it was clear that McAbee had arranged this library to square within his perception of reality.

Behind McAbee was a low credenza that matched the mahogany desk. In a distinct section of the large office was a circular table with three chairs. There were three pictures: El Greco's View of Toledo, Homer's Man on a Raft and Raphael's The School of Athens. He imagined that they all represented special moments for McAbee, but was disinclined to ask for fear of the question leading to relationship nuances. As with everyone else, Barry Fisk was off-limits to McAbee.

McAbee took him to the circular table where they both sat.

"Can I get you anything to drink, Barry?"

"No. Let me explain what I have. We are blessed, as always, by record-keepers and the bureaucrats who run them. In this case, we have the Illinois Racing Board. Their oversight is thoroughbred and standardbred racing in that state. There are two kinds of standardbreds: pacers and trotters. The distinction is simply a matter of gait and how they race. Pacers and trotters don't race against each other, but harness or standardbred tracks have both kinds at their stables. Races are written for each. However, over 90 percent of the standardbred races in Illinois are written for pacers. This Cassies Ruler, for example, was a pacer. Every parimutuel track in Illinois has a backstretch - which involves barns where the horses are kept. I've seen the blueprint layouts of some of them. There are rows and rows of stables with each stable or barn holding between twenty and about eighty horses. Usually the barns or stables are lettered. Thus, Erin Tobin was stationed in Barn Q. At any rate, you can't get into a backstretch without some form of identification."

McAbee raised his hand at this point. Fisk stopped. "So, do you know anything about the security? Is it tight?"

Fisk looked at McAbee, trying to telegraph to him that he would answer this question in due time. He thought the better of doing so when he saw McAbee's mouth tighten in response to Fisk's look. Fisk said, "The Illinois Racing Board meets on a monthly basis. I read their minutes for the past fifteen years. About every three years, there's an uproar about backstretch security. When the Tobin incident occurred, there had been no problems for two years and three months. This would tell me a scandal was coming due and security was probably weak. In fact, one year and two months after Tobin died, there was some screaming and yelling at the Board about security. This led to a crackdown at the tracks for about a year. Then, the slow let-up until the cycle played out and another began."

"So, how exactly, could someone get on the backstretch?" McAbee queried.

Fisk approved this question because it got them back on the point. "You need a license or a sign-in by someone with a license. Licensees include track personnel, vets who work with track horses, trainers, drivers, grooms and owners. They get licenses by filling out an application, paying a fee and getting their fingerprints taken."

McAbee exploded, "Fingerprints? My God! A potential murder scene and no take on prints! I can't believe this!" Fisk was taken aback by the emotion shown by McAbee.

"Well, there's something good about this whole thing. There was an extraordinary data base developed by the state, so to one of your ends, you're well served. We know everyone who was licensed to be on that track on May 23, 1987."

"OK, Barry, but if security was problematical, what good does it do us?"

"Yes, there's a chance that someone did it from off the track or that someone broke security, but don't forget the retarded guy, a track backstretcher. This seems to me, to increase the likelihood of another backstretcher. To pull off what he did would demand some background with horses and a knowledge of the backstretch. But I admit, it's not a 100 percent overlay."

"I suppose it's not possible that they'd have kept the records of the sign-ins?"

"They're not in any database that I've scanned. They may be on paper buried in boxes somewhere at the track, but you didn't want me to make one-on-one contact," he said with a slightly caustic tone.

"No, that's right. I'll make a run on that, Barry. OK, keep going. May 23, 1987, what about the particulars?"

"You already got the good news - there's a database, and I was able to get into it. Then, the bad news is that there were 1,132 licensed applicants who could access the backstretch on that particular night."

McAbee sat back and looked at Fisk in exasperation. "Great!"

Fisk stared down at his data. What he had done from this point forward, he thought, was a tour de force.

"So, I've taken some logical liberties with the data and I've come up with some variances. First, of the 1,132 people, I eliminated all women. Your case summary talked about the two different semen specimens which led me in that direction. That knocked off 302. I eliminated any owners who did not have a horse in that night because their presence would be a bit suspicious. That cut out another 378."

"That's reaching a little, but I'll buy it," McAbee stated.

"So we've got 680 off the list. Just another 452 to go. Now, here is where it starts to reach, but not doing so is a big problem. I eliminated everyone else who didn't live on the backstretch -that takes in a lot of trainers, drivers and track personnel. I know that it's a big leap, but I needed to give you something that you could live with."

"OK, well, let's hear it anyway."

"One hundred sixty-one is what I have left." He was very proud of this number, but he wasn't finished. He loved to surprise the infidels.

"Well, that gives us a better handle, although some of your assumptions are a bit shaky. But, I can see that you're not finished. Go ahead," McAbee said.

Fisk wondered how he knew he wasn't done.. "Now, here's the kicker. Before you can get any kind of license you must register with an organization in Columbus, Ohio, called the United States Trotting Association. Yes, another form and another fee. They have a superb database also and, like the Illinois Racing Board, their file security is third rate. In your report you said the potential murderer was still alive. Using the USTA, the IRB and the Social

Security Administration, I have eliminated another 31 due to death." Even Fisk realized that he was getting into his most pedantic mode. "Of the 161, I eliminated anyone who was at that time over the age of 60 on the ground that a rape was unlikely. That caught me another 27. Now we're down to 103. That's what I could get to without going so far out on the limb that I'd fall."

"Do you think it is likely the murderer left the Quad Cities Oval after the event? Could you access that data?"

"I did a run for that. Illinois would have no record of that nor would the USTA. Individual states and Canada would. So I ran my list against all subsequent licensures in race tracks around the country for the three, two and one months following the May 23 death."

"And?" McAbee asked brusquely.

"Going out to three months, I have twenty-seven names; two months, nineteen names; and from May 24- June 22, I have eight names."

"Your conclusion?"

"These eight are my best guess."

"Now what?"

"Let me pursue these eight real tightly and I'll get back to you."

"Why not. It sounds as though you did a tremendous amount of work."

"I did - many hours. Here's my bill." He nervously handed McAbee his bill. For work that took twenty-three hours, he charged $690. McAbee looked at him as if he wanted to say something, but he didn't.

"I'll get on these characters right away."

"Barry, this is great work - incredible! By the way, your bill is quite modest. A check will be in the mail tomorrow."

Fisk left. McAbee pondered that he was given the kind of work that was worth a good $5,000. He compared it to Scholz. Muscle over intellect: $5,000 a night versus $30 an hour. McAbee scanned the list. He didn't have a clue about any of the eight's identity. The names were Otis Aronson, Pete Damien, John Harbitt, Cal Lansing, Tommy Lee, Pat McDermott, Les Smith and Thad Yates.

Eddie Fox left Forest Park for East Moline and the Quad Cities Oval at 2:00 p.m. sharp. From Rockford Avenue, he drove to Harlem and then drove out the Eisenhower Expressway until he picked up the East West Thruway, or Route 88. Traffic was still fairly light. Once he got beyond the Aurora toll plaza, there was little traffic on the road as he headed west.

He stopped at a McDonald's in De Kalb where he bought two double cheeseburgers and a large Coke. He figured that he wouldn't be eating again until he got home. By 5:00p.m., he made his first brush of the Quad Cities Oval. He slowed down and kept his eyes peeled for anything unusual in or near the area of the drop, which was clearly visible from the highway. He drove west for about two miles and turned into a Jewel Food Store. After walking around the store for fifteen minutes, he bought an eight-ounce package of M&Ms. Then, he went to a bar that was in the shopping plaza. He drank two double Beams and headed off again for another pass at the Quad Cities Oval. It was now 6:30 p.m. Still, he saw nothing of alarm.

He decided to go into the Quad Cities Oval betting parlor and hang around there for a while. He watched a few intertrack races until 7:45 p.m. It was starting to get dark. He left his car parked at the Quad Cities Oval. He decided to walk from the betting parlor to the security gate of the old backstretch. This was about a half mile and would put him about 200 feet from the actual drop site. He kept his eyes open, proud of himself for upping his vigilance. He saw nothing untoward and proceeded back to his car. The darkness of the night was about 90 percent present.

At 8:15p.m., he drove from the parking lot back across the highway to a frontage road to the south. He went east on that road for about an eighth of a mile where he pulled into a tavern parking lot. He sat in the car and watched the old feed building until darkness smothered its visibility. He went into the bar and sat with a double Beam watching the Chicago Cubs playing at the Astrodome. At 10:00 p.m., he intended to drive back to the security gate, run quickly, pick up the bag and get out of there, just like the other times. He had a good feeling as he ordered another double Beam.

Scholz was in an old barn about 600 feet east of the drop site. He had told the farmer that he was on surveillance and gave him $500 for the night. The farmer was elated. He was intending to tear the barn down come October.

Scholz couldn't believe his luck. At 7:50p.m., he picked up Fox walking up the lane nonchalantly, as it were, but all the time peering to his right and left for the suspected trap. By the time Fox started his walk back away from the site, Scholz and his men had twenty five stills and nearly eight minutes of video of this disingenuous crook. His men, keyed up for a complicated game of chess, were now seeing it as a tic tac-toe game with a simpleton.

Their view of the area enabled them to see Fox drive over to the bar across the road. Scholz gave a thumbs up to Umberto Gonzalez. Gonzalez, clad entirely in black including his blackened face surrounded by a balaclava, was already moving across the field and heading toward Fox's car. Scholz scoped the bar entrance and gave him the green light on his mobile. The transmitter was placed on Fox's Chrysler New Yorker and Gonzalez was back at home station in a matter of ten minutes.

By 8:40, all of the men moved out to their preassigned places. By 8:50, the area was encircled by Scholz's men. Scholz sat in the hay berth, night scope rotating back and forth under his steady but excited hands.

Orville Tobin drove up the backstretch road at 9:00 p.m. sharp. Scholz radioed the men to stay low and let him be. They did. Tobin dropped the bag, got into his car and drove away. Then, there was nothing. The wait began.

Scholz saw the bar door open and Fox, stumbling slightly, fell into his New Yorker. Scholz immediately gave the one word they were all waiting for -"Rabbit." Each man signified his understanding by using a pre agreed number. "One," "two," "three," "four," "five," "six," "seven," "eight."

The New Yorker went across the highway and turned toward the backstretch area. Halfway to the drop site, the headlights were turned off. The car made a U-turn. The rabbit parked close to the feed building. He came out of the car quickly but sloppily and trotted to the front of the feed building. Another 100 pictures were shot. A live video with clear head shots was also successfully shot.

The rabbit grabbed the bag and footed it back to his New Yorker. He turned on his lights and drove from the scene. Everyone of Scholz' men now proceeded to their own cars as the trailing of Fox began. One car was west and one was east of the drop site. The remaining six, coming from the west, would tail him and play a number of games as would a pack of wolves on a prey.

Scholz called McAbee.

"Bertrand, it's done. Good footage and pics. Will be in your office tomorrow, late a.m.? Should have an address whenever he lands. Easy as pie."

"Good work, Jack."

Within five minutes of the call, Orville Tobin called. "Bertrand, I did it. Let's hope he calls."

"Orville, one way or another, we'll get to the bottom of this, I promise you."

"Yeah."

Tobin went out of his house, sat on his swing and looked out into the dark, star-filled night. He said lowly, "Ah, Erin, my Erin." He could almost hear the pacing hooves across the field.

CHAPTER 9

That night, the two blacks had him cornered in the backstretch at Northfield. During the day, they had been cursing at him because he had cut off one of them on the track while jogging a pacer. The verbal exchanges got to be vicious and the threats and warnings weren't far behind. Tommy Lee, at twenty-one years of age, was a fine specimen. By just looking at him, most people backed away from any direct confrontation. For whatever reason, the two blacks didn't.

"OK, white boy. You been lookin for it," the fat black guy with the Georgetown sweatshirt said.

"Yeah, we're gonna take you out, motherfucker," the tall one with the Bulls cap drawled.

The fat one had a knife and the tall one had a chain. Tommy Lee looked at them. He figured he could take a direct hit from the chain, but the nigger with the knife had to go first.

"Needs two of yuh shits- and yuh still gonna lose," he said in a low and controlled voice.

The two blacks separated to a distance of about twelve feet and crouched down to an attack position. He'd let them make the first move. The tall one on his left suddenly swung the chain. Tommy Lee let it catch him in the back. He went down to a low crouch, feigning a worse injury than he felt as the knife man flew at him. He brought the knife back so as to come in sidearm and ram it through Tommy Lee's cheek, his teeth, take a slice from his tongue and maybe go all the way through to the other cheek. Whatever it was, it required far too much windup and concentration on momentum.

Tommy Lee's right fist caught him full flush on his jaw. The sickening thud sent him sprawling. The chain was being released by the tall nigger, who was still processing the information and just beginning to feel fear as he saw his ally fall into a heap. Tommy Lee ducked under the descending chain. He came up with a thunderous right and left to the nigger's crotch.

On the ground gasping for breath, Tommy Lee caved his left cheekbone with a vicious right cross and then broke his nose with a flush left. He went back to the unconscious knife-man, took his right arm and broke it at the shoulder over his thigh. He did likewise to the left arm. He never saw either one of them again.

About a week later, a large, head-shaven, black man who was about fifty came up to him while he was eating in the backstretch cafeteria at Northfield. When he entered the cafeteria, he stationed two hulks at the door of the place. Of the twenty or so customers, only one stayed longer than two minutes. That was Tommy Lee. The black guy immediately realized that word of the fight last week was common knowledge across the track, otherwise the customers wouldn't have left.

"Mind if l sit down? Name's Jonas Fielder." He didn't hold out his hand.

"What do yuh want?"

"Just wanna chat with you, man. Those two brothers at the door are just for decoration. I'm not here to start trouble with you. Hear?"

"So?"

"So, my name is Jonas Fielder. I'd like to know your name before I present a proposal to you."

"Tommy Lee."

"I got two brothers in a serious way; broken arms, broken jaws, broken cheekbones, broken nose, broken balls - broken men. Now I know that shit happens and I happen to know these two ain't angels, but, man, do you realize that these two were boxers in their heyday?"

"Look, what's this gotta do with me? I didn't have a fight with anyone. I did defend myself against two hoods who were trying to rob me, but I'll tell yuh, they weren't fighters. These two were weasels with weapons. So, I don't think, Mr. Fielder, we're talking about the same men."

Fielder gave a low growling laugh. "OK, man, maybe we're lookin' at the same picture, but we're wearing different lenses. What you did has impressed a lot of people. Where I come from, they just don't make tough white guys anymore. They're only produced in black factories, it's like TVs, they're not made here anymore. We're the Asia of toughness like they're the makers of TVs." He chuckled again, all the while watching this white bastard. He was trying to get a semblance of respect from him. He wasn't sure if Tommy Lee even understood what he'd been saying. But he realized that Tommy Lee wouldn't back down from Satan. He liked that.

"Man," he continued, "I don't expect you to know who I am. I own Fielder's Gym in downtown Cleveland. Ain't no boxer in the fuckin' Midwest doesn't know my gym. When I heard you got the drop on those two, I had one question - Who? Fuck their jaws and balls, I want to know who got the best of them. And then I hear it's some white guy and I'm sayin' you give me a good white fighter and it's millions for everybody. That's what I'm here about, brother." He reached into his jacket pocket and pulled out a card. He placed it in front of Tommy Lee. It had Tommy Lee's name on it. It said, Complimentary Membership - three months. He continued, "When you come in, the dates will be written in."

"I thought yuh didn't know my name?"

"Man, where I come from, names are changin' all the time. I didn't want to say Tommy Lee and be told you were Johnny Smith, if you get my meanin'."

"So, if I go, how do I know I won't be ambushed by fifteen of yuh nig ... guys?"

Fielder laughed and slapped his thigh. "You can call us niggers anytime you want, honky. Nobody's got thin skin in my gym. If they do, they show it in the ring. Nobody'll ever touch you in my gym or my parking lot. That's my kingdom, man- nobody fucks with me, hear? If you're as good as they say you are, we just might make a lot of money together. How about it?"

"I'll think it over. If I'm coming, I'll call yuh."

Fielder left. They had never shaken hands. "Racist bastard," Fielder muttered to himself as he left the cafeteria.

On the way back to the gym, his driver asked him, "How'd it go down, boss? He's a mean looking bastard."

"Surly honky. Got a good look in his eye though. Ain't no ethics between his ears. No put-on with him. He's a straight nigger-hating fucker. We'll put him in the ring, see what he can do and we'll bring him along. He'll probably hit a wall. All the whites do. He'll start bleedin' all over the fuckin' mat or he'll low punch or something else. It's like buyin' a horse- most of them never make it to the track."

Ten days later, Jonas Fielder grabbed Mavis Brown's arm and took him into his office. Mavis had been a professional fighter up to three years ago. He was now a bit flabby and a bit punch-drunk. One of many hangers-on in Fielder's Gym. As a professional heavyweight, his record was 17-13-1. He became fodder for up and comers when he couldn't get that sacred fifth win against another has-been, who he was intending to climb on top of.

"How you feelin', Mavis?"

"Yeah, OK, boss."

"Still workin' out?"

"Oh, yeah. Gettin' better. Thinkin' about a comeback. I miss the glory, ya know, man?" He smiled.

"You sparrin' with anyone?"

"Yeah, yeah. I'm in there once or twice a day. But I wear the helmet. Anything wrong?"

"No, man, no. I got a favor to ask you. Some fuckin' honky is coming down here in about one hour. I wanna see him in the ring. I'll give you fifty bucks to have a go at him. I want you to give him a go - no breaks. If you kick his ass, that's cool. I wanna know how good he is." He took a fifty out of his pocket and handed it to Mavis who couldn't hide his joy. Getting money and fighting were the joys of his life.

"I'm ready," he smiled, a mouth full of pink emptiness.

Fielder had his guys looking for him. When he drove into the parking lot in a beaten-up and dirt encrusted pickup, they went out to escort him. This was not a white man's haven and the few who came here were warned to be careful. They took him to Fielder's office, who asked for the complimentary pass and filled out the starting date for the three-month offer. He was trying to make this cracker feel good, but was unable to get a read off of him.

"Don't know how you want to start this, man. I got a guy who's been around the block a few times. Maybe you'd like to spar with him? Otherwise, I'll put you into some drills for strength and speed, or maybe we can do both?"

"I'll spar, then we'll see."

"Show him where to change, you guys. Do you have a lock? Shorts? Jock with cup?"

"Shorts are just running shorts, got the jock and cup and yuh better believe I have a lock."

Fielder caught the inflamed eyes of his two men, but nothing was said.

"Well, why don't you change and warm up for a few minutes. We'll get some gloves on you and we'll see what happens. The guy you're sparrin' with is called Mavis. You guys come and get me when Tommy Lee here is ready."

There were thirty-two guys in the gym at this time. The deteriorating place had three rings, the full complement of weight equipment and numerous bags. Twenty were in varying stages of training as either trainer or boxer, while twelve were either sitting or standing around. Tommy Lee's presence was marked because Mavis had left Jonas' office and had chatted up his comeback against this white chump. When Fielder was told that Tommy Lee was ready, he came out of his office. The center ring was being used by two youthful nothings. He yelled up to the referee that after this round, they were to find another ring. The two boxers heard him and looked at him crossly, but thought the better of it, finished and vacated the ring.

Jonas had one of the oldtimers go into the ring to referee. Tommy Lee had never been on an apron of canvas from the way he warily walked around the ringed rectangle.

Jonas yelled out, "Are the seconds all arranged?" The two bodyguards gave their respective thumbs up.

"Mavis, Tommy Lee, you guys ready?"

Mavis yelled "yup." Tommy Lee nodded. Jonas took up the hammer. Just as he was prepared to gong the bell, he realized that the entire gym had fallen silent, even the two young jerks that he tossed out of the center ring. Jonas Fielder was doing something that he had rarely done before and they all knew it. He hit the gong and Mavis and Tommy Lee approached each other.

As Fielder watched them, he conjectured that Tommy Lee, untrained, would probably get his ass clobbered. Even though Mavis was a has-been, he was still a professionally trained fighter. The difference was immense between one of them and a neophyte such as Tommy Lee, no matter how fast his fucking fists were supposed to be.

Mavis caught him with two quick jabs over his right eye. Mavis' best punch was his left jab. He was setting Tommy Lee on notice right away. He hit him again and closed as if to clinch. As he got in close, he uppercutted the unsuspecting Tommy Lee and hurt him. Tommy Lee threw an undisciplined right and left at the escaping Mavis, who pushed out his mouthpiece and said, "You in for a long day, white boy."

By the end of the round, which Jonas cut short by a full half-minute, Tommy Lee had taken over forty punches and had landed two on Mavis' arms. Jonas noticed, however, that he was hard to hurt, was game and that he was calculating something. It was as though he was willing to take scores of punches to prove a point or spring a surprise. There was a bit of feigner in Tommy Lee.

The second round opened. Within a minute, the same pattern as the first round was fully established. Tommy Lee was slow afoot and was a sitting target for the hyped-up Mavis. And then, it happened. Mavis came in again, as if to tie him up in a clinch. On the other three occasions when he employed this tactic, he had used it to deliver a crushing uppercut to Tommy Lee. Simply, he was going back to the well again. Jonas almost missed it because Tommy Lee's right fist moved inversely to his feet. His right cross came from nowhere and caught Mavis flush, sending him flying across the ring, through the ropes and onto the padded floor. In Jonas' take on the scene, Mavis was unconscious by the time he fell through the ropes. "A hard way to make a fuckin' fifty bucks," Fielder said to no one in particular.

He studied Tommy Lee for a few minutes after the knockout. He was calm. And by Jonas' reckoning, he was the only one not surprised by the outcome of this battle. He thought of the two guys in the hospital. He now understood why the assholes were mincemeat with this mean fucker. He figured he could go far enough to make it to the "Young and Upcoming Heavyweights" section of Ring Magazine, but once he ran across disciplined speed, he would be a dead man. But it would take a lot of training to even get him to that point. Unless he saw a pretty sure return on investment, he wasn't about to encourage this white bastard for whom he felt a visceral hatred.

Tommy Lee maintained a grueling two-month training program, besides staying on at Northfield Harness Track. In two months, he had made tremendous progress. Even Jonas Fielder was surprised. When Mavis had come to and shaken off his latest of many concussions, he had one comment, "He's slow, but that right is as fast as they come- it explodes."

Fielder would have him spar, but not be in any match such as with Mavis. He reaffirmed his original analysis: quick hands, no legs. After two months he signed Tommy Lee to a contract. He scheduled his first professional fight, fifth down on an undercard against some dumb, down-on-his-luck Mexican who needed to make $300. Tommy Lee dispatched him in forty-five seconds of the first round. Fielder said to his two men, "That spic was a slower piece of shit than the honky."

After that, Tommy Lee fought three more times in less than two months. None of the bums that Fielder found could survive past the first round. With a record of 4-0, Fielder stepped up his marketing and gave Tommy Lee the sobriquet, "The White Shark of Lake Erie." No matter that words "fresh" and "Lake Erie" were problematical. When a reporter asked Fielder about the compounded oxymoron, Fielder said, off the record, "Hey, man, you want me to call him 'the mother fuckin' carp of Lake Erie'?"

Tommy Lee picked up the usual following of insecure whites around the Cleveland area. They saw it as a matter of pride, race consciousness and whatever other bullshit they needed in order to get through each day of their miserable lives, Fielder conjectured. He knew there was nothing better to whet the appetite than see this hulk whip the shit out of a few over-the-hill niggers. His scheduling reflected that insight.

When Fielder got together with Clovis Hagen, who ran the Cleveland Arena, the discussion was about Tommy Lee, who had made the sports section of the *Cleveland Plain Leader.*

"Jonas, what gives with the honky?"

"He's got a few more fights in him. If he had legs, he'd be brutal, but he doesn't and you know as well as I do, you can't give a man a pair of fast legs. From his head to his upper thighs, he's a champ; from his upper thighs to his toes, he's a chump; and chump and champ don't mix."

"So, what do we do? Can we make some money off him?"

"Hell, yeah. But not for long, like I said, man. People see through this. Even the fuckin' skinheads will smell a rat. I want to take him out of the undercard stuff and feature him. I got the perfect fighter for him. Then, we get him another joker and then we send him up against someone in the top ten. I want to send the fucker off on a stretcher. And believe me, man, anyone in the top ten will dismantle him, especially someone with a good pair of legs."

"OK, let's do some dealing," Clovis Hagen said. Neither of these men would reject the thesis that fighters were no different than pit bulls, fighting cocks or whatever. Another man's body was the urinal of opportunity.

Mavis Brown's comeback was ballyhooed in the papers. It was to be a ten-round featured fight between him and The White Shark. Rumors were spread that the two men hated

each other and that it would be a no prisoner-taken battle.
Mavis had a quick warmup with a stumble-bum honky who
had to be carefully led into the ring - he was so drunk. Much
to the delight of the brothers and sisters, Mavis dispatched
the moron in two rounds. His jabs had left a bloody pulp.
When his corner led the dumb shit out of the Cleveland
Arena, anyone within earshot heard him pleading for some
whiskey.

The ad had Mavis holding a picture of the blood
drenched white that he had just beaten in his hand and
pointing to Tommy Lee, who scowled at him. Clovis Hagen
and Jonas Fielder chuckled at the ad. They figured that the
honkies would be pissed off at still another white getting his
ass pounded, and blacks would be pleased to see the white
man get his due for all the shit they had to put up with.

Much more accomplished now, Tommy Lee didn't get
jabbed quite as easily as on that first day with Mavis and his
punches were more focused than Mavis remembered. Mavis
tried to stay clear of him and box his way to a ten-round
decision, or a TKO if he could get him to bleed. He had
only knocked out two men in his career.

Tommy Lee waited for his chance. Mavis gave it to
him in the third round. He had come under Mavis' jab
while Mavis was backing away just a shade too slowly. In
one brutal punch, the fight was over. Mavis was still on the
canvas being attended to when Tommy Lee left the ring.
His sneer caught Jonas in the nearly full Cleveland Arena.

They set him up with another Mavis-like black who
Tommy Lee dutifully clobbered into unconsciousness in
the second round. The Cleveland Arena was jammed. Some

ugly racist brawls were averted by a highly vigilant Cleveland Police Department.

Fielder was waiting for this moment.

He took great pleasure scheduling Tommy Lee against Mohammed Khali, AKA, Jimmy O'Neal, an up and-coming black street kid from Pittsburgh. He had an eight ranking in Ring and was clearly the better fighter because of his leg speed. He was 13-0 with twelve knockouts and one TKO. No one had gone beyond five rounds with him.

Tommy Lee fought Khali two days before his twenty-second birthday. Fielder saw in his eyes that he knew he was beaten within thirty seconds of the first round; too much speed and too much firepower. He was game for three rounds as Khali brutalized him, slicing large chunks of flesh off of his eyebrows, cheeks and forehead. His vision was blurred by the dripping blood when Khali came in to close. In one final lunge by Tommy Lee, Khali just barely avoided getting clipped. He hammered brutally on Tommy Lee in a sequence of eight straight combinations before the ref broke up the fight. Tommy Lee had gotten his comeuppance. Jonas Fielder was pleased, as were the high-fiving blacks in the Cleveland Arena.

At about 1:00 a.m. that very night, Tommy Lee stopped his pickup near a black whore standing alone on East Ninth and Euclid in downtown Cleveland. He showed her a $100 bill when she came over to the truck. "I want the whole night."

"You got it, man." She entered his pickup. Seeing no one around, he motioned as if to place his arm around her. He clipped her jaw with a quick right fist. She collapsed down into her seat. He raped and strangled her to death. Then he dumped her into Lake Erie, behind the Rock and Roll Museum, where she was found by fishermen two days later. Already, Tommy Lee was in Vernon Downs outside of Syracuse- a stable groom.

CHAPTER 10

FBI agent, Bert Pauerhorst, was nearing retirement from the Bureau after thirty years of service. He had worked in a number of field offices, all east of the Mississippi River. For the past twelve years, he had been assigned to the Multiple Murder Division in Arlington, Virginia. The office had grown over the years, from two persons to one that now housed twenty three agents.

As he headed down Interstate 95 on his way to Norfolk, his mind wandered. He had personally taken down two serial killers in his twelve years. In addition, he suspected that his pressure had led to the suicide of another. A serial killer was defined as, an individual who murdered on more than one occasion, where the apparent goal was principally driven by the murder itself and the associated psychological goodies derived from it.

Although usually a male thing, it was not unknown for women to engage in it also. In fact, one of his two arrests was the capture of a female who would pretend car trouble, allow herself to be picked up by a male and manifest sexual desire. As the male would make his move toward her, a knife would find its way to his heart. She became known as the "Vengeful Princess" who, upon the death of the victim, would then engage in a ritual castration. At the time of her arrest, five penises were found in her basement freezer, along with a notebook detailing the crime and a Polaroid of the crime scene. Victims ranged from a Baptist minister to a bank loan officer.

Pauerhorst had worked exclusively on this case for three years. The murders had occurred in Northern Florida, Alabama and Georgia. She struck about once every eight months; thus becoming predictable and giving Pauerhorst a chance. About one year after her life sentence in Georgia, she was murdered in prison by another lifer who tried to fondle her and was punched for her efforts. The next day her throat was cut in a work area. The lifer didn't give a damn; she wasn't going anywhere anyway. Pauerhorst said, "Good riddance," to anybody who'd listen.

One side effect that Pauerhorst would mention in his public talks was that hitchhiking crimes were down an average of 65 percent in the affected states over this period. Any woman next to a stalled car was seen by some as the "Vengeful Princess."

His other case stopped a trucker after two successful murders and what appeared to be the beginning of a heinous career in the Delaware-New Jersey area.

He was going to address the Noon Rotary Club of Norfolk and take care of some business in the Norfolk Field Office of the FBI. His talk was entitled "Serial Killers." He had been giving it for what was now becoming an almost weekly event in the Virginia, Maryland, and D.C. area. In fact, it was becoming clear to him that he was being eased out in this manner. Things could be worse, he thought.

Pauerhorst, ruddy complected, with a nose that all too manifestly showed the effects of alcohol, was about six-foot-three with a large frame that enabled him to carry his 235 pounds with, if not grace, some proportionality. He was introduced by Agent Tim Morton who focused on his career with the Multiple Murder Division. Morton had whispered in his ear that the attendance at this meeting was terrific. This didn't surprise Pauerhorst who knew that people were drawn to the topic, like the peekers who would gaze at a grotesque highway accident.

"Our office receives over 7,000 police reports a year that tell us of murders and unusual disappearances. Two thousand of these are usually resolved in the community, but the rest are live wires needing careful tracking and manipulation. Let me explain." He went on to tell of his experiences with the "Vengeful Princess" as he watched the 90 percent male audience squirm. When told of her eventual murder, he heard a deep, collective sigh. It never failed. It was so different with a mainly female audience. Although they weren't supportive of the woman, there was a certain sympathy at some level in those groups.

He spoke of the problems on which he worked and a few of the world-famous cases that had been part of the Division's work. There was no doubt that everyone would leave the banquet hall worried about their loved ones and aware that the world was a dangerous place. Congressional representatives who in any way fought against the budgetary requests of the FBI, would hear it from groups like the Noon Rotary Club of Norfolk.

When Pauerhorst allowed for questions, a sea of hands went up. "How specialized is this Division? What I mean is, do you go by a geographic region or a certain kind of murder or victim?"

"Good question. We do have regions, but we check each other's work. It's not impossible for someone in Maine and New Hampshire to have set a pattern to move to another region, e.g., Louisiana. Sometimes it's because of a job change, a divorce, or he just plain feels that it's getting too close for comfort. He might see a police car in a strange place and decide that they're after him, when in fact nothing's happening. It's very important that we talk to each other. An odd fact, a clue, could turn out to be the clincher in a case. So we cross-expose our work to each other at all times."

"Agent Pauerhorst, you mentioned that you'll be retiring in about six months. Is there some case or situation that has you particularly frustrated or that you're upset about?"

"Well, as you know, we can't comment on any ongoing investigation. I will say that everyone works terribly hard; it's house-to-house combat. But the answer to your question is yes. There is a murderer out there who uses an M.O. that is very consistent and who has escaped every net we have put out. We have run every conceivable check and correlation, used every profile matrix available to us, yet I feel that we haven't made progress. We know that he uses his right fist to knock his victims unconscious. He then rapes and strangles them. He has struck in a number of states across the country, but primarily in the East, South and Midwest. So, in answer to your question, if I could get my hands on him, I would feel that my career had been fulfilled."

Pauerhorst answered a few more questions and left the hotel banquet room with Tim Morton. While they were driving to the FBI headquarters in downtown Norfolk,

Morton asked Pauerhorst, "So just how bad is it with this guy you were talking about at the meeting?"

"It's a downer, Tim. The computer kicked out the trend about three years ago. We started to backtrack through the states and put it together. It looks like a range of maybe even fifteen years. He's dropping women at a rate of about two a year. Same goddamn thing - a clean punch, a rape and a clean strangle. We know the size of his knuckles, we have pubic hairs, we have semen samples, we have a lot of useless information unless we can get the creep in action. We thought he was pretty much East Coast, except for some stuff six years ago when he did a woman in Provo and later one in Sacramento. He's hit in Massachusetts, Maine, New York, New Jersey, Pennsylvania, Kentucky, Ohio, and Florida. And since he does sometimes make an effort to conceal his victims, God knows how many others are out there someplace."

"Any men?"

"No. But except for the sex, this guy could flatten anyone. Our M.O. says that he has grades of punches-almost as if he was a trained fighter."

"Suspects?"

"Some of the guys think that he might be a carny or in sales, some occupation that lets him float around the country. It's frustrating. I keep my fingers crossed hoping for a break. But the guy's no fool."

"Well, Bert, you know as well as I, it'll come when you least expect it and probably from some incidental avenue that you're not even aware of yet." Morton patted Pauerhorst on the shoulder and the conversation shifted elsewhere.

Scholz came to McAbee's office, not his preferred approach, but at conclusions he liked to go to the official place of business. He presented McAbee an envelope. "This is my bill, no surprises. It involves setups, meetings at the whore's place, two full nights one actual, one set up and incidental expenses – total $11,800. Problem?"

"No problem, Jack. I'll have a check on its way by tomorrow. What do you have?"

"I have a name, an address and phone number. Why don't you put your nasty little midget on him?"

"Let's see it, Jack."

He handed him an envelope. McAbee opened it and found a 3"-by-5" index card. It read: "Edward Fox, 102 Rockford Avenue, #301, Forest Park, Illinois, 60130; phone: 708-771-4371." McAbee looked at him and said, "Jack, this is great work. I couldn't ask for better work from you. No suspicions on his part?"

"None. He's one of the dumbest slobs I've been up against. He gave himself away, but you could see that he thought he was being real cagey. So, he gets to Forest Park, but instead of going home, he goes to a liquor store in River Forest first. This is not good. We have eight cars tracking the stooge. He comes out and heads home. He pulls into his parking place and goes into the building. In a minute, my men see his lights come on and there he is, framed in his blinds. Can you believe it? He's one dumb rabbit. If you want, we could bust him wide open and get to anything he knows probably in a matter of minutes. I know you don't want to do that, but that's my offer- $3,000 when you give me the word." He left McAbee's office.

After calling Barry Fisk and telling him about Edward

Fox and the need for a full profile, McAbee sat back, took off his glasses and thought about the case to this point and the tantalizing offer given to him by Jack Scholz.

He was relatively certain that Erin Tobin was, in fact, a murder victim. He also believed that Edward Fox actually did know something about it, up to and including the name of the murderer. The double semen sample from Tobin's body and alleged suicide of Rickie Crocker constituted too much inside information. Fox was probably in some sort of financial bind and saw Orville Tobin as his best chance out of the mess. On the other hand, the facts may just simply be what they are and McAbee and Tobin were being led down some imaginary road that went nowhere by an all-too-clever man. Fisk would uncover the needed data that might put the legitimacy of the information into perspective.

Scholz's offer to break him was another matter. If it wasn't for the deal that he had cut with Orville Tobin to not impair the relationship between him and Fox, it would be quite tempting for McAbee, whose philosophy on the matter was that this agenda was set by the crook and definitionally that meant that there was already a violation of ethics in the treatment of another human being. This, in turn, gave leverage to McAbee to jump ethical bars that he would never even consider in his conduct of business in day-to-day matters.

His brother Bill, a pragmatist, had told him on numerous occasions that he wasn't ruthless enough. Bill said that to reach the next level, he would have to suspend some of his "cute little tenets." McAbee was, in fact, a fairly avowed follower of Aristotle's vision of ethics, which involved the pursuit of four virtues: temperance, bravery, prudence, and justice; a cultivated inner life and the acquisition of a few close friends, Beth's departure being a sore test of this latter ingredient. What he liked about Aristotle's ethic was that it was not tied to any universal formula that blocked particular actions, yet it still had the touch of prodding him to aspiration to a better life and a sense of searching. His brother's ethic was akin to that found in the heroic age of Homer, where you simply out-powered your adversary using any means at your disposal. This was probably the key to his success with governments whose attention to ethics was tied to spheres of interest and not aspiration to a higher good. So, McAbee had built-in restraints that he would let go of very unwillingly and only under unusual circumstances. Whereas, his brother was essentially without restraint except for his consideration of not getting caught, an old Sophist argument attacked by Socrates, Plato and Aristotle.

Still, Scholz's offer stood there. McAbee knew that he could probably break Fox in twenty or thirty minutes and if Fox was tougher than he thought, he'd work on him for a month for the same fee that he requested-$3,000. McAbee had used Scholz once for this kind of job. Scholz did indeed get the information that he needed. He got it in two-and-a-half hours, from a drifter who had defrauded an eighty-year-old lady out of her $70,000 life savings. Most of it was recovered and the drifter was sent on his way. McAbee was very uneasy about the mind-altering drugs that were used by Scholz in the pursuit of the drifter's hiding place and accomplice. He was particularly bothered by Scholz's ordering a severe beating of both of them since it never became a police matter. The last he had heard of the pair was their being ticketed by the Iowa Highway Patrol for going eighty-five miles per hour in a sixty-mile zone near the Nebraska border. Scholz's justice had, at least, gotten them out of the area, but who knew what vengeance would be wrought on their next victims. McAbee heard his brother's voice, "Bertrand, you think too much!"

Pat came to the door and said, "You know, Bertrand, you have a racquetball game with Lou at the St. Anselm gym in twenty minutes."

"I'm on my way. Thanks."

Kodowsky had come to St. Anselm from the Polish south side of Chicago as an eighteen-year-old football and basketball player. It was the early fifties. At the time, St. Anselm had a powerhouse football team. As a player/student, in that order, he had excelled in sports. Upon graduation, he was named an assistant coach and went on to get a master's degree in physical education from the University of Northern Iowa in Cedar Falls.

He had just celebrated his forty-second year at St. Anselm as a faculty member, in addition to his sixty sixth birthday. He was bald, overweight by a good thirty pounds ("I'm a disgrace to the Polish flag"). Yet, still a fierce competitor and an estimable racquetball player, who in the last six years had been regularly entering the sixty-plus division of national racquetball tournaments. In his sixty-third year, he was a semifinalist in a national tournament held in Houston before being beaten by a "thin, little, sixty-year-old bastard from Los Angeles."

As McAbee was changing in the locker room at St. Anselm, Lou came down, sat across from him and started what McAbee called "the Kodowsky cant." This typically involved a long list of Kodowsky ailments from a bad knee, to a sore elbow and shoulder, to being overweight, to not having had a good night's sleep.

"Lou," McAbee interrupted him, "if I listened to all this crap, I'd play you with my racquet on the end of my foot. You haven't had a good night's sleep in years, by your reckoning. As for the rest of your miserable body, why don't you schedule a visit with Kevorkian. I think that he has just the right medicine for you."

"You think I'm kidding, but this is real. I don't stand a chance today."

"Well, on that score, you're right. You truly don't stand a chance."

They had been playing fairly regularly for about twenty years. Kodowsky rarely beat McAbee. Even during a two-year period when his right shoulder forced McAbee to play with his left arm, Kodowsky had his troubles with the ambidextrous McAbee.

Kodowsky's biggest problem, in McAbee's view, was his weight, his faltering ability to move laterally and his lack of imagination. McAbee's serve, low, fast and accurate, forced Kodowsky to compensate and lean to his backhand, where most of McAbee's serves went. He kept Kodowsky honest by going to the forehand of Kodowsky about every seventh time. Lou's mastery, however, of other parts of the game was fine, plus he never quit. McAbee wondered what it would have been like to play against this tough Pole from Chicago's south side, when he was a young man.

Once, at an alumni dinner, McAbee sat next to an ex-teammate of Lou's who said that he was blessed with tremendous speed, spirit and was the dirtiest player he had ever met.

He knew that Lou had been relieved of his coaching duties for the men's varsity basketball team because he threatened to kill a referee in an awkwardly silent gym of about 1,000 fans. McAbee had heard it clear as bell on a cold, quiet morning-"I'll kill you, you dumb, fucking son of a bitch!" The then president of St. Anselm, was entertaining three would-be contributors to a new library building fund. At dinner before the game, he had spoken about what a good Catholic university St. Anselm's was. The game was the denouement of the sell. The president's face showed the entire spectrum of redness for the remainder of the night. Unceremoniously, Kodowsky was sacked from coaching the next day. This otherwise stupid president was wise enough, however, not to challenge Lou's tenured teaching appointment, his being a sort of legend at the University. It wasn't long before the President was unceremoniously fired himself.

McAbee beat him in the first game with a serve to Kodowsky's right, which he never got to- 15-11. The second game was very one-sided- 15-3 McAbee. He had seen this tactic before from Kodowsky, who would consider it a big victory to win even one game. The second game played had been relaxed to take the edge off of McAbee. At the water fountain, McAbee realized that the third game would be given an all-out effort from Lou, who was now complaining about a sore pinky, of all things!

Kodowsky was elated! McAbee had missed three straight returns by beating them into the ground, albeit just missing two killer shots by less than an inch. He served, again to McAbee's backhand, figuring that McAbee would try the same shot and would keep doing so until he missed. To Kodowsky, McAbee was a hopeless perfectionist who would constantly work on a shot, even if it might cost him the game, not that that happened often. McAbee was always a tough competitor who could play to the level he faced. So, Lou figured that the quick three points would lead to a stiffening by him.

His next serve was taken on a low hop by a charging McAbee, who ripped it across the court and by Kodowsky's right hand. He had been leaning to his backhand and was caught off guard by McAbee's change of tactics.

McAbee as server was Lou's nemesis. He had a low serve that had enough speed to keep him on his toes and also, guessing. McAbee had developed a serve that was without a hint of divulgence. He had two points in fifteen seconds, but on his third serve, Lou managed to get it up to the ceiling and ran McAbee deep to his backhand. McAbee's shot was down the middle of the court where Lou buried it for a kill.

Lou picked up four more points on his serves. McAbee, once again, aiming to perfect his return, finally succeeding on Kodowsky's fifth serve. Lou reflected that McAbee was unusually quiet for all of his misses; McAbee was not a quiet player and was given to some mean-sounding yells.

Kodowsky successfully fought off McAbee's serve again. He was pleased to be sitting on a 7-2 lead. The game seesawed at this point. It was at 13-8, Kodowsky, when McAbee looked at Lou and said, "OK, Kodowsky, get ready. I'm coming after you."

"Yeah, well, you can go straight to hell. I've got you in this one!"

"How's your pinky?"

"Fine! Now you just serve!"

Lou shut him down at 13-12 and took the ball for serve. He picked up one point, but McAbee, going across court again on a serve, caught Lou leaning. It was 14-12. McAbee went to his right and caught him sleeping- 14-13. He sent the next serve across the front wall and the side wall. The ball came out at Lou's feet with a mean spin that Lou couldn't handle- 14-14.

McAbee stared at Lou for about fifteen seconds. He had that habit. He'd catch your eyes and see through you. Lou didn't like it, but it was a McAbee trait. Kodowsky wondered where he'd strike- low left, low right, across court, where? McAbee went to his backhand. Lou lifted it high off of the ceiling sending McAbee deep to his backhand where he in tum, sent the ball to the ceiling and sent Kodowsky deep. Lou decided on a low percentage shot, figuring McAbee wasn't thinking that he'd try it. He attempted to bury a low killer backhand across court. He missed. McAbee won 15-14.

"Next week I'll get you, you skinny, little bastard!"

"Right, Lou! Right!"

CHAPTER 11

At Vernon Downs, Tommy Lee was hired on as a groom by trainer Mitch Christensen. Tommy Lee was good with horses, but he had a mean streak that worried Christensen, who himself wasn't a particularly gentle man. He paid Tommy Lee $200 a week to care for five horses. The job meant being at the barn by 6:30a.m. Each horse had to be exercised, which involved relatively leisurely four-mile jaunts around the seven eighths-mile track. Then, the pacer would be washed down, walked, his stall cleaned, water changed and food given at two scheduled times. The process had a ritualistic quality to it. Tommy Lee was usually done by 1:30 p.m. He worked six days a week, with the duty of once a month cleaning the stable and feeding the horses on Sundays when there were no workouts.

If a horse was not in a race that particular week, he would be trained, which meant that he would be subjected to the equivalence of a race.

On nights when the track was in session, Tommy Lee would be the groom for any of his five horses who might be racing. This meant that he was on duty for about five hours, because the pacers would have to be brought to the detention barn where they were officially monitored before the race. Tommy Lee would stand and, occasionally, chat with other grooms as he waited for the actual race. Then, after the race, he would be responsible for washing down the horse and walking it until it was relatively dry. They could be long nights, but they had their rhythm. When he groomed on a race night, he was given $25.

Christensen, like many small-time trainers, used cash only. He never reported his transactions to the IRS. Tommy Lee, therefore, was a cipher of sorts to the IRS. Over his grooming life span, where he was exposed to twenty-one trainers in all, he only had three who had required his social security number and who played according to the book. Tommy Lee was consistent with the track etiquette by disliking any medium of payment that wasn't in cash.

About two months after arriving at Vernon Downs, he and a fellow groom went out on a Saturday night to hit the bars and night spots. They ended up at the Bare-It-All in downtown Syracuse. The place was packed. The strippers were hot. He was on his fourth Bud at the place and was just beginning to relax, when a stacked, bikini-clad blonde came over to his table and offered a private show. He looked her up and down and said, "Why not." She did her thing. In about three minutes she had her bra off. Tommy Lee followed her swaying breasts as she moved them within six inches of his face.

She tucked her right hand inside her bikini bottom and simulated masturbation. Tommy Lee was getting a good show. He knew that it was getting close to the time to stuff a ten-dollar bill into her crotch and let her get on her way. The rules were known to everybody in these places. More than two seconds was taboo and no going between the legs. Tommy Lee didn't abide by them. He slid his hand down past her triangle of public hair and tried to insert a finger into her vagina. She raged, pulled away, and screamed at him "You fucking pig! What the hell do you think you're doing?" The ten-dollar bill had fallen to the floor. Tommy Lee moved to pick it up and also yelled out, "Screw you, bitch- you pig!"

The exchange brought an eventual hush to the entire night club. Even the three fully nude strippers on top of the stage behind the bar stopped dancing; finally, even the band quit.

A bouncer was there in seconds. They looked at Tommy Lee and his friend, who was now looking around sheepishly.

"OK. You two, get the fuck out of here or I'll put you in the hospital." He was about 6-foot-3-inches tall and a good 280 pounds; a serious weight lifter by Tommy Lee's reckoning.

A waitress came over to the bouncer and whispered in his ear. He said, "You owe $43 - let's have $50 - I know you want to leave a nice tip for Wanda, here."

Tommy Lee sat there. He tried to make himself seem smaller than he was because he had decided that he would destroy this fucker at the right time, this muscle bound freak.

"I'm not paying a nickel to this shithouse if I have to leave. I'm either here for the night or I'll go, but I won't pay you."

At this point, the apparent owner or manager came over to the table. The stripper had been whining to him, Tommy Lee observed, ever since the incident began.

"Are we having some trouble here, Patrick?"

"No, sir, I'm sure these two will pay and leave peacefully; otherwise, I'll deal with them as criminals needing to be arrested."

Tommy Lee heard his fellow groom nervously say, "OK, OK, I'll pay for us and we'll be on our way." He reached for his wallet. Tommy Lee grabbed his arm and said in a low voice: "Shut the fuck up and just sit there, you asshole." The groom put his hands up and just sat there in resignation.

The owner looked at Tommy Lee and said, "You heard Patrick! Let's have the money. Then, let's see your back out the front door."

Tommy Lee was fully aware that the scene was being watched by around 300 people. It felt like the Cleveland Arena again. He glared at Patrick, saying: "Where I come from, muscle-bound assholes with names like Patrick are fucking queers. You big, useless pile of shit. Try to put a hand on me!" He summoned up a cross smile and stood up.

Even years later, Tommy Lee could not figure out what was in the jerk's mind, because he sauntered over to Tommy Lee and grabbed his arm. It was as if he had no fear of Tommy Lee. He imagined that he was accustomed to dealing with drunken businessmen, men who crossed the line with these whores and who were easily intimidated by Patrick and the fear of getting their names in the *Syracuse Post-Standard*. His grip was hard; a weight lifter's vise.

Tommy Lee said, "Take your fucking hand off of me or you're going to the hospital."

"Shiiit," Patrick said sarcastically.

Tommy Lee immediately went into action, pounding down on Patrick's arm with his right fist and breaking the lock. He went into a boxer's stance and squared up against Patrick, who came toward him with a sneer, arms out like a wrestler. Tommy Lee flashed a left jab which fully engaged Patrick's attention. The savage right fist caught Patrick full on the lower jaw and cheek. Patrick's face caved terribly; surely a broken jaw and crushed cheekbone were in his future. He went down on all fours, tried to make some effort to get up and then, collapsed. The blood was beginning to gush from his disfigured mouth.

Tommy Lee immediately went to the owner or manager, grabbed him by the lapel and said, "Are we even?"

"Yes . . . yes . . . just please leave," he said tremorously. Tommy Lee gave him a shove that sent him back about three feet, then, signaled to his friend to come. They left unchallenged from the silent nightclub. The next day, Tommy Lee headed east/northeast to Saratoga in New York State. He would spend the next bit of time in Saratoga Springs at the harness track. He figured that the Syracuse Police Department might be on his ass.

The experience engraved a few lessons into Tommy Lee. He could destroy most people, he could make money as a bouncer and, he could begin to explore the role of enforcer. Getting paid to beat the living hell out of people sounded pretty good to him. His exhilaration from the Syracuse experience gave him a strange sense of relaxation. The women in upstate New York were indeed safe, since when Tommy Lee was relaxed and feeling good, his need to murder abated.

Barry Fisk got Eddie Fox's Social Security number from the database in the Illinois Motor Vehicle Bureau. It took him about forty-five minutes of intense work to break into the system. From there he pulled up Fox's records from the State of Illinois' system. Fox was born in 1950 in Cairo, Illinois. He had attended Southern Illinois University in 1968 for two years. He dropped out in 1970 at the most intense times of the student-protest movement.

Fisk stopped at this point and accessed the Selective Service System. He found out that Fox was given a 4-F classification because of a heart murmur. He then buried himself into the records of Southern Illinois University. He found out that Fox was a declared business major, with a cumulative G.P.A. of 1.73, when he left Southern Illinois. Fisk thought this was pretty hard to do in those days when profs were skittish about giving any student less than a C and, thereby risking them to a draft call. His ACT score was a cumulative 17, which threw him into the lower end of the normal range.

Fox's driving record showed two DWIs, one in 1980 and one again in 1991. On both, he was convicted with alcohol counts of 2.5 and 2.6, respectively.

His employment record was pursued in the files of the United States Trotting Association and the Illinois Racing Board. It was clear that his entire work history involved racing, primarily harness, but some thoroughbred. The two big facts that he knew that McAbee would want was that Fox had worked at the Quad Cities Oval in 1987 when Erin Tobin was killed and that he was presently employed at Sportsman's Park, which was engaged in its harness meet.

His credit record showed a man who was broke, with credit card balances on Visa for $10,771, Mastercard for $9,310, Standard Oil for $971 and Discover for $6,413.

Every card, except for Standard Oil, had put an end to his charging. He was probably beleaguered by collectors. Although he couldn't find any way to get at his gambling proclivities, Fisk inferred from what he saw that Eddie Fox was a troubled creature.

He backtracked through his records to 1987. He was showing signs of trouble even then. In 1989, he filed bankruptcy, which successfully got him out from under $22,000 of debt. Fisk felt anger at the derelict credit card companies which encouraged debt and eventual bankruptcy, only to make the honest ones pay for characters like Eddie Fox.

Fox had been married once. It had lasted two years. There were no children. Chalk that miracle up to modern contraceptive methods, he thought to himself, while shaking his head in disgust. To Fisk, Fox was simply an irritant in society; essentially a useless man playing rogue elephant and probably hurting all sorts of people who came into his path. But he felt, for reasons that he couldn't articulate, that Eddie Fox was probably not a murderer. He phoned McAbee, who was not there so he gave the information to the peppery bitch, Pat. The fact of the matter was that she scared him, he admitted to himself.

When McAbee got back to his office, he was gladdened by the work of Fisk. To his mind, Fox's motive was apparent - he needed money. When that itch came, he was prepared to do some dirty things. How and if Erin Tobin got into his cross hairs was still unknown, but a possible picture was beginning to emerge.

In the meantime, McAbee found out that the Quad

Cities Oval did not keep any records of gate sign ins. They were disposed of within the week of their usage. Accordingly, there was no way to access any data about arrivals and departures on the night of Erin's death.

If, in fact, Eddie Fox was in some way associated with Erin's death, perhaps it was due to betting processes at the Quad Cities Oval. McAbee thought back to his visit with Jim Panayotounis and decided to make appointments with the two men that Panayotounis had recommended he visit.

Ray Ashburn was Panayotounis' saint. If all the harness horsemen were like him, it would forever remain a sport and be honest, was Panayotounis' contention. Ashburn lived just south of the small town of DeWitt, which was about twenty miles north of Davenport, in Iowa. He was a farmer. He told McAbee on the phone that he could just spare little time, but he was welcome.

Ashburn was about seventy years of age, white haired, wearing a green, sun-bleached, Deere baseball cap. He sat on his porch watching McAbee come toward the house.

"Morning."

"Ray Ashburn?"

"That's right. Grab a seat. Takin' a break right now, so this is a good time, but a short time. I've got to get back in the fields again; busy time around here now. What can I do for you?" He pushed his bifocals up to his eyes and squinted across to McAbee.

"I'm looking into a possible crime at the old Quad Cities Oval. Frankly, I'm trying to ascertain a motive. I've come up with one main candidate- money. As I mentioned on the phone, Jim Panayotounis recommended you highly. So I'm here."

"Jim Panayotounis! A shrewd man." He sat back, took off his glasses and stared at them as though they were some kind of crystal ball. "You know, I was no big bettor. I'd usually put five or ten across on my own horses and just stop at that. If they were going good, I'd show a little profit. I didn't stable there. I'd ship in from out here. But I was aware of all the crap that went on at that backstretch. To me, it was always the joy of watching your animal perform. It wasn't a money thing. You know, farmers are exhibitionists at heart. That's what county fairs are all about; I grow better stuff than you do. A horse is just an extension of that. Harness racing goes all the way back to the nineteenth century. It is not that far off from chariot racing. Where does that put us: 2000, 2500, 3000 years?"

McAbee knew what Panayotounis meant. This guy was one of the 20 percent, a lover of the sport and probably honest to a fault. "I guess it's the backstretch I'm interested in. What crap are you talking about?"

"Drugs and race fixing."

"I understand that the State of Illinois is pretty vigilant about drugs."

"They are, but trainers are pretty vigilant about staying on the end of the curve. At any rate, they'd catch some of the dumber ones and hang 'em up by their balls!" He chuckled. "But it was the fixing that really irritated me. A drug is a drug, after all. Sometimes a bozo would spend his entire waking week trying to figure out how he could beat the urine and blood samples, only to find out that the drug had no impact on performance anyway. But fixing is another question. I saw it sometimes and so did the fans."

"Fans? You mean bettors."

"No, I mean fans!" His adamant response caused McAbee to straighten up. "There were a lot of people out there who watched the beauty of this sport, its rhythm, its skill, its sheer simplicity. They were the fans. The bettors!" he said acidly. "They would bet on rats if you were racing them. They're the addicts who'd sell their wife and children for a tip on a sure thing. When they started to infiltrate the backstretch, we were in trouble. They were the fixers."

"Who drove for you?"

"My son, Larry. He's out of the business now. When the Oval closed, so did we. Larry's a mechanic in Kansas City. They'd approach him, tell him to duck his horse and finish out of the money. You know, if you know the favorite is a non-factor, you can make a lot of money betting the gimmicks. We always told them no, but that never stopped them from trying."

"You say 'they.' Who's that?"

Ashburn put on his glasses again and looked at McAbee. "The trick in the backstretch is that you never knew who was speaking for whom. But, there were some trainers and drivers who were into it heavily, which meant one or two races a night. Most of the races weren't fixed."

"Let me see if I understand this. Let's say they wanted you in and you refused to participate. How could they fix the race?"

"Let's say my horse was a 2-1 favorite. Let's say he was a front-ender, which means he'd take the lead. Larry would send him flying out of the gate. Now, you can get a lead real quickly or you have to work for it and use your horse. Most horses usually have only one good move. When you use it, he's done. If Larry has to use his horse hard to get the lead, he's taken something out of him. Now, let's say he gets the lead, but instead of slowing down the race to preserve his horse's energy, another horse immediately challenges him. Our horse is getting worn down. By the time we hit three-quarters of a mile, he's exhausted. The horses that have been coasting in the pack now make their move and probably beat us at the finish. So, my point here is this, if you had three or four drivers in on a fix in an eight-horse field, they would sacrifice one or two to get you out also. As a bettor, if you know how the race would go, you could make $70 or $80, let's say, by having an exacta. You put that bet down ten times and you've got $700 tax free. That's why the State of Illinois is so vigilant. If the fans and bettors get the idea that the sport is rigged, it's all over. But the crooks could care less."

"You mentioned drivers and trainers. How about track management?"

"Panayotounis? No, he was honest. But there were some others ... I forget their names, but I had the feeling."

"Eddie Fox? Remember him?"

He hesitated and then said, "Look, I don't have any direct evidence, but he was one of the characters I heard about. He never bothered me, but I heard some stories."

"One more question, Ray. Do you remember Erin Tobin?"

His body snapped to attention. "Jesus! I hope that she's not part of this inquiry. I only knew her by reputation, saying "hi," chatting with her once in a while, that sort of thing. Nobody would ever shake her down. A gritty woman! You're not suggesting anything about her death are you?"

"I'm looking into it."

"Look! I only heard of one incident when someone was beaten up over supposedly violating some arrangement. Panayotounis got rid of all of them in a snap! I just can't believe it. Murder?"

"What if someone came to threaten her. How would she react?"

"Well, there you have a point! She'd be tough. She'd probably fight back! But I thought that Cassies Ruler got the best of her. Jesus, I hope this isn't going anywhere."

"I don't know yet, Ray. I'm still nibbling at the corners. There may be nothing to it."

"Well, I'll just repeat my rule of thumb to you. You never know who's speaking for whom on a racetrack. Good luck!"

McAbee drove off the farm and headed back on Route 61 to Davenport. Eddie Fox was still hanging around the killing scene that was in McAbee's mind. The more he heard, the more he wanted to go to Orville Tobin, who was probably sitting near his phone anticipating this bum's call to him. For $3,000, Scholz could break him like a twig. His promises to Tobin and his desire to get at Fox were in direct opposition to each other. He figured that he'd take a trip to Springfield, Illinois and speak with Tom Barley, the trainer/driver that Jim Panayotounis said was half angel and half devil. He also remembered that Rickie had worked for Barley.

Fisk continued his work on the eight names that he had tabbed as potential suspects. It bothered him that the entire investigation lacked a smoking gun, that it was still based on conjecture.

He ravaged the database of the Illinois Racing Board, the United States Trotting Association (USTA) and the principal state agencies where harness racing existed. These included Maine, Massachusetts, Pennsylvania, New York, New Jersey, Delaware, Maryland, Florida, Kentucky, Ohio, Indiana, Illinois, Michigan and California. He also tapped into Canada, namely, Ontario and Quebec.

Three of the names simply disappeared. He ran their Social Security numbers and found that one of them was in prison in Joliet. He noted that McAbee thought that the murderer was free and alive. So he put that name aside. One of them was in a terminal cancer ward in a state facility in Tulsa, Oklahoma. He put him aside. He still had six. Of these, five were still active in the business. He noted that two of them typically left the Quad Cities Oval every late May or early June. Thus he excluded them. They seemed to be in the yearling business and would go back down to a farm in Georgia until the next spring when they would bring up some new stock for sale. One left the business and disappeared from the USTA. Checks of his Social Security number indicated that he was in Las Vegas, a blackjack dealer. He excluded him. He was down to three. He felt stymied; however, three names weren't bad. He dug into the backgrounds of each but to no effect. He decided to stop for the night. His computer had been hacking at all day. He figured that they were both exhausted. He wrote the three names on his pad: Otis Aronson, John Harbitt and Tommy Lee. All three of them were interesting.

When McAbee arrived back in his office, he sat down and thought about the case. His mind went around and around then he reached his conclusion. It was time to level with Orville Tobin and get his OK to move in on Fox.

Eddie Fox was jubilant- $50,000 to the penny. He couldn't believe his luck. But he felt angry at himself. This money was easy-getting. He wondered how much more he could stick the old man for. It would take some thinking.

CHAPTER 12

Tom Barley stabled in Springfield, Illinois, at the County Fairgrounds. Except for the Great State of Illinois Fair, which occurred for ten days in August, there was no parimutuel racing in Springfield. Barley had a ship-in stable. This meant that he would haul his horses to the Chicago harness meet north on U.S. 55 into Chicago and, occasionally, to Fairmount Racetrack in Collinsville, Illinois, south on U.S. 55. It was a five hour trip each way to Chicago, but only about two hours each way to Collinsville. Barley worked about eighteen hours a day on average. He was born in Paris, Missouri, and was proud of that, his individualism and his extraordinarily thick accent.

Barley was always armed. He carried a derringer behind his right ankle and a knife behind his left ankle. His territoriality was respected, he knew, because of his willingness to take up any gauntlet thrown down to him. His third wife, a full-blooded American Indian of Navajo origin, was a little too flirtatious for his blood. Because of this, three horsemen had been subjected to serious beatings by the wiry, 5-foot-10-inches, 160- pound Barley. "If you're fooling with my wife, you're fooling with me." This thinking extended to his stable, which was successful but hampered by the constant hauling back and forth to the harness meets. He chose not to stable in Chicago because there were "too many niggers, spies and lowlifes hanging around the backstretch up there."

It was 12:30 p.m. when McAbee came into his barn. He had called and because he used the name of Panayotounis, Barley had consented to speak with him-"off the record or not talking."

"Tom Barley? Bertrand McAbee."

"Yes ... OK ... got one chore to do. Just make yourself comfortable." Barley knew that this city stiff could never make himself comfortable in a barn with grooms walking around with shovels of straw and horseshit, horses rearing up, horses kicking stable walls and a few, if you got too close, trying to take a bite out of your shoulder. Barley kept an occasional eye on him. For a newcomer, he was handling it OK. Eventually, McAbee took the wisest course. He walked out through the open barn doors and stood outside.

McAbee was watching a vet across the path at another barn inspect a horse's foot. The vet was saying: "Looks like I'll have to X-ray. I can't feel anything unusual, but she's definitely favoring the leg. The way she walks it looks like the foot."

"So you're from the Quad Cities." McAbee stiffened as Barley knew he would, having been caught off guard.

"Yeah, yeah, I am."

"You haven't been round horses, have you?"

"No, not really. I used to watch the Lone Ranger and Tonto. Does that count?"

Barley laughed loudly. "Good line. I like that. Good line. Let me show you a few of my stock."

He took McAbee to the middle of two long, parallel rows of stalls, eighteen on each side. Barley had each stall filled and was damn proud of it. The Barley barn had, in fact, forty-seven horses in all and had monthly billings of over $37,000 to various owners and partnerships. He was running a small but successful business. No one was to screw with him.

"Let me show you something." He went into a stall, led out a big, beautifully proportioned horse and put him in the ties. He went forward about twenty feet and took out another horse. It was the smallest one that he had in the barn and by Barley's norms, the ugliest and most awkward-looking beast he'd been around in some years. He was put in another set of ties.

"Take a look at these two. What can you tell me?" McAbee moved behind the first. Barley said, "Now don't you get too close to those hind feet; the big boy kicks sometimes. If he catches you, he can kill you or break a leg or make a gelding outta you." McAbee backed up quickly.

He watched McAbee walk around the first one. Finally McAbee said, "Well, he looks like a champ to me; beautiful face, aggressive eyes, conformation looks terrific. I don't know. I guess he's the star of your barn."

"You know what he cost a partnership two years ago at a sale?- $73,000! Can you believe that? And then you look at him and you see champion. Everybody was smelling the roses! We didn't cut him either; thought he'd make a big time sire for us."

McAbee said, "That is a lot of money. How old is he?"

"Three. Now take a look at this one. You can walk close to him. He doesn't kick."

After about thirty seconds, McAbee said, "Well, he's pretty small. He's real tame and gentle." McAbee ventured to pet him on the nose, "I'm not sure about him. I think though, if it were a beauty contest, he'd only win if it were for the homeliest."

"You got that right. I got him for $2,000 from an Amish farmer in Kalona, Iowa. He was three. The guy swore to me that he'd be pretty handy, especially on smaller tracks, like Maywood in Chicago. Now I don't trust nobody in this business. I mean, they'll sell you their filthy pig and tell you the horse is the next Beach Towel." He paused, aware that McAbee was probably thinking about some towel on a beach. "Oh, by the way, Beach Towel was a great pacer. So, I don't know. I always feel sorry for those bearded bastards trying to live in the nineteenth century in these times, so I bought him. They raced him five times in some dinky little fairs around Iowa. His name ...," he laughed in a short and sarcastic way, "his name is fucking Mr. Good. Can you believe that? And once they're raced, you can't change their name. Imagine me with Mr. Good?" He laughed again and hit his thigh. "But, I know something else. Those Amish don't usually lie. So anyway, I got him down here and started training him. Good on small tracks ain't the half of it. He turns out to be so quick and maneuverable, I can't believe it. He also had three moves in him. Almost every pacer has one good move. For some of them, it's five seconds. The good ones have two, the great ones three and the champs, well, there's just one big move all around the fucking track!" Barley noted that McAbee had good eyes and knew how to listen.

"So, Mr. Good, I take him up to Maywood and put him in an $8,000 claimer, figuring that no one would touch him and they didn't. He takes the lead outta the seven hole, so he's way outside. I had to use him once just for that. So, some dumb shit comes up and challenges us as soon as the quarter mile's done. I'm not going let him get in front of me, 'cause I think Mr. Good might quit if I let this asshole by me. I didn't know him well enough then, so I worried about that. So, I have to use him again to hold off that charging son of a bitch on my outside. You know, Maywood is just a half-mile track, so you go around it twice. It's almost a circle. Because of that, if you're on the front end, you always have the advantage. And, if your horse is handy, since you always seem to be turning at that track, you're in a great situation. When someone has to pass you, they always have to run extra feet, so you keep them out there if you can. It's called parking them. You park a horse, you keep him outside and let him suck air. Well, anyway, we put that bastard to rest, but we hit the half in 57.1; that's brutal for $8,000 claims. So, I figured we're done. Right away, we got challenged again. He puts that bastard away and I haven't even touched my whip. Well, to make a long story short, we win by eight lengths and he cuts the mile in 1:55 flat. That's the last fucking time I ever exposed him to a claimer. You know how much he's made me over four years?- $271,000! Breeding stinks, looks like crap, warms up like he's gonna fall over, but he has the heart of a goddamn lion." He patted him on the flank and walked back to the looker. "Now this one, $73,000, you know what he's made the partnership?- $250! The big piece of shit." He proceeded to slap the big pacer's face. "Useless. Has the heart of a worm. Best breeding money can buy-useless! He's like one of those empty-headed fuckers in a gym, lifting weights, real cute, useless!" He laughed. "Now, what can I do for you, Bertrand?"

"When the Quad Cities Oval was still open, how much race fixing was there?"

Barley's head went back for about three inches. He wasn't about to share this with McAbee. McAbee must have seen this because he said, "Look, Tom, whatever you say to me is confidential. I'll never use it or report it. I'm not wired. You can search me if you'd like."

"OK, I want to search you." He did a thorough job. After all, he thought, if it was itching him, he might as well scratch it. After the search, he said, "Why you want to know this?"

"Fair enough. I'm looking into the killing of Erin Tobin. Some information has been handed over that suggests she was murdered. I'm looking into motive. Also, I'd like to have your thoughts about Rickie."

Barley pointed to a closed tack trunk and said, "Sit down. In my judgment, about one race a night was fixed and there'd be different people in on it. I wouldn't do it, but I'll tell you, I wouldn't interfere with it when I saw it. So I was a passive participant, I'd guess you'd say."

"How come you didn't tell anyone?"

"Cause you'd get run off the track and where the hell would I go? Springfield wasn't an option for many of those years."

"How about Panayotounis?"

"Nah, he wasn't in it, but he had to know."

"Erin Tobin?"

"No way. She was a tough little babe. She wouldn't do it. We all know who they were."

"Didn't anyone ever say anything?"

"Yeah, back in the late seventies or early eighties a guy named John Rawls ... he was a trainer and a driver... went to the stewards and complained. Next morning, he came to his barn and two of his horses were dead; poisoned. That night his pacer was tested for illegal drugs. The test showed the pacer was full of some illegal shit; automatic suspension for six months. Listen, the barn areas are unprotected and open all night. If someone wants to fuck you, they can. Rawls never recovered. Everyone knew why it happened! Someone had drugged that horse. Rawls was honest!"

"And Erin Tobin?"

"I talked with her once in a while. She was a straight shooter."

"Could she have run afoul of these characters?"

"Sure, easy. Especially for a young idealist."

"If I told you that maybe she was murdered, would it surprise you?"

"Yes and no. Cassies Ruler was a crazy-assed bastard, but she was no fool. If you work around a horse like that, you're always on your toes. I was surprised when I heard. But, intimidation is one thing; murder is something else. Can't help you there."

"Tell me about Rickie, your groom. Apparently, he suicided on that same night."

"Never could figure that out. It was just too damn complicated. He was dumber than a fucking board. I had

to think, and still do, that someone helped him. I felt sorry
for the bastard. What can I say?"

"I have one more name that I'd like a reaction
to -Eddie Fox."

"Toilet paper! He was one of them. Anything else?"

"No ... oh, by the way, you told me Mr. Good's name.
What about Adonis over there? What's his name?"

Barley laughed. "You got me there. I was too embarrassed
to tell you. Money Mongrel!"

McAbee drove back from Springfield and arrived in
Aledo at 7:00p.m. Orville Tobin was rocking back and forth
with a beer in his hand when McAbee walked up the three
steps to the porch.

"Grab a seat, Bertrand. Beer?"

"No thanks." McAbee saw him as pretty relaxed. He
wondered how many beers had been consumed.

"Hear anything yet, Orville?"

"Not a word."

"Orville, you told me at the outset not to interfere with
your relationship with this guy. And I told you I wouldn't
but that I was in charge of the situation. Now, neither of us
are fools. We both know that there's a gray area in these two
positions. Would you agree?"

"Of course. You hit it right on the head. I would have
said no if you said you'd interfere, and you would have
walked out if I said you weren't in charge of the investigation.
So, I don't know why you're bringing this up, unless there's
been some tinkering in that gray area. I know that I haven't
been doing that. So, I guess the ball's in your court." His

look told McAbee that it was his show. Orville had nothing more to say.

"Orville, you know that there's a very good chance that this guy will never call you again or that he might try to hit you up for more money and still never give you anything."

"Yup. It's a possibility. But, it's my money, like I told you." He had stopped rocking.

"Just out of curiosity, would you give him any more money?"

"I just don't know. Maybe. But I know that I'd deal with him more strongly than I have. Why do you ask?"

"Because I have his name and address. In fact, I have his phone number, too. He's working right now and he has an answering machine. Would you care to hear his voice?"

Tobin looked at McAbee through very narrow slits in his eyes. After some twenty seconds, he said, "Well, I thought as much. I just wasn't sure what you'd do. Yeah, I do want to call this number. I should be able to ID his voice."

They went into the house. Orville dialed the number that McAbee gave to him, but only after accepting McAbee's advice to hit *67 before dialing so as to defeat any caller ID system that Fox might be using. Tobin listened, then hung up the phone. He gave McAbee the closest thing to a smile that McAbee ever saw from him. "Well, I'll be damned! You sure do have him. But my question is this - does he know you have him?"

"No, we're about as certain as you can be. It cost you a lot of money to get those probabilities. At this moment, I have a great deal of information about him. McAbee recounted to Tobin the data that Fisk had managed to come up with, especially emphasizing the bankruptcies and the heavy indebtedness. When he was finished, Tobin said, "So, what you're saying is that he just might come back and hit me for more?"

"No, not necessarily. Look, Orville, maybe he'll be true to the deal. Maybe he'll call you tonight and hit you with the name of the murderer. But, I don't think so. There is no evidence to support this guy as being a noble person. What he did to you is extortion and if, in fact, there was a murder, he's an accessory. He's in big trouble. You could argue that his best move would be to shut down his transmitter right now and disappear back into the mountains. If he fingers the murderer, after all, he himself just might be fingered in turn."

"So what are you saying to me?" Orville asked impatiently.

"I said that I wouldn't interfere in your relationship with this guy. But, Orville, he's a small time crook."

"It's important to me to be honest!" Tobin said brusquely.

"Honest with a dishonest man?" McAbee was getting angry and caught himself.

"Look, I know that this sounds strange, but I made a deal and I think that I should keep it. Even now, since I've been involved with you, I've made inroads on the relationship, taping his calls, and now this? I feel like I'm cheating him."

McAbee could not get his mind around what Orville was telling him. It seemed to McAbee to be honoring some code that was indefensible and outlandish. Tobin continued. "Look, let me put it this way. We're into an investigation, and we've opened up possibilities due to one single occurrence - this guy called me! I feel a certain debt to him. Don't you see my point?"

"Yes. Grudgingly, I do. But here's my rejoinder to you.

Myself and a few of my associates would like to go up and visit with him. We think that we could break him and get from him whatever he might know about Erin's death."

"Me and my associates? Will you beat him?" McAbee was flustered by this severe moralizing.

He moved close to Tobin. He looked the old man in the eye before saying, "Look, Orville - what happened to your daughter? To Erin? If it was a murder, it was pretty gruesome and vicious. Why are you playing sponge ball with a hardball man?"

Orville Tobin went into his house and fetched another can of beer. He sat down. "So, if I give you a green light, you go to him and ask him questions? And what if he says no? What if he says I never did this? I don't have his money -you're a liar!"

"Do you have a VCR?"

"Yup."

McAbee went to his car and drew out a briefcase. He said to Tobin, "Let's go in and watch a little television." McAbee gave Tobin the tape for his VCR. The first minute showed, in a greenish overlay but with very good picture fidelity, Orville dropping money at the site. Orville sat forward as he viewed it. There was a break. Then, he saw twelve minutes of tape introducing a car coming from a bar across and up the road, to the same car driving away from the scene.

"And, who is this man?"

"The same- Eddie Fox!"

"Wow! They said you were good. What can I say?"

"Say, Bertrand, go up and talk with him."

Tobin was silent for a good bit of time. Finally, he said:

"If and when he calls and he wants more money, I'll be in touch. We'll make the decision then. I feel right about that. Let's do it that way, Bertrand."

Gloria Power heard McAbee drive into his garage. It was almost 10:00 p.m. She heard Scorpio let out an anticipatory bark, then a low whine that was a mixture of relief and anticipation. She turned on her light and went out outside to meet McAbee as he closed his garage door.

Gloria was sixty-four, a widow with a very narrow, solitary life. She had a sister who lived in Omaha who she would visit once a year for about three days. She had two children, one of whom she lost to cancer two years ago. Her daughter lived in Dubuque and would occasionally visit. Her only real friends in the complex were McAbee and, before she left, his estranged wife, Beth. She worried about McAbee, who she felt was in the wrong business.

Her deceased son had taken McAbee's class in Ancient Philosophy. He had loved it and had remarked that McAbee came alive when he talked about the old sages. Gloria had seen her own husband make a job switch from being a manager at the local Sears store to a salesman for filter systems at a local company. She put down his fatal heart attack to that dubious job switch.

She didn't see McAbee fitting the dirty world that he had to navigate as a PI. But, he never asked her opinion and she wasn't about to say anything, although she did say a few things to Beth, who became, as she grew older, crustier and edgier. Beth had picked up an attitude and it sure showed. The more she became involved with bicyclists, the more she started to measure her life by speed and endurance and, abandon McAbee to his own life. Although Bertrand might have been surprised at the abrupt departure, she sure wasn't.

She thanked God for the dog, because McAbee had sunk into himself. He became less and less forthcoming, in her judgment. She observed that he seemed to be going through the motions, waiting or hoping for some new message to appear on the horizon. She met him at the run.

"Bertrand, I've been with him a few times. Don't let him fool you. He's not as sad as he lets on."

"Gloria, I don't know what I'd do without you. I'd have to give him up. No one's going to take on a neurotic, four-year-old German Shepherd. So, literally, you're a life saver. How are you?"

"Oh, everything is the same. My daughter has a new boyfriend. I didn't think that there were that many possible boyfriends in Dubuque, but she finds them."

"That's a problem with beauty. It draws the hunters."

"Yes. Well that's a nice, polite way to say it," she said ruefully.

McAbee hadn't opened Scorpio's locked cage door. The dog was beginning a demanding barrage of barks while galloping up and down through his run, leaping loudly against the wire fence.

"I have some leftover stew. Would you like it?" She already knew the answer, but just in case, she thought she'd ask. McAbee was very perceptibly becoming a vegetarian of sorts. Meat meals like stew, although she knew that he was tempted, were probably seen as evil temptations. She knew that he was a fanatic about his weight, even more so with Beth's departure.

"Thanks, but I've already eaten, Gloria." She suspected that he was lying, but what could she do? He continued, "I guess I'll have to walk this big guy and then hear all about the many intruders that he chased away all day." He smiled. Gloria knew that it was his way of saying, get lost. He was typically polite, but if you didn't get the subtleties of his messages, he could be abrupt.

"Now you take care of yourself, Bertrand! You worry me." She felt obligated to, at least, say that to him as she walked away. She heard Scorpio's gate open amid the joyous barks and yaps of the big white shep. Just as she was about to close her door, she heard McAbee say, "Damn it, Scorpio, down." She figured that the good dog had done in another pair of McAbee's pants.

CHAPTER 13

Doctor Dan Dugan worked for the California Corrections Department. His job involved pre-trial assessment and recommended placement of violent offenders. He had been with the Corrections Department for twelve years and in this California program had dealt with thousands of violent offenders. He was confident that within a half hour he could get enough of an angle on a prisoner to make a reasonably solid and defensible recommendation. Dugan had a doctorate in Counseling Psychology from Southern California University. He figured that his being an ex Marine captain made him an ideal choice for the job.

He had left the Atascadero area two years previous for Sacramento where he oversaw the work of two other counselors. It was 1991. Dugan had had a long day dealing with the animals sent to him. His recommendations were usually adhered to by the judges, but not always. Dugan felt that California was still dealing with the liberal freaks who were nominated over the years. The last appointment on his calendar read, Tommy Lee. He picked up the thin file and scanned it.

Tommy Lee was in California because he was a groom at CAL EXPO, a harness track in Sacramento. He had been there for seven months. He had been arrested on June 4 for having severely beaten a man by the name of Jimmy Smith who, supposedly, had come to the rescue of Letoya Mills, a prostitute. An addendum had straightened out the relationship - Letoya was being protected by her pimp, Jimmy.

Tommy Lee had claimed that Letoya had taken $25 from him, but refused to perform. He then claimed that she tried to scratch him, at which time, he hit her in self-defense. She was now missing five teeth. Tommy Lee said to the arresting officer, "I barely touched her." As he tried to drive away with the unconscious Letoya, he was confronted by Jimmy Smith who had pulled open the passenger door of Tommy Lee's pickup in order to free Letoya. At this point, Tommy Lee rushed from his truck where he encountered the now knife-wielding Smith who had placed the unconscious Letoya on the sidewalk. Jimmy Smith succeeded in slicing Tommy Lee's left arm, but it was costly. Tommy Lee broke his jaw, snapped his right arm and severely incapacitated the man's genitals through several brutal kicks, before a police car happened by. When asked why he was leaving the scene with Letoya, he claimed that he was taking her to a hospital for emergency treatment.

Both Jimmy Smith and Letoya Miles had long records of petty crime, shakedowns and robberies. It was in Dugan's mind that here was a typical pimp whose relationship was marked by drug addiction and violence. Dugan's first instinct was to see it as a deal gone awry; they had shaken down the wrong john and got a good beating for their trouble. Now, it was a matter of how to dispose of Tommy Lee.

Tommy Lee entered his office with a swagger and a look that went right after Dugan who wondered if he missed something in the file about Tommy Lee having been a Marine. Whatever, as far as Dugan was concerned, he was in charge and no convict was going to set the tone of the meeting.

"Sit down," Dugan said coarsely, as he pointed to a soft, low chair in front of his tall rocker. When Tommy Lee sat, he appeared to become much smaller, almost as if he had the power to diminish himself. But Dugan could see the coiled qualities of this man. He wondered how the two streetwise blacks could be so stupid.

"Let me explain what this session is all about. You've been charged with a felony. I'm to prepare a pre-trial profile about you which will go to the trial judge. It will influence his jury instructions and also your sentencing if you're found to be guilty. It pays to cooperate with me. Do you understand?" Tommy Lee had stopped giving him eye contact after his mention of a felony.

Dugan let the silence between the two sit until finally, Tommy Lee said, "I understand. Is that what you wanted from me?"

"Yeah, but with an emphasis that tells me you'll cooperate. Will you or won't you?"

"I said I would when I said I understood." Tommy Lee drove his eyes into him.

Dugan wrote down "Smart-assed punk" next to Tommy Lee's name.

"So, tell me about yourself."

Tommy Lee looked at him as though he were from Mars. Dugan figured that this man probably had no idea how to answer such a personal question. He wrote down "constipated Neanderthal."

"I work at racetracks. I'm a groom and stable hand."

"Graduate from high school?"

"No, and I'm not interested in a GED, if that's going to be part of this horseshit deal!"

"Well, let me put your mind to rest. It's not. What it's about is sending you to jail for a few years, buster. Am I clear?" He wrote down "has balls."

"So, you dropped out of high school? From where?"

"Cazenovia, New York."

"And?"

"And what? I got a job grooming and that's what I've done."

"We have a police report from Florida, 1981. Says you were arrested for a double rape. They think you intimidated the two girls." Dugan let it sit, seeing this as one of his great tactics.

"Don't know anything about that. Never did."

"You mean that you didn't do it?"

"Of course. Why would I rape someone when I can get anything I want for free. Give me a break!"

"What about the whore you punched out? Was she free?" Dugan was trying to anger this character.

"That was nothing. Just a quick screw and home to bed."

"Nothing? I thought you paid."

"Twenty-five bucks! A nothing bitch, a nothing price."

"So, why did you beat her?"

"I told her what I wanted when I paid. She said OK. Then she starts to fuck around with me. She wants more money and she tries to scratch me. I defended myself. I just tapped the whore once. What was I supposed to do? Let her have her way because she's a nigger?"

"Racist" got on Dugan's pad, as he asked tauntingly, "I still don't understand. If you're so hot, why are you paying for it?"

"Because every once in a while I like it that way; down and dirty; fuck 'em and leave 'em. Is that some big problem?" He was starting to bulk up a bit. His eyes were beginning to challenge Dugan's again. He didn't seem to know fear.

"You ever in the Marines?"

"Why, so I could have some crazy DI fucking with my head? No way!"

"I was a Marine. Just thought I'd ask." Dugan couldn't believe the audacity of this guy. "What do you mean fucking with your head?"

"Just like what yuh trying to do right now?"

"I'm trying to help you, mister, and you're just digging a hole for yourself."

"I told yuh about the whore. The pimp was no different. He came out of the shadows and pulled a knife on me. And I did what any self-respecting Marine would do - didn't I? I beat the shit out of him. And nothing would have come of this if a cop car hadn't come onto the scene. And yuh know it." His voice had risen along with a new intensity.

"What else would you have done to this couple if the cops hadn't come?"

"Couple! What fucking couple are yuh talking about? Do yuh mean would I have hurt these two crooks anymore? No!" He was almost screaming now.

Dugan sat there and tried to keep his composure. He was quite sure that he wouldn't be able to beat off this freak if he came at him. The level of violence and anger in Tommy Lee's whole being was extraordinary. "So, this was pure self-defense?"

"Yuh got it, mister! And I'd do it again. Those two fuckers were lucky that I ... forget it."

"No, no, no. What?"

"Forget it."

"You were going to say kill, weren't you?"

"No! There's nothing else to say."

Dugan wrote on his pad: "Lethal! Watch out for this guy. Keg of dynamite." He sat for about forty seconds before saying to Tommy Lee, "Is there anything else you'd care to say to me? Is there anything the judge and jury should hear?"

"Fuck 'em all!"

Dugan was on his PC within a minute of Tommy Lee's departure.

> *Interviewed subject about crime. He's convinced that it is entirely the fault of the two disabled parties, as he sees only self-defense in his own self-analysis.*
>
> *He is a high school dropout with no marketable skills except for cleaning racetrack barns and helping around horses. His attitude toward women is primitive. There is undoubtedly a high amount of sexual aggressiveness and probably violence in him.*
>
> *In my judgment, he's a sociopath, incapable of experiencing guilt and*

> *without a clear and visible police*
> *presence, he would see the entirety of*
> *society as being fodder for his work*
> *and ambitions.*

> *I ask the court not to extend any*
> *largesse to this man and recommend*
> *hard time and perhaps a visit to*
> *Vacaville for further examination.*

On the eve of the trial, Tommy Lee's court appointed attorney, Nora Diego, came to the meeting area in the Sacramento Jail Building. The Assistant DA had taken a long look at the arrest report and was ready to deal. Diego told Tommy Lee that she made the Assistant DA realize that he'd look the fool for punishing a man who defended himself from a shakedown. The Assistant DA was prepared to make it a misdemeanor-solicitation for prostitution, a $250 fine and thirty days probation. She recommended it highly.

Nora Diego had just graduated from law school a year and a half ago. She received California licensure two months ago, having failed the bar exam on two separate occasions. She was quite proud of herself. She had just gotten this man's exposure taken from a possible four years imprisonment to a virtual nothing.

Tommy Lee agreed. The next day the deal with the Assistant DA became a reality. The Assistant DA and Nora Diego had dinner that night followed by celebratory sex with each other. Tommy Lee went back to the track and resumed his job, which was held for him. Dan Dugan's report was appended to Tommy Lee's file. It had never been read.

On the same night that McAbee was soliciting Orville Tobin to OK a direct move on Eddie Fox, Eddie Fox was in the clubhouse area of Sportsman's Park eating a steak and nursing a double Beam. He was troubled and anxious. He knew that there was more money out there and if he played it right, he could get some of it. The old man was a ripe target. Unconsciously, he would gulp a large drink of whiskey whenever he thought of the deal between him and the old man. The more he drank, however, the clearer the choice- screw the old man!

He was looking at the program and handicapping the eighth race when he peripherally saw a figure sit across from him. He had decided to bet on horse number two, Ancient Mariner, which he circled. He then looked up. Jesus, he thought, Tommy Lee. Does he know something? Could it be possible? Look at the sneer on the bastard.

"Mr. Fox. Yuh surely remember me from the Quad Cities Oval. Nice to see yuh again." He extended his right hand and sent shudders of pain through Fox's returned hand. Fox knew that he was sweating and probably turning pale. He saw that Tommy Lee was observing it all.

Oh, shit! Don't show fear to this madman. It's probably just coincidence and has nothing to do with calling Orville Tobin. "Just bluff it out," he told himself.

"I do remember you. What are you doing here?"

"Just grooming for the Grandino stable. No big deal. I thought I saw yuh the other day at the qualifiers, but yuh disappeared by the time I turned around. I was wondering if yuh saw me?"

"No, can't say I did," Fox lied, as he was beginning to regain his composure. "I thought you were gone from Illinois for good. In fact, I thought that I assisted you in that direction," he said sternly. Fox would use any tactic to get this fucking drifter out of the state. No one had to tell him how dangerous he was.

"That's not my understanding." Tommy Lee now shifted into a louder voice that surely he knew could be overheard by other diners. "Yuh paid me to get me out of yuh hair. I got out. But that deal's off."

Fox put his hand up. He was embarrassed as he looked around to estimate the potential damage done by this goon.

He leaned forward and said with low intensity, "Shut the fuck up. Don't you dare come up here and pull this crap on me." Fox was furious but knew that he was dealing with someone with no sense of shame and perhaps, he conjectured, no sense of guilt.

"I thought we were friends?" He said it sarcastically, telegraphing his knowledge that Fox wanted nothing to do with him.

"Friends, my ass. You had a job to do and you fouled it up big time. You already robbed me of some bucks back at the Quad Cities Oval. You're not getting anything else."

"I don't want any money from yuh. I just wanted to tell yuh that I was back and I'm willing to do odd jobs for yuh, if yuh'd like."

"Listen, I'm manager here. I can get you run out of here if I have to. As far as I'm concerned, you don't know me and I don't know you. That's what I prefer. So keep your distance."

Tommy Lee reached across the table and took the plate with the apple pie. He started to eat it and didn't say anything. Fox knew that he was in trouble. This guy would not go away unless he was paid to do so, but if he did that, he feared that Tommy Lee would forever be on his back.

Fox waived to the waiter, who came over instantly. "Yes, Mr. Fox?"

"Put this on my tab, AI, and give yourself 20 percent. Show this gentleman out when he's finished eating the apple pie." Fox didn't like the look that he got from Tommy Lee. It was at that point that he firmly decided to give Tommy Lee's name to Orville Tobin, if Tobin would give him another $50,000. Playing both ends against the middle sounded like a good tactic. Furthermore, he was only slightly drunk. He didn't see it as a rash decision.

By the time he got home, it was 11:00 p.m. He called Tobin. It rang four times before he answered drowsily.

"Yes?"

"Tobin, it's me. Everything went well the other night."

"Wait a minute, please." Before Fox could stop him, Tobin was gone but came back again after about thirty seconds.

"Yes? Yes? I'm here," Tobin said. "What was that all about?"

"Prostate, had to go to the bathroom," Tobin said.

"Well, something's come up. I can't give you the name unless you give me another $50,000. I guarantee you'll have it by tomorrow night at midnight. In fact, I'll tell you something else. I just talked to the bastard, so I can tell you where to get him. So, you're paying extra, but I'm saving you a lot of time. I want it tomorrow night, same time, same place."

"Yes ... one big problem. I thought that we had a deal."

"We did ... we do. It just is going to cost you more. Yes or no?"

"There may be a problem with that kind of cash."

"Just have it done!" He hung up.

Orville was proud of himself. He had gotten to the kitchen phone and taped the call. He had lots of problems, but his prostate wasn't one of them.

He called McAbee and played the tape, after which he asked McAbee, "What do you think?"

"Play it again for me, Orville."

When it was done, Orville said, "Well?"

"I think that you should let me have him tomorrow night. He violated the agreement. I think that he's just making a fool out of you, quite frankly."

"Yeah, yeah. I think you're right. Should I place a bag there?"

"Yes. Do everything as you would. Just put some newspaper in it. I'll get in touch with you as soon as I come up with something. OK?"

"You got it."

McAbee called Scholz and told him the situation. He wanted to pin down the flat $3,000 price. He also wanted to be present during the questioning.

Scholz said, "Are you sure about that? This won't be pleasant. And, if you interfere, I won't guarantee anything."

"Unless you're going to murder him, I won't interfere."

"Very well. I'll call you tomorrow with details. If I need to, I'll meet you at the whore's place."

"Just name it."

Immediately, after calling Scholz, McAbee called Fisk. "Yeah?"

"Barry, Bertrand. Hope you weren't sleeping."

"No, I wasn't. I'm still on these three characters. What a threesome. Could be any of them."

"I have some more news. This should help. The caller, Fox, claims he saw the guy tonight. Physically saw him. That means Chicago. Does that help?"

"Help? That does it. I think that it's a guy named Tommy Lee. He's in Chicago at Sportsman's right now."

"Great! Why don't you get me everything you can on him. This looks promising."

McAbee liked the way things were beginning to fit. He sat as Scorpio came to rest his head on his knee. McAbee had one commitment tomorrow, a guest lecture on Stoicism at St. Anselm University. A former associate, Paul Davidson, was out of town. McAbee had promised to cover his class. Davidson had asked him to spend his time talking about the Stoics and in particular, Marcus Aurelius and Epictetus. McAbee picked up his well-worn *Meditations* of Marcus Aurelius and the *Discourses* of Epictetus. He glanced through them and read some of his own notes on some passages.

After a half hour, he had isolated three passages, around which he would direct discussion and comment.

From Book VII of *Meditations*, he chose:

> *Consider thyself to be dead, and to*
> *Have completed thy life up to the present*

> *time, and live according to nature*
> *the remainder which is allowed thee.*

The Stoics, McAbee thought, were pictured by many as yielding to fate and throwing their hands up to forces way beyond them. His spin on the passage could argue that if we commit to a life of reason (live a life according to nature), we can change our entire life and not yield to the past and the mistakes of the past. It was never too late to change.

From Book XII, he chose:

> *If it is not right, do not do it.*
> *If it isn't true, do not say it.*

He intended to refer the passage to the politicians of America and ask whether a Marcus Aurelius would do well with the American electorate.

And finally from Epictetus' *Discourses*, he chose:

> *The difficulties of all men are*
> *about external things, their*
> *helplessness is about externals.*

He was prepared to speak to how the Epictetus saw the perfidy of external matters. The trick was to control your inner environment. He put the books away and played with Scorpio, who unlike the Stoics, was in no frame of mind to sit around. The old tennis ball rested between his teeth as he gnawed at it, waiting for McAbee to come to his senses and play with him. Each time McAbee looked at him, Scorpio would make a feinting move with his head, urging McAbee to throw the damp ball.

CHAPTER 14

McAbee entered the old building. It smelled like any old school building smelled, a mix of chalk, dust, creeping moldiness, wax and assorted other aromas that he didn't pursue because a student bumped into him, presumably on his way to another class.

The class had always been his favorite - "The History of Ancient Philosophy." Its continued offering at the university gladdened McAbee, who knew that its days were numbered in the coming ahistorical age. It was being taught in the appropriate building, at any rate.

Davidson, a philosopher by training, had assumed the course and was an effective teacher. This meant, of course, that he was removed from the classroom and placed in administration, the quirky logic of the current provost prevailing in the placement of "assets" as he would refer to them. Davidson felt compelled to teach one course per semester. He thus protects the birthright of philosophy.

As McAbee entered the classroom, he saw that there were six students in the room, a bad sign; still another arrow for the cost-cutting president to shoot at the indulgent humanities. They didn't look like the happiest of students, as they eyed McAbee in a way that suggested that all substitute teachers are scavengers and perhaps worse still, when found in electives. McAbee didn't have a class list. He asked each of the six students to put their names on tent cards that he had brought along.

"Thanks. My name is Bertrand McAbee. I'm subbing for Dr. Davidson who is out of town today. We're going to talk about Stoicism. In particular, the brand espoused by Marcus Aurelius and to a lesser extent, Epictetus. I used to teach this course here some years ago. It's good that it's still being offered. Comments about the Stoics?"

The silence that came over the room was uncomfortable, but McAbee let it sit there. After about twenty seconds, McAbee said, "I guess that I'd like to hear your thoughts first."

Judith offered: "They both seem to be so passive and remote. In my management course, we'd call them reactive and not proactive. They're like spectators."

"You mean in terms of the outside events that happen to them?"

"Yes. It's like they're waiting for the next stimulus so that they can say it was destiny and wash their hands of it."

He was about to call on Kathy when Travis said, "I think they're both jerks. They have nothing to say to me. Maybe some monks would like them, but not me."

"Jerk? Tell me what that means."

"They're just into themselves. Epictetus, especially, doesn't give a damn how he's perceived by others. In fact, he almost makes it an ethical obligation to piss on other people's observations."

"Both of you have read them. Interesting and timely comments. Let's explore." He pointed to Kathy who looked as though she was interested or at least thinking. His judgment on the other three was anchored into the body language that they emitted, which went from non-caring to hostility. At least the opinionated Travis spoke his mind.

Kathy said, "I think that Travis is off base when he picks on Epictetus for not being concerned with the perception of others. It seems to me, Travis, that that's what you're all about personally. You've been giving Davidson a hard time all semester with off-the-wall comments that I personally don't appreciate. But do you care?"

The gauntlet was tossed. Good for her. McAbee said to Travis, "Reaction?"

"Yeah, go straight to hell, Kathy; screw your opinion."

"That's my whole point. You just proved it. You don't give a damn about what other people think. It seems to me that Epictetus should be one of your heroes."

"I don't need some old Greek slave telling me about how to deal with other opinions! Snoop Doggy Dog tells me this stuff. So stuff it, Kathy." She shook her head and looked down.

"Let me understand you. Is it your aversion to antiquity that drives your opinion, or is it what he's saying?"

"No. I guess what he's saying isn't all that bad, really, but who needs this old crap? It's a world that's gone and their views are no longer relevant. They're like old dishwater, not much use to anyone."

McAbee asked the class, "Comments?" He waited. When it was clear that he would get nothing, he went back to the Judith, "When you say that they're reactive, is that true in all regards?"

"Yes, I think so."

"The inner life, too?"

"Well … OK … I see your point. Yeah. They're very proactive in the study of the inner world of thought and ideas. I buy that. But, they're active in a way that shuts out the outside world. It's like saying I can't control others, I can't control the material world and events and thus leave me to my garden, myself."

"Would you say they're reactive to the world outside or inactive?"

She paused awhile. "You know when they talk about proactive and reactive, I guess they don't talk about that, I mean your distinction between inactive and reactive. I don't know. I have to think about that."

McAbee said, "You know, I think the words 'I don't know' are extremely well-taken in a philosophy class."

McAbee managed to draw out the taciturn three, but only barely, as he took the class through an analysis of the three passages that he had selected from Marcus Aurelius and Epictetus. He concluded with the passage from Marcus Aurelius about not doing what is wrong and not saying what is false. He tied it to politics and quickly to interpersonal relations, finding that the cynicism toward politicians was so profound that the only discussion involved how much lying and bad things they did. In the personal relations category, there was more interest, because they had to live with the concept of truth telling and doing right on a daily basis.

It appeared that the more they could relate the material to their personal lives, the more enthusiastic they became. He entered the door of their feelings by asking, "Is it ever right to lie?" From there the conversation flew and the class became spirited. McAbee always felt the tug of not teaching and engaging in what he thought was the great profession. He wondered, however, if the students would ever think again of Marcus Aurelius or Epictetus.

Eddie Fox drove toward the Quad Cities, figuring that there was a 75 percent chance that Orville Tobin would come up with the money. Although he went back and forth, he was determined to call the old man and give him the name once he got back home and counted the money. He'd love to see that vicious bastard, Tommy Lee, squirm under a police investigation.

Jack Scholz was only going to use two other men for the busting of Eddie Fox. He considered that the breaking down of Fox would be comparatively easy, given the sloppiness of the man, which correlated with Scholz's sense of success. In his conversation with McAbee, he would call McAbee's mobile the minute Fox was taken to a safe haven. If Fox was true to form, his car would be removed to the Quad Cities Oval parking lot. When Fox had been broken, he would be driven back to his car for what Scholz saw would be a memorable trip back to Forest Park.

Pat came into McAbee's office and said, "Barry Fisk is here, as usual, unannounced. Do you want to see him?"

"Just give me about two minutes."

McAbee came out of his office and saw Fisk sitting uncomfortably on one of the chairs in the office.

"Barry, all set?" He scampered down from the chair and brought along his valise. To McAbee's eyes, the man was brimming with excitement.

When they were seated, Barry looked at McAbee and shook his head. "I have some disquieting news."

Fisk stopped, thus demanding that McAbee ask him, "What?" This was Fisk's way of developing an air of excitement and mystery. "What news, Barry?"

"I've been centering most of my work on this Tommy Lee.

I'll say right now, I don't know if he's a murderer or not. So you have to know that. But he is a working hypothesis and the more I get involved with him, the more I see a likely candidate.

"Explain."

"Well, for one, he was a professional boxer once. Although he didn't last long, he was clearly enough of a fighter to show that violence was compatible with his personality. I think that's important. He weighed in at 240 pounds as a heavyweight in the Cleveland Arena.

He won a bunch of fights before he got clobbered in his last. He disappeared only to show up back at the track again. He seems to have been committed to the track throughout his life, from the age of sixteen on. "How old is he now?"

"Thirty-three."

"OK, but, Barry, this in itself is interesting, but you've got more than this?"

"Yeah, I do. It's very speculative, but it's curious. Here's his history." He handed McAbee a sheet of paper that was, in effect, a vita of Tommy Lee.

Tommy Lee-b.	December 3, 1962, Baltimore, Md.
1977 Age 16:	Cazenovia, New York; high school dropout but licensed as a groom at Vernon Downs (NY)
1977-83 Age 16-21:	Pompano Race Track (FL), Northfield Harness Track (OH) (traveled back and forth to both)

1984 Age 22:   Northfield, Professional
Boxing

1984 Age 22:   Last fight; on to Vernon
Downs

1985 Age 23:   Vernon Downs, Saratoga
Harness Track (NY)

1986 Age 24:   Vernon Downs, Saratoga,
Pompano

1987 Age 25:   Quad Cities Oval (IL),
Northfield

1988 Age 26:   Meadowlands (NJ),
Vernon Downs, Bangor
Raceway (ME)

1989 Age 27:   Vernon Downs,
Buffalo Raceway (NY),
Pompano

1990 Age 28:   Big Red Mile (KY),
Pocono Downs (PA),
Vernon Downs

1991 Age29:   Woodbine (ONT),
Pompano, CAL
EXPO (CA)

1992 Age 30:   Vernon Downs, Hazel
Park (MI)

1993 Age 31:   Pompano,
Meadowlands (NJ)

1994 Age 32:   Pompano Vernon
Downs, Foxboro (MA)

1995 Age 33:   Pompano, Sportsman's (IL)

McAbee studied the sheet carefully and finally asked Fisk, "What am I supposed to make of this, Barry? We know from this that he's a gypsy of sorts and that he's been all over the U.S.A. Where are you going with this?"

"Well, the first thing I went after was any unusual barn deaths like Erin Tobin's. I didn't find any. So, if he killed her, he did it in a way that I couldn't pattern elsewhere. Then, I looked at barn deaths period. There was a questionable one in Pompano in 1982, but I let it go. Of course, this makes the whole thing look to be kind of unstable." He was continuing to clutch some sheets of paper as though he were Moses with the tablets. McAbee knew that he had other information up his sleeve.

"So, it looks as though you've hit a dead end?" McAbee asked coyly.

"Well, I did and I didn't. From what you said about the murder scene, Erin's skull was pretty much crushed. The contusions and bone damage were enormous. Nothing says, therefore, that the guy couldn't have punched her. After all, he's a trained, professional boxer."

"I agree with you. He could have beaten the daylights out of her and we wouldn't know it. A good M.E. could have probably picked it up but not after the screw-up. So, what did you do at this point?"

"I started to troll in some of these areas of the country, at the precise dates when he was in these areas. He has some arrests, but no convictions."

"How many?"

"Well, I looked and he's been in trouble with the law six times."

"And?" McAbee asked impatiently.

"I have a copy of the reports here." He handed them to McAbee who noted that he still had paper left in his hands. "I call your attention to Sacramento and Fort Lauderdale in particular. The others in Lexington, Cleveland, Boston and Toronto are of note, but the fullest of the two are as I noted. In every arrest there is violence attached and in five cases with women. The Lexington, Kentucky, one involved a beating of another stable hand. Maybe you should scan these."

McAbee did. He saw that Tommy Lee wasn't resistant to throwing his fists around, a dangerous man by any standard, an intimidator of the first order. But still, there was no smoking gun as to Erin Tobin.

Fisk sat there with that ever expectant look on his face whenever he was hiding something. There was more to this whole thing. "Anything else, Barry?"

"Yes. This is the thing that I'm most interested in, but in a way that leaves me stymied, but also, enthused. I need to crash the FBI system, but so far I haven't been able to do so. Here's the thing. I looked for unsolved crimes against women in the police files of the states where Tommy Lee was, just on the off chance that there was something there. Besides finding that there were a lot of unsolved disappearances and murders of women going on all over America, I became interested in MOs. I began to pick up a pattern of sorts; it's most disturbing. I know that the FBI does the tying together of all the reports on this stuff. I need to get into their database."

"What MO are you looking at?"

"Simply, a knockout punch, a rape and a strangulation. It's like there's an art of murdering out there that has been mastered by some guy, but no one has put it all together. And it may be true that the FBI has nothing on it. I don't know. But here's my point, Tommy Lee fits the profile except for those two college students in Davenport that the Lauderdale PD says were intimidated. By my reckoning, he should have murdered them. That California incident with the prostitute and the pimp could well have been the precursor to a knockout, rape and murder. The psychologist's report is incredible. He thought Tommy Lee was a psychopath."

"OK, so it sounds like you're going to persist on the FBI thing, but I should put someone on the ground, as it were, to get some background on Tommy Lee."

"Yes, that's the way I see it. We may be on to something very big here."

"The problem here is, why did he go to such pain to conceal the murder, if it was, of Erin Tobin? It wasn't his usual MO."

"I don't know," the little man said, shaking his head.

McAbee sat and mulled before saying, "Perhaps, he was on a job enforcing, a lot of these ring types do that and he felt obligated to do it. Well, I'll talk with Augusta and see if she can spring some time. Maybe I'll get her to Cleveland, Chicago and perhaps she can find those two Harcrest College coeds. Tonight, we're going to try to catch this caller and do some work with him. We don't know what he knows."

"Are you going to use Scholz?"

"Yes."

"The man is certifiable, you know." He grimaced and left.

McAbee met Augusta Satin at the Olive Garden in Davenport. "I like that place. The soup and salad keeps me thin," she said. Augusta was 5' 9" and weighed 130 pounds. She was a picture of health, an athlete who was practiced and an eater who was fastidious. Her dark brown eyes held an air of skepticism, but the crinkling around her thin lips suggested a sense of humor, which McAbee always admired since she had been through a lifetime of rough waters.

"So, what great occasion calls for Bertrand McAbee to spring for lunch?"

"You mean, you don't think that I just take you out to admire your beauty?"

"Well, you may be admiring my beauty, McAbee, but it seems odd that over the five years that we've known each other, you've always wanted something other than my beauty. But, I guess there's a first time for everything." She looked at him with a shy smile. "Let me just sit here and feast on the food and your company with the knowledge that there's no agenda to this meeting. What a pleasant change. Oh, my!" She took a buttery garlic bread stick out of the basket, broke it in two and chomped down on one piece with an air of finality.

McAbee knew that she was pulling his string but, for a fleeting second, read an offer to more than just a business friendship. Perhaps, one of these days he'd explore that. After Fisk and Scholz, Augusta Satin was a joy to be around.

"Now, Augusta, ..."

"Here it comes. Eden interrupted by the devil's treachery. Go ahead, don't bow your head in shame, just let it out," she said smilingly.

McAbee gave her a full briefing on the case. Augusta was a quick study and as he spoke, her face became somber, almost deadened to the pain around the scenario.

"So, I need someone to hit the ground, as it were. But I know about your kids. It would mean, in part, leaving town for a day or two."

"No, that's all right, Bertrand. My corrosive ex husband is getting his two weeks with the kids, even though it's school time. He's throwing big money at them and undercutting me at every step. But there's nothing I can do about the turkey except recover the kids when they get back to me. I could use the work."

"Augusta, I'm always hesitant about these out-of-the-state jobs, but you're the best. I wanted to give you the whole thing, or at least the two Harcrest women. However, I don't know if they're even in the area anymore. Everything that I have is in this folder, including a picture that Barry downloaded from the *Cleveland Plain* Dealer when this guy was a boxer."

She looked over the material letting her minestrone get colder and colder. The waiter came and asked if there was anything else needed. McAbee, seeing Augusta totally monopolized, asked him to get another bowl of soup that was hot. The waiter looked at the current, mostly uneaten bowl, then scanned McAbee as if to let him know that he didn't approve. It was as if he were saying finish this and then I'll get you another. McAbee said, "It's cold." He relented and left with the soup bowl.

Augusta came out of her study holding the picture of Tommy Lee. "Looks like a mean sucker to me. But, all those boxer-types are off-key somewhere. I see that he got his off-key white ass, kicked thoroughly by an off-key, black brother. That's good for the morale. Blacks unite around entertainment and athletics -but don't you be getting into anything serious," she said acidly. "So let me see if I have this straight. This guy may be doing women all over the country. This is way beyond that little baby he may have snuffed at the Quad Cities Oval."

"Yes, exactly. Wouldn't that be an irony? Caught by misdirection. Erin's revenge. But the fact is, this is all circumstantial. We have a lot of coincidence, but no real surefire facts, except that he's been in all these places at the times mentioned. But, presumably, so have thousands of others."

"What do you want from me?" She was now all business; this was the pro.

"Three fronts, for now. Talk with the Harcrest women if you can find them. Go to Cleveland and talk with his manager. Maybe visit Northfield Harness Track to see what you can find. Then, you may have to go to Chicago, Sportsman's and just poke around. But Augusta, be really careful. If this guy's who we think he is, he's ultra dangerous. By tonight, I should have a confirmation on Tommy Lee's identity, at least in reference to Erin Tobin. I'll catch up with you- if and when it connects. I was hoping that you could begin with those two Harcresters right away, like right after this lunch."

"Yeah, I will. Is it OK to finish my lunch - Doctor No-Agenda McAbee?" She laughed.

McAbee slid across an envelope. "There's $5,000 in cash, if you need to buy information. Orville Tobin has deep pockets, a bad heart condition and a need for closure. Same deal. Expenses and $1,000 a day. OK?"

"Nobody pays like you." She smiled.

They spoke of other things but her world reverberated

around her two kids. Toward the end of the meal she said, "So, McAbee, what's up with you? You over Beth, yet?"

"It's not that easy, Augusta."

"Yeah, I know. The nice thing about my situation with the ass I was married to, is that I was overjoyed when he left for that hussy-bitch up in Madison. He just didn't want to support his kids. But my closure was pure joy. I couldn't believe how nice it was to have lost the SOB. We now have a perfect relationship. He sends me the money I need to raise the kids and I never see him, except when he gets the kids for two weeks."

"Well, I've got my dog, at any rate."

"You mean that big, white creature. He ain't no dog," she laughed "he's a midget polar bear. And by the way, those times I came over for those parties that you and Beth used to have ... my question ... how did that psycho dog become a racist? He barked and snarled much more at me than he did others. Racist mutt!" She had a great laugh, full and generous.

"I never bought that theory. With you, he'd bark right away. With everyone else, he'd let them in the house and then he'd go after them. Which would you have preferred? The point is, he's territorial. But I do love the guy."

She touched McAbee's hand and said, "I know you do. I know he's important to you. Don't worry, this'll end."

"I wonder sometimes, Augusta. But then, you've been through much- I listen carefully to you. If you say so- OK."

Under the eyes of Scholz's night scope, Orville made his typical drop and left. Eddie Fox, apparently superstitious, did everything that he did before, a ritualistic freak, a stalker's dream. Scholz stayed behind the grove of trees. He had positioned one of his men in the Quad Cities Oval parking lot with a fully enclosed van and the other was in a ditch to the east of the old feed building. As soon as Scholz saw Orville leave the area, he crept forward across the field until he came to within twenty feet of the drop area.

He heard Fox's car driving up the backstretch road. Scholz radioed the van to leave the parking lot and start moving to the pickup location. Fox turned his car around and left it running as he trotted out of his Chrysler and headed toward the newspaper-filled bag. As he was picking it up, Scholz's man in the ditch hid behind the building, and Scholz started to move stealthily toward him. They both converged on Fox when he was within ten feet of his car. The van was just arriving as Fox was hurled into the back of it. One of the men got into Fox's car and drove it to the Quad Cities Oval parking lot. The van followed. After parking and locking the Chrysler, the ex-SEAL jumped into the back of the van to be with Scholz. The van was driven to a safe farmhouse about three miles away in Hampton, Illinois. McAbee was tersely notified by a "Done." Eddie Fox was in for a long night.

CHAPTER 15

Fox sat in the back of the van like a trapped animal-scrunched down with his covered head close to his upraised knees. His struggle when they cornered him was almost comical, Scholz thought. Fox had swung the bag at Garcia who in less than a second had Fox's arm doubled up behind his back and a strangle hold around his throat. Garcia whispered, "If you say a word, I'll break your arm, and if you say two words, I'll break your neck." After about ten seconds in this pose, Fox relaxed enough for the next stage. "I'm going to let you go, but I want you to be absolutely still while we put a bag over you. Don't be suicidal. Now whisper yes if you understand me."

"Yes," he croaked.

Scholz had a large black bag over him, tied, and had him pushed into the back of the van in less than ten seconds. He knew that what had transpired from the money pickup to the closing of the van's back door was the highest exposure that he faced from third parties. Time, therefore, was of the essence. By his calculation, the operation had taken exactly thirty-eight seconds. As they drove to the nearby farm, the chastened Fox was told by Scholz what was in store for him. "We don't appreciate people like you. You made a deal with the three-phone-call bit and then you violated it. That's just not ethical, even in the world of crooks, which you are. So, now you have a bag of newspaper, and you're in big ass trouble. I know you're listening and you can comment through the dirty laundry bag that you're wrapped in, scum."

Fox didn't say anything. Scholz looked at Burke and nodded. Burke was a former SEAL also who had become a chiropractor; in fact, he had a very successful practice in Moline, Illinois, but like many former special forces types, he couldn't let go of the thrill of special assignments. Scholz had a market for his product. Burke went over to Fox, stood in front of him, and kicked him lightly in the groin. Fox went over and started to moan. "Oh, oh ... oh." Nothing was said. Scholz now had the proper environment in place- fear, and he chose not to do anything else until they arrived at the farm.

The farm was owned by Burke's brother, who by eight each night was safely tucked away in bed. He religiously adhered to the principle that he didn't want to know what was happening out in his barn. "Just tell me you're coming so if I wake up, I don't think you're rustlers; clean up after you finish and be gone by dawn when I get up." Scholz had used the place on thirteen occasions. He had never stayed beyond dawn and had never failed to secure what was needed.

He had an array of drugs, besides a physician's bag of elementary instruments. He would make his judgment about which to stress after he got a sense of the subject. His opinion of Eddie Fox was already formed: a stupid, arrogant, overweight, drunken and cowardly cretin. On a scale of one to ten with one being an easy breaker to ten being a difficult breaker, he figured Fox to be a two. Only women, in his mind, could achieve a one.

When the barn doors closed and Garcia turned on three 1500 watt halogen lights, which gave the outsized edifice an eerie ambiance of shadowy darkness and intense light, they rolled the again-quiet Fox out onto the barn floor. Scholz nodded his head toward the barn door and Garcia responded by slipping outside to await the arrival of McAbee. Scholz wanted to get some of the rough stuff over with before this reluctant detective arrived. He didn't want to hear what Socrates or some other prissy-assed philosopher might think of his methods. And even though McAbee said that he wouldn't interfere, he was always hoping for repeat business. Three thousand dollars for a few hours work paid a lot of bills. McAbee took the deal, Scholz conjectured, because he figured that he might need days to sweat Fox; Scholz knew better- he'd have Fox in quick order. It would be a coup to get access to McAbee's brother, who was a legend in the business and who saw the world for what it was, and didn't bother with the pretentious questions of what it ought to be.

Scholz noticed that Fox now kept his thighs tightly closed so as to insure that no kick could come home in quite the same manner. "So, tell us about the scam, Fox."

"I don't know anything." His voice was low and had a pleading sound to it, a good sign to Scholz.

"What were you doing behind the feed building picking up a bag?" Scholz shrugged toward Burke and shook his head.

"A guy was paying me $500 to pick it up. Honest!"

While reaching into his bag, Scholz said with a humorous fatigue to his voice, "And who would that be?"

"I don't know. Some guy from where I work. His name is Tony."

"Tony. I see. Well, I guess we should let him go. What do you think?" He said this to Burke.

Burke's response was, "Yeah, I guess so, but I have one more question. Did you do the other pickups on the other nights?"

"No, no, no, no ... this is my first time. Look, I don't know anything about this." He was trying to look around, the bagged figure turning in different directions as he futilely struggled with his blindness.

"You sure that's your story?" Scholz asked as he moved closer to Fox with a cattle prod in his hand.

"Yeah."

Scholz clicked the switch and let the end of the prod touch Fox's knee. Fox yelled out, "Jesus! What's that?" Scholz brought his left hand up into the air and yanked it downward twice toward Burke. Burke went over to Fox and pushed him back so that he was prone on the floor. He tried to tum so that his head could be facing the floor, but Burke said, "Don't move." He removed his pants and shorts as Fox tried to slither away unsuccessfully.

To Scholz, torture was mostly mental. He felt that he had already established the prod and that he'd let Fox lie there for a few minutes and think through the possibilities. Finally, he said calmly, "Sir, I want to know everything that you know, and please be aware, I'm on to an awful lot about you already. If you lie to me, I will apply this mechanism to your testicles, and, if I must, one of the boys will sodomize you. So, why don't you just come clean and maybe we won't kill you at the end of it. What do you say?"

Fox didn't respond at first, but after ten seconds or so, he said stubbornly, "I told you what I know."

Burke, getting a hand sign from Scholz to say his line, said, "Do you want me to fuck him now?"

Scholz said, "No. He's just testing us, and I guess we'll just have to teach him about truth." With that he placed the prod onto Fox's testicles and kicked him in the ribs. The rib kick would produce a nagging pain for days and would keep Fox on his toes for the remainder of the meeting.

"Now, sir, let's start from the beginning. Don't lie, because if you do, there's only pain at the end of it. And, please, stop whining. What's your name?"

"Fox ... Eddie Fox."

"And where do you live in Forest Park, Eddie?" Scholz liked to give information to Fox and thus have him guess just how much was known.

"102 Rockford Avenue."

"How many rooms in apartment 30 I, Eddie?"

"Three."

"And if I called you at 708-771-4371, what would happen, Eddie?"

There was a silence. That piece of information could not have been gotten from his car registration. It was Scholz's way of getting inside his head. "My answering machine."

"And what do you do at Sportsman's Park?"

"I manage the inside of the track, the restaurant, customer service; things like that."

At this point McAbee came through the door with Garcia. Scholz put his finger to his lips and motioned to

McAbee with a waving hand to sit or stand wherever he pleased but away from the action of the lighted area. He couldn't help but notice McAbee's teeth clench at the sight of Fox's nakedness below the bag sashed around his waist.

"Congratulations, Eddie. You're telling us the truth. That's wise."

"Are you cops?" Fox asked.

"No, and that's the last question you get to ask. You have a lot of debt don't you, Eddie?"

"No, just normal."

"Any credit cards putting a freeze on you?"

"Nope."

"I'm sorry, Eddie. You just don't know how bad you are." He clicked the voltage regulator up to the second level and touched his testicles. Eddie bolted backward.

"What did I tell you about lying?"

"Not to. Yeah, most of my cards are frozen." He said this through tears and obvious fear.

"So you need money?"

"Yeah."

Scholz felt that he finally got a breakthrough. "So, where's the $100,000?"

There was a long pause. "I paid $30,000 to my bookie. There'll be another $30,000 to pay down the credit lines and the rest I'm going to use for a car and some other things."

"OK, I think now we're talking."

"Hey, look, I made a deal with Tobin."

"The deal, Fox, was to give a name. You hear? Why didn't you?"

"OK ... OK. I thought I could get another hit."

"So, Fox, give me the name and some particulars. If

193

we let you live, we may even let you keep the money and enjoy it. But don't screw with me. There's one more prod, a sodomy, then I start breaking your fingers, and if all that fails- I have drugs here that'll leave you a basket case for months. You understand, Fox?" Scholz glanced at McAbee whose face was somber and still.

"Look, I'm scared shitless about this guy. He's up at Sportsman's right now, and if he gets wind of this, I'm cooked. There is no doubt in my mind that he's a murderer. Can you keep me out of this?"

"Fox, you're an accomplice after the fact, but that's not my mission. I'm here to right the scales between you and Tobin. I could give a damn about you, but I will say this, I'm not going to the cops if that's your concern."

"The name is ... Tommy Lee."

Scholz looked over at McAbee and put his thumb in the air. McAbee nodded. "Now, let me tell you something. We already know the name. So you saved your balls a touch of hell. We know more, too, so don't play. What was the deal with the murder of Erin Tobin?"

"I don't know. I just heard about what he did." Scholz looked at the three standing men and shook his head as if he was saddened.

"Fox ... Fox ... you'll never learn will you?" He pushed the prod to the highest level and zapped Fox's testicles. He cried out in pain and then started to sob, his quaking shoulders giving off the impression of a spasmodic ghost wrapped in black until Scholz's eyes found the irony of his nakedness.

"Now, let's try again. What was the scam, Fox? Put your zipper up." The last remark was to let the threat of sodomy creep into Fox. Burke gave a quirky smile to Scholz and raised his eyebrows as if to say, "You'd better break him now because I'm not laying a hand on him."

Fox responded, "Tobin wasn't playing ball with some fixes. She cost me a few wads of bills, and she was also blowing me off when I'd make a move on her."

"And?"

"So, this Tommy Lee had let me know that he did some enforcing. So, I told him to scare the hell out of her. He killed her, and he also killed Rickie, a track retardate who for some reason he brought along. Tommy Lee said the idiot let my name out to Tobin, so he murdered her, supposedly to protect me. That's what he told me. He said he used Cassies Ruler to kick the life out of her. The goddamn horse obliged him. Look -that's it. That's all I know."

Scholz turned to his partners and thrust his hands out and upward. He had done it again. He signaled to McAbee, inviting him to ask any questions. McAbee stepped into the light.

"Eddie ... Tommy Lee still on the track?"

"Yeah, he lives there."

"Why did you call after all these years?"

"I needed the money, that's why I called, and then I saw the bastard. I hadn't seen him since the day after he murdered Tobin. I don't need him hanging around, you know."

McAbee said to Scholz, "I'm done." He walked out of the barn.

The computer files at the Multiple Murder Division of the FBI had a layer of protection, codes, and warnings that sent most hackers packing in short order. In fact, explicit warnings of arrests and fines were the first screen event that any strangers ran into as they tried to get into the storage system. Barry Fisk approached the files with great care, knowing the FBI's penchant for security and punishment, especially in terms of making examples of would-be violators. Accordingly, he felt like he was playing a real-life video game where the stakes were high and where his obsessive/compulsive disorder to uncover the hidden drove him beyond common sense. On top of it all, was his desire to put his data to a test and find out if Tommy Lee was possibly more than just a murderer of a young woman at the Quad Cities Oval.

He broke through the first level of FBI security in two minutes. Fisk figured that this was a "gimme" for the brave souls who ventured near this byzantine agency. His screen read:

> The Federal Bureau of Investigation is
> Serious about stopping crimes like you
> are presently committing. In fact, right
> now you are committing a FELONY.
> The FBI prosecutes to the maximum of
> the law. It is normal for offenders to be
> sent to a special wing of Leavenworth
> Prison where no computer access is
> allowed because it has been established
> at trial that you, the criminal hacker, are
> a threat to national security. In no
> uncertain terms - cease and desist
> immediately.

Fisk didn't doubt the warning or the Leavenworth bit. What greater punishment for a hacker than having access to a computer taken away. Comparing himself to Bilbo Baggins in the J. R. R. Tolkein stories, Fisk set out in his dangerous adventure.

He could feel, as he wandered around the complexities of each step, that a shadowy presence was tracking him, trying to get a fix on him. Each level of security in the Agency's database fought with him and eventually time was forgotten as he became one with this ethereal reality.

Three hours later, when he hit the sixth distinct level, a verbal message was run at him. It was from a convicted hacker, Myron Golden, who spoke in a Brooklyn accent about the horrors of life in Leavenworth without a computer. Fisk wondered how much time off for good behavior old Myron got for that act of atonement.

Ruefully, he wondered about the level he'd have to reach to find all of the blackmail goodies that the FBI had on the illustrious House and Senate members, and the JFK assassination, where would that be, FBI scum!?

Each level became more and more difficult. The traps and ploys utilized by the FBI to protect its databases were extraordinarily elaborate and sophisticated. It was like going from high school work to post-doctoral work under a great scholar. He knew that he was finding minds equal to his own. Fisk, of course, would never accept that there was a mind greater than his.

When he hit level eight and typed in serial murders, he found the motherlode. It was now five hours from the time that he had started. In one half of an hour he had gotten to the data relevant to what was probably Tommy Lee's file. He knew that it was in the downloading of these data that he was most vulnerable. It would take two minutes. He threw the dice and did it.

He immediately disengaged from the FBI and scanned what he had and within a half an hour said out loud, "Unbelievable." It was 4:00 a.m. and he was totally exhausted. He went to his living room couch and collapsed into a deep sleep.

Agent Bert Pauerhorst was called by FBI security at 4:00a.m. Eastern Time.

He then called his superior and told him the news and requested a Lear from the emergency fleet. He was cleared and was in the air at 5:00 a.m. heading for the Moline, Illinois, airport where arrangements had been made with the field office in Davenport, which covered the Quad City area. Bert Pauerhorst read the disappointingly brief file on Barry Fisk. He knew right away that the fist that killed the women could not be the fist of a tiny person like Fisk. So, he wondered about the man's curiosity and whether or not he knew anything about the murderer. Pauerhorst figured that this might be his last good chance at this case before retirement.

Field Office Agent Anthony Scorze drove Pauerhorst to the home of U.S. District Court Judge Henry Water, where a warrant was made out to search the home of one, Barry Fisk, who lived on 3214 Division Street in Davenport, Iowa. Because of the one hour time difference, it was only 7:50 a.m. Water looked at the warrant and asked just one question, "Gentlemen, you assure me that this is on the absolute level?"

Unflinchingly, Pauerhorst said, "Yes, sir. Absolutely!"

Pauerhorst and Scorze parked a block away from Fisk's house. They walked up to his door quickly and silently. Pauerhorst knocked as if using a feather, but for some prying eyes across the street, it would look normal. He did it again, while Scorze sized up the door frame and hinges. He took the crowbar from under his coat and with two swift pries, the door gave way. A tiny man on a couch looked at them through sleep-filled eyes. The warrant was served, and Pauerhorst started to look around. He placed the CD into the computer and before his eyes the all-too familiar files came up on the screen.

He turned back to Fisk and said, "I hope you're going to talk, Mr. Fisk, because if you don't, dreadful things will happen to you. Those warnings in the system are serious." Fisk never said a word. He struck Pauerhorst as a rancorous little character, but yet, there was something terribly sad about him. Pauerhorst felt that it had nothing to do with his physical deformities. He was just a sad, little man.

CHAPTER 16

Augusta Satin stayed in her car and waited outside the parking lot of Fatima Elementary School in Davenport. She caught a break in the investigation when she visited the alumni office of Harcrest College and sought the whereabouts of Alice Windham and Barbara McNally. Barbara was in Seattle, but Alice was a third-grade teacher at Fatima, which was barely a mile away from the Harcrest campus. Satin ran a check through a friend in the Davenport Police Department and found out that Alice drove a 1992 Geo with a vanity plate that read PAX. Satin parked right beside the Geo and waited.

Alice Windham came toward her car warily, probably seeing Satin's blackness. People were so spooked by black violence that well-meaning blacks came under racist nastiness on a regular basis. She despaired of that changing in her lifetime. And the whites wondered why some blacks weren't all that friendly. It was like whites saying, "Let my dog sniff you for bombs and then, after you clear, maybe I'll be your friend."

"Miss Windham, my name is Augusta Satin. I'm a licensed PI in the states of Iowa and Illinois." She took out her IDs and showed them to Windham. "I was hopeful of sitting and talking with you for a few minutes."

Alice Windham was about five-feet six inches, could lose about twenty pounds, dark blonde with some noticeable white hair beginning to make its presence. Her pear-shaped face carried a deep frown and some fear was in her eyes. This was a woman who was spooked, and Satin knew that just about anything that was introduced around it could set her off.

"I'm in a hurry. What do you want?" Her voice was very high pitched and Satin detected a tremor.

She noticed that Alice's sport coat had frayed cuffs and put that down to the disgracefully low salaries that parochial school educators received.

"Miss Windham, I'm in a hurry, too, so I won't keep you long. I'm investigating a series of violent crimes and your name has come up." Alice sagged and threw her weight to the door of her Geo.

"Yes?" she asked guardedly.

"The person I'm investigating has probably damaged hundreds of people, directly or indirectly, since any victim in turn causes agony for those around them. I'm not exaggerating, really, if you think about it."

"And?"

"I was wondering if we could sit in my car or yours. It might be easier." Satin was sure that Alice knew who and about what the discussion was to be. She decided to play another card. "This conversation is private. It's not being taped, and it will only be used within the confines of the firm that I work for, I promise you that. And I'm prepared to give you $500 in cash for your trouble."

"Is this about Florida, years ago?"

"Yes."

"I thought so. You know, I've put it behind me. It's very hard for me. It's going to cost me some nightmares," her eyes were swelling up with tears.

'Yeah, babe, you really put it behind you,' Augusta thought as she stood there in the fall sun.

"Let's sit in your car," Alice said.

Augusta peeled off five Franklins and handed them to Alice who sat in the passenger seat of her Celica. She put the money into her purse. Sometimes people would make some kind of protest about money being handed over. Alice dealt with it as if it had never occurred.

"What do you want to know?"

"Look, I don't want to drag you through all of the details. You don't need them and neither do I. OK? But, tell me about this man."

"He's empty. I never saw anything like him. He's pure viscera. It's like he reaches conclusions the way a wild dog would. I believe that he thinks only to serve his own pleasure; there's no sense of another person. I used to feel that you could always get through to someone, either intellectually or emotionally, and get them to be human and responsive. I'm convinced that that could not happen with him."

"So in all of this - pure violence, ruthlessness - not a touch of kindness or sensitivity?"

"No, just the opposite. The more I hurt, the more he wanted to hurt me. It was as if he could only have pleasure with a hurting individual."

"And what about Barbara McNally."

"We broke up. We tried to deal with it, but we were

too much of a reminder to each other. I know that she's in the Northwest somewhere. I just don't ever want to deal with her."

"When you say you broke up ... you mean as friends?"

"No, no. We're both gay. We were lovers. But that ended when he nailed us."

"I had no idea, I'm sorry ... so you filed charges with the Fort Lauderdale Police Department in Broward County. Why did you drop them?"

Alice went silent. Except for the lesbianism, she pretty much had just recounted the police report. After a wait, she told about the night that she and Barbara were picked up near the Harcrest campus. During the description, she started to sob and eventually bawled for several minutes. Augusta didn't need to speak with Barbara McNally or the Fort Lauderdale Police Department. This was just a case of arrogant and vicious brutality. Whatever ill came to Tommy Lee would be well merited.

"Would you mind looking at a picture? I have to confirm that we're dealing with the same guy." She took out the grainy picture that Fisk had pulled down from the Internet and showed it to her.

"Yes, that's him." Alice looked away hurriedly.

"So, what has he done over the years?"

"I'm looking into a possible serial killer, Alice. You know, it looks like you and Barbara were spared from what usually happens to his victims."

Alice turned in her seat to look at Augusta for a few seconds and said, "Yes, I guess that's one way to look at it, isn't it?"

Augusta wanted to kick herself for her well meaning,

but what now laid out there as dumb and callous comment. "I'm sorry, I didn't mean it that way, Miss Windham. I know that you're still carrying this."

"It would really help if you brought the bastard down. Would you be kind enough to call me if you do?"

"I promise I will."

The next day, Satin took a United Express from Moline to O'Hare in Chicago at 6:30 a.m. From Chicago, she took a nonstop to Cleveland at 7:45 a.m. on her way to see Jonas Fielder, the owner of a gym in downtown Cleveland. He sounded like an interesting dude to Augusta.

As soon as she parked her rental car, she noticed that two brothers were moving toward her car. Their sweatshirts read "Fielder's Gym." An escort service in this pitted out neighborhood made a lot of sense to her. The taller one said: "Augusta Satin? Jonas is waiting for you. Your car will be safe, don't worry."

As she walked toward him, she looked up and noticed that a window had been cut into the side of the building. Through the window she saw two long-legged stools. Presumably, this is how they monitored the lot. Jonas Fielder had a sense of class.

She was brought to his office and told that he would be there momentarily. His office was a running commentary on boxing. He had autographed pictures from Sonny Liston, Ali, Sugar Ray Robinson, and a host of other names with which Augusta had some acquaintance. She didn't notice anything with Tommy Lee's visage. She became aware that only black fighters were on his walls, even though Mexican and Cuban fighters had dominated some of the ranks in the more recent years.

He came through a side door noiselessly, only her peripheral vision picking up on the movement. She stood up and said, "Mr. Fielder, I'm Augusta ... Satin. Thanks for seeing me."

He gave her a slow eye up and down as if he were assessing a piece of steak. "Yeah, well, as I said on the phone, always pleased to help a sister. Name's Jonas." He sat down and waved at her to do likewise.

"I'm part of an investigation team back in Davenport, Iowa."

"Yeah, I know exactly where it is. Used to have a good friend across the river in Rock Island. Been there a few times. Not the best area in the country for a nigger."

Augusta smiled and said, "No, you're right, but I could do worse. I'm trying to get some background on a guy who you managed. I ..."

He put his hands up in the air and then started to point at Augusta. "If this is police stuff, forget it. I don't deal with those pricks, and if it's a totally private investigation, but you're out to hurt a brother I like or respect, you're out of luck. Sorry you had to come all the way to Cleveland to find that out, but that's the way it is. You get it?"

Augusta smiled at him and said, "Listen, Jonas, understand. There is no brother involved here."

He leaned forward, "It's pretty hard to find a honky or a spic down here. Who you after?" He was very interested.

"Do you remember a honky by the name of Tommy Lee?"

He looked at her with wide eyes for a few seconds and then leaned back in his chair and started to laugh. But it wasn't a genuine laugh. It was a laugh of knowledge, a confirmatory laugh. "Do I remember Tommy Lee!" He spat out the words. "He's from hell, that fucker. If I had to picture him in a previous life, he would have been a mean, fuckin' overseer on a plantation. If you ever want to meet a nigger hater, he's one."

"How did he end up down here? This isn't exactly a honky-friendly place." Satin wasn't given to the white/black patois but was practiced enough to use it when she had to.

"He worked out at Northfield, the harness track. Got into some trash talking with two brothers who used to train down here. They weren't the nicest of dudes. They could handle themselves pretty good. Well, they ambushed Tommy Lee and he beat the living shit out of both of them. Thought I should take a look at him. The long and short about this racist bastard is that he has white man's disease-he can't move fast. Whities could never have survived in the jungles. The goddamn tigers woulda eaten every one of them. That's why they left Africa and headed north where speed wasn't as important. They're genetically defective, I say."

Augusta had heard this biobabble bullshit before but shook her head as if agreeing with him. The fact was, both Tommy Lee and Jonas Fielder were cut from the same racist rock, and they probably really understood each other. "OK, so why did you manage him?"

"Well, he impressed me. I put in a slug against him the first day he came here. Now this slug was - then - still pretty handy with his fists. Mavis, Mavis Brown. When you leave, say hello to him. He pushes a fucking broom all day. He's in la-la land, but he wasn't that bad then. So I tell Mavis to beat the shit out of him. He's doing it real nicely, and then this white mother fucker lands a shot on Mavis like he never saw before. He's on the floor- out of the fuckin' ring, out cold."

"What's the deal? I thought he was too slow!"

"That's relative, babe. He's too slow for the league he wanted to be in, but I'll tell you right now, he's not too slow for any other league. So, I worked with him and we brought him along. I even gave Mavis, who was cryin' for a rematch, a clean shot at him. Poor bastard got his clock cleaned again, this time for keeps. Meanwhile, all durin' this, the fucker is out at that goddamn harness track, Northfield. Me and the promoter, he's dead now, decide to put him up against a real pro who beats the fuckin' daylights out of him. Never saw the mean fucker again. So, what're you lookin' into?"

"There have been a number of killings and his name has come up more than it should. Do you think he's mean enough to kill someone?"

He paused for a few seconds. "Yeah, I could see it, but he'd beat them first."

"How about a punch to the jaw?"

"Well, yeah, I suppose so. You know he had one great punch, a right cross. As right crosses go, this guy was a champ. Never saw a better one, and he knew how good it was."

"Rape?"

"Sure, why not? If you're goin' to beat someone senseless, you might as well rape for good measure."

Augusta didn't look at Fielder for fear that he'd pick up on her disgust with some of his thinking. "Could he strangle someone who was probably unconscious?"

"I'm tryin' to tell you this, the son of a bitch is capable of anything. There ain't anything behind his eyes. He's like one of those machines at the hospital that go ping - ping - ping, except he goes piiiiiiiiiing. He's dead in the head."

"What else should I know?"

"Well, he's a bad nigger hater, and he's a very good boxer - don't you be alone with him. You get anywhere near that right hand, which he uses as a slip punch, and you'll be cooked."

Augusta was leaving the gym when she saw the broom man. She went up to him, "Mavis?" she said.

He looked at her but didn't respond. His eyes were glassy and weren't registering.

She said again, "Mavis?"

"Huh?"

"Mavis, do you remember fighting Tommy Lee?"

"Huh?"

There wasn't any Mavis left. She took out a $100 bill and gave it to him. She had been prepared to pay Jonas Fielder, but he didn't hit her up. Mavis put the bill in his pocket. She hoped that no one would take it away from him, but looking around at some of the sharks there, she didn't like the odds.

McAbee was working with an executive from the John Deere Company in Moline, Illinois. The issue involved the compromise of new research designs by a French engineering company. Deere's surveillance program had been caught short and they wanted to cut their losses, and also, discover how their system was broken into.

It was unusual for Pat to buzz McAbee during an interview of this type. He knew that it was important. "Bertrand, it's Barry Fisk. The FBI has arrested him. He wants to speak with you."

McAbee asked the Deere executive to step out of his office, then took the call.

"Barry?"

"It's me. They broke into my home this morning. They've seized my files and my computer and whatever else their dirty hands wanted to take. You're my first and only call. They're threatening to put me in with some drug gang. Can you do anything? I'm at the County Jail." Barry Fisk sounded terribly desperate.

McAbee asked the Deere executive for another meeting. He wasn't happy, but he accepted McAbee's dilemma.

McAbee immediately called Dan Ledbetter in Chicago, all too aware that Fisk was in trouble because of this case.

"Bertrand, Dan Ledbetter."

"Dan, how are you? I have a problem. I've been running an investigation on Erin Tobin's murder."

"Right. Orville told me he'd use you. He called me about you. My father and he grew up together."

"Well, let me cut to the quick here. I've got a bonafide suspect, and I've been using a great computer man to put together a profile of this suspect. In that process, he began to see a pattern for the murders, and he began wondering whether or not we had a serial killer on our hands."

"Wow! Great! When are you going to meet with me?"

"Well, actually, I was going to meet with you in pretty short order, but we've hit a wall. He was just busted by your FBI."

A silence hung on the telephone for about twenty seconds. Ledbetter finally said, "So, let me guess. He tried to invade some FBI database."

"I haven't talked with him yet about the details, but I think that's a good guess. I'm on my way to see him now."

"That's serious business, Bertrand. Let me talk with my boss and see if I can drive in to Davenport. You guys are in the Chicago region. Meanwhile, start thinking about cutting a deal with your information."

"Gotcha. Thanks, Dan."

On his way, he called his brother Bill who was in Atlanta. He was put through by a series of convoluted relays.

"Bertrand, I'm in a meeting, but what's up?"

He explained his dilemma to his brother concerning Barry Fisk. After he had explained, Bill said, "I'll call Louie right now. All I can promise you is that he won't be treated harshly, but he's in a jam." He hung up.

The Scott County Courthouse was a fifties building, designed to exude the ultimate in bureaucratic efficiency. In fact, it was a jumbled building of offices with long counters, small doorways, narrow hallways, and salt and pepper marbled floors. It stank of overuse, frustration and stagnancy.

Pauerhorst had seen more than he needed to. The lousy midget had broken through the FBI net, and it didn't gladden him to be looking at a screen that had the same information on it that he looked at in his own office back in Arlington.

He pounded the table and looked at Scorze who had adopted the reasonable cop pose in their interrogation of Fisk, who continued to look at Pauerhorst in steady hatred. "I say we put the runt in with the addicts. They'll sodomize the little turd and then, maybe he'll cooperate."

"Well, it may come to that, but I suggest he'll tell us what he's up to, won't you, Mr. Fisk?" Scorze said.

"You're both Nazis. I can't believe that you broke into my house. Is this the United States of Jefferson, Adams and Washington?"

"Yes, it is, Fisk. And who gave you the right to break into our files? Do you think you're God?" Pauerhorst shot back. Just as he finished, his cellular rang. He left the room and went out into the hallway.

"Agent Pauerhorst?"

"Agent - Simon Strauss. Do you know who I am?"

"Yes, sir." Pauerhorst knew that he was number four in command of the FBI and a man who had a reputation for being an SOB. Pauerhorst had never met him, but had seen him on a teleconference screen on several occasions.

"You have a suspect there, a Barry Fisk?"

"Yes," Pauerhorst said slowly.

"Louie is interested in his well-being and health. Let's see what we can do to resolve this thing peacefully. There's a man coming down by the name of Bertrand McAbee. Try to work with him. I think a win win situation is possible for all of us. Am I clear?"

"Yes, sir. Is there anything else?"

"Yes, here's my number. Keep me informed." He gave him a Washington, D.C., number.

Pauerhorst saw a bench about forty feet down the hall. He went to it and sat down, feeling like a stunned bull probably feels on its way to being killed. This wasn't the first time that Headquarters or a higher up had intervened, but it hurt because of this lousy little midget's insolence. If he had his way, he'd kick the little bastard through a window.

211

McAbee followed the deputy sheriff from the fourth-floor elevator and headed to the west end of the building, which he knew was reserved for the feds for emergencies, interrogations and whatever else they deemed to be important.

He saw a big man sitting on a bench, staring straight ahead. McAbee saw drinker and intensity, maybe anger, in his face. The deputy stopped in front of him and said, "Sir, you're with the FBI?"

Pauerhorst looked up and said, "Yeah."

The deputy left and McAbee introduced himself. Pauerhorst didn't shake his hand. He pretended not to see it. McAbee figured that he'd already been called and was irate.

"So, is there any reason I shouldn't feel like you're coming on to me like a rogue elephant?" Pauerhorst said.

McAbee saw that it wouldn't take much for this agent to explode and thus said very gingerly, "Look, I assume you've been called."

"Yeah, that takes a lot to see, doesn't it?"

"I also know that Barry Fisk has a difficult personality."

"Really?" he said caustically.

"I'd like to be present at your interrogation."

"Can you tell me why he's invading an information base on serial killers?"

"I'm prepared to tell you a lot of things. Believe me, our interests are common, if we can take this whole matter out of the criminal context."

Pauerhorst looked at McAbee closely before saying, "Look, McAbee, I'm going to retire in less than six months. In fact, I may be retired tomorrow if I don't treat that lousy, little, anarchist shrimp in there as if he were a god. All I do anymore is look for more murders by some cretin who's been doing it for years, and give talks to service clubs. Once in awhile, they'll ask me what I find frustrating. My answer is - retiring before I nail this serial killer. Now, I find someone rampaging through my files- on this exact case. What's up? Does he have something or is he some creep who works for some junk TV show?"

"It's not that at all. I want to know, are you willing to forget this if I give you some data and a name? You'd have to do the investigation on your own, of course. I won't help you with that, nor will I tell you how I came onto the name. In fact, I don't think that you'd want to know."

"I don't think I have a choice, thanks to you and your clout, wherever you got that from."

Two hours later Dan Ledbetter came to the courthouse from Chicago. He spoke with McAbee who had been busy calming down the runt who sat there with a mean and sullen stare on his face. Ledbetter figured that he didn't realize the gravity of his offense. McAbee was conciliatory.

Pauerhorst was another story. Ledbetter tried to get him to focus on the information. This was his chance to break a case that had been screaming at him for years. Pauerhorst eventually relented, but only after some violent epithets and threats that he directed against Barry Fisk. In Ledbetter's view, he had let it become personal.

After a long and gruelling day, peace was made. All of Fisk's material would be returned to him. Fisk would conveniently forget what had occurred, all charges would be dropped, and the name would be given to Bert Pauerhorst. By 7:30 that night, the deal was set. Pauerhorst was given the name of Tommy Lee. McAbee told Ledbetter that he respected his ability at negotiations. Ledbetter, in no uncertain terms, told both McAbee and Fisk that there would never be a deal if it happened again. Ledbetter finally got in touch with Pauerhorst's anger when the runt, Fisk, threw him an insolent stare. A professional, he disengaged.

CHAPTER 17

When Augusta Satin arrived at Northfield Harness Track at 1:00 p.m., she went directly to the security office of the track, which was situated in a one story building near the gate to the backstretch. The closed door was opened by a man who was probably related to Boris Karloff, thick, Slavic features on an extraordinarily elongated face. She introduced herself, showed him her Illinois license, but disregarded her Iowa license on the assumption that this immobile face was already unimpressed with life. His name was Frank Protsky.

"I'm trying to track a Tommy Lee. He's worked here off and on for about twelve years. Right now, he's in Chicago."

"I know who he is," he said tersely. "What exactly do you want?"

"Would he have acquaintances?"

"Maybe."

The white stiff wants money, she reflected. She opened her purse and handed him $200. She didn't have the time or interest in playing games with him. She noticed from the slightly upward movement of his eyes that he was impressed. It was probably the biggest explosion in this dolt's life in twenty years. She caught herself; it was PMS time and she knew that she could get into trouble.

"I appreciate the contribution. He had one good friend here as best I could tell, a guy from Kentucky … name … Jerry, Jerry Lynch. I believe he's probably around here. Let me see if l can raise him for you."

He called a number on his mobile and said in a low monotone voice, "Get Jerry Lynch here in my office, ASAP." He turned back to face her.

"What do you remember about him?"

"Tommy Lee?"

"Yeah."

"Good worker, mean, and treated horses like shit. You know, he was a prize fighter for a bit. I never had any big trouble with him, but he could be sullen. People pretty much didn't bother with him, but if they did, he'd teach them real quick not to. There were a few incidents, but nobody would talk."

"Incidents?"

"Yeah- beatings that I'm sure he gave to some people."

"Did you take action?"

"No. If they're too dumb not to complain, why in hell should I get involved?"

"He have problems with blacks, Hispanics, women?"

This drew a chuckle from Protsky. "Everybody's got trouble with everybody. This is a very immediate place. Emotions are raw. I don't know if l want to call him a racist or whatever. I think I'd call him a mean, down-home bastard who hates anybody who gets in his way and who works on tracks because he's got nowhere else to go. I get lots of people just like him, and some of them are from your race, too. We have equal employment opportunity here; if you want a job someone will give you one. It's miserable, low-paying, but if you want to shovel shit all day, it's yours."

"What if I told you Tommy Lee was into some really bad things like rape and murder?"

"It's not my problem. He doesn't work here."

"No ... but would it surprise you?"

"Hell no. I gave up a long time ago hoping that people would be good. It's original sin and most people are going straight to hell as soon as they die," he said morosely.

It sounded like Catholic crap that some wild-eyed nun had put into this maniac's head a long time ago. "I guess if I were doing your job, I'd be a little more concerned about who was working here." That was a PMS comment. She was concerned that she had gone too far with this screwball.

"Yeah, maybe you would. My job here is to guarantee that the races are run cleanly. That's it. We have virtually no theft on the backstretch; if you're trying to treat the horses with illegal drugs, I'll take your head off. As long as you don't damage the sport," he spat that last word, "I won't bother you. I'm not out to transform people, you hear? I'm not the pope or Billy Graham. You're an Illinois black. Are you preaching morality?" He frowned. The door was knocked on and a security man who was dressed as though he borrowed his clothes from someone twice his size ushered in what had to be Jerry Lynch.

Lynch was potbellied, stood about five-foot-nine inches tall, but weighed a good 220 pounds. When he sat, his undersized tee shirt rode up to uncover his hairy belly. He had an unfiltered cigarette in his twisted mouth. He looked like he hadn't shaved in three or four days, and his forty-something face had a perpetual snarl to it. He also smelled like horseshit, which to Augusta's way of thinking was a step up for this pig.

Protsky dismissed the security man and told Lynch to sit down. "This young lady has come all the way from Illinois to find out about a friend of yours. I'd like you to help."

"Who's that?" It sounded as though he was pissed off at being accused of having a friend. Augusta thought that this guy needed an incubation period before being introduced to another human being.

"Tommy Lee," Protsky said.

"Don't know him," Lynch responded abruptly.

Protsky waited for about ten seconds, dolefully staring into the belligerent eyes of Lynch. Augusta said to herself, this is where Boris earns his 200 bucks. Protsky got up and walked around Lynch's chair three times. Finally he said, "Pack! You're out of here."

"You can't do that."

"Oh, yeah? I've thrown plenty of shit off this track, and the Ohio Racing Board has never once questioned my judgment. You have fifteen minutes!" He started to punch in some numbers on his mobile when Lynch responded.

"OK, OK. I remember him."

"Answer the lady's questions."

Lynch sat back in an appraising manner as he gave the once-over to Satin. She felt like taking a shower.

"Tell me about Tommy Lee."

"What's to tell. He's on a circuit. He comes and goes. I've seen him at other tracks. I went out with him once in a while. What's the problem?"

"Nothing, as far as you're concerned. It's Tommy Lee I want to know about."

"Yeah?"

"Tell me about him with women?"

"How the hell do I know. I didn't room with him," he smiled, his front teeth showing a sickening glossy, dark brown. They were a product of chewing tobacco, rot, or probably, both. He continued to smile searching for confirmation that he was funny. The chilling look of Protsky ended that hunt. Protsky picked up his mobile again, and Lynch seeing that said, "Look, what do I know? He's a good-looking stud, and he's had his bitches."

"Was he violent?"

"Violent? You mean was he rough? Yeah, he was rough. Hey ... listen ... if you think I'm rough, and I can see by your face, you do, I'm an angel," he laughed and slapped his knees. Augusta knew that he had all sorts of stories, but she'd never be able to get at them because she was black, a woman and a non-trackie. But she had the principle and she could well imagine the practice. She asked him some questions on how Tommy Lee treated horses and his betting behaviors, all by way of distraction. She was leading to one thrust and she had seen McAbee do it with great effectiveness. She watched him now with close attention as she sprung her central question. "Which times were you with him when he committed murder?"

Lynch went wild-eyed and looked at Protsky and stood up, "What the fuck is going on here with the nigger bitch? I can't believe this. I don't know anything about murder. What goes here?"

Augusta put it at ten to one that Lynch knew anything

about Tommy Lee, the murderer. She looked at her watch; it was 2:30 p.m. and she had a flight to catch from Cleveland to Chicago at 4:00 p.m. She said to Protsky, "I see what you mean. I'm finished with him." Lynch stormed out of the office.

"Sorry you couldn't get more out of him. These track people are tight. By the way, did you mean that about Lynch being around a murder?"

"Maybe, maybe not, Mr. Protsky." She left, feeling that Tommy Lee had all the right stuff to be a serial killer.

The racing secretary's office was empty and Lynch went back there to use the telephone. There was a listing of all harness tracks in North America on the wall, and he dialed into Sportsman's in Cicero, Illinois. It took ten minutes for Tommy Lee to be raised out of the inefficient backstretch to answer a call from his brother who wanted to tell him about the death of his mother.

"Tommy Lee. Who's this?"

"Jimmy Lynch, Northfield. You listening?"

"Yeah. What is this?"

"Nigger babe in here asking questions about you. Don't think she's a cop. She's from Illinois, tall, thin, good lookin' for a nigger babe. Wanted to know how you got along with women and whether I was with you when you murdered people." The sentence hung on the wires.

Finally, Tommy Lee said, "When?"

"Twenty minutes ago."

"Anything else?"

"No."

"Thanks. I owe yuh one." Jerry Lynch lit up another smoke and headed back to his barn. He still had to change the drinking water for twenty-two horses.

Pat Trump had been trying to raise Augusta Satin throughout her turbulent day. McAbee had been in touch with her as soon as he had found out about Fisk's arrest by the FBI. "I don't want Augusta Satin going anywhere near Tommy Lee. Tell her to bypass Sportsman's Park and head home directly from Cleveland."

Pat had failed to make contact with Satin's mobile number. She was beginning to assume that Satin had inadvertently let her battery run down. She tried calling Fielder's Gym, but some insolent black guy stiffed her, "Ain't nobody like that here. Now you stop calling. We don't take calls from honkies; you dig?"

"This is an emergency- please?!"

"Forget it, babe."

"Let me talk to Fielder," she pleaded.

"Ain't no Fielder here," he lied. "Now back off bitch and don't call here again, hear?"

"Her life is at stake!" Pat screamed in exasperation.

"Yeah, right, babe." He hung up with a low and disgusting laugh.

Her call to Northfield Race Track was taken by an operator who promised to page Satin and tell her to call Pat. Pat had called the track three times. The operator said that she was trying and that the loudspeaker was heard all over the track, "Just fixed this summer, dear. If she's here we'll find her, now don't you worry."

The black guy at Fielder's Gym, who took the call from Pat, was proud of himself. He figured that he just protected Satin from some goddamn bill collector or some other kind of fucker who was screwing around with blacks. She had been in Fielder's office when the first call had come through. From then on, whenever Pat called, he just hung up saying, "Bullshit, bitch!"

The operator at Northfield was diligent as she continuously paged the name of Gus Lavin. It didn't help that she was addicted to daytime soaps, that she found messages and paging to be a bore, and that this edgy bitch from Davenport, Iowa, already didn't trust her to get the job done right. There just wasn't any Gus Lavin on the track grounds that day. Augusta Satin had been, however.

Augusta returned her Avis at the Hopkins Airport in Cleveland. She was running late, but fortunately, she was only carrying an athletic bag. She got into the terminal at 3:30p.m. for her flight to Chicago's Midway Airport and went right to Gate B-18. They were starting to board the Southwest plane when she finally got to the counter. The airline rep was asking those in rows twenty to twelve to please board. She was processed without incident and got on the plane. As she was walking toward the tunnel entrance to the plane she thought she heard a page for a name that sounded like hers. She dismissed it; they probably would have said something at the check-in counter. She wavered ... she almost turned around ... but in the end, she didn't.

The flight took one hour and with the time change, she arrived in Chicago at 4:00p.m. In one of those rare instances of luck, Sportsman's Park and Midway Airport were separated from each other by three miles along Cicero Avenue. In fact, Augusta remembered the Harcrest graduate.

She had had luck on that one, too. Some investigations are just luck-prone, she thought.

Lynch's call to Tommy Lee didn't sit well. Handling frustration was not a strong suit in his psychological profile. He tended to handle it by quick, physical, and immediate responses, as if the removal of the stimulus meant the end of the problems. It was that simple. He walked around the backstretch for a short time. He had no idea who the nigger bitch was, and Lynch was too dumb to find out.

He thought in bursts. For long stretches, he became one with his environment and wasn't conscious of time, or even of himself, as separate from what he was doing. It was as though when he hitched a pacer up to a sulky, he became the straps and ties themselves. But then, something would jar him and remove him from his merged self and force him into his separateness and, ultimately, his alienation. It was that alienation that he fought to end so that he could return to his world. Stress, therefore, was the threat to his unified world, which was anchored to simple tasks and simple pleasures. The murders had become simple and more and more became the panacea for his stress removal.

His world was best with inanimate objects or animals who presented problems that could be resolved by direct action. The world of human affairs, however, was always futile with the possibility of disunity and incoherence. So, Tommy Lee saw himself as a nice guy beset upon by many enemies.

Lynch's call had brought him into very troubled waters. Lynch had said that she was from Illinois and didn't seem like a cop. But if she was from Illinois, what was her reason to be in Ohio? What was she looking for? And then it hit him- Eddie Fox. He had approached Fox a few nights previous and now suddenly this bitch is tracking him down. Fox did it. It was 1:45 p.m. in Chicago as he sat in his narrow, small room. Tommy Lee did not have to be on the track until 6:00 p.m. when he was responsible for taking a pacer to the detention barn, the safe area where horses are watched closely by security to foil any last minute drug dosing.

He went to the racing office, which was not now open for business but which could be traversed through. He went into the racing secretary's area and scanned the top of the desk but didn't find what he was looking for. He opened the top right-hand drawer and saw an address book. He opened it to "F" and found Fox's address and phone number.

Forest Park was not hard to reach from Cicero, Illinois. He drove west on Cicero Avenue and took the ramp onto the Eisenhower Expressway. He exited at Harlem and drove until he saw Rockford Avenue. He took a left and found himself at Fox's apartment building by 2:30 p.m. He parked on a side street about two blocks away and went into the vestibule of the building. Fox's name was on a panel that held the names of all the residents along with a buzzer beside the name to request a signaled entry through the inner security door. He rang it and Fox's unmistakable voice screeched out, "Yeah?"

"UPS. I have a package."

"OK, I'll buzz. Just take a right, you can't miss me. I'm at the end."

Tommy Lee quickly climbed the narrow stairs, pausing only at the entrance to the third floor. He suspected that

Fox would have his door open and be ready to accept the package. Tommy Lee would have to be poised to catch him by surprise before he could close his door.

When he opened the door to the corridor, it was just as he had imagined it. Fox was standing beside his door, which stood open about twenty feet from the corridor door. Tommy Lee had to make it through those twenty feet before Fox could realize what was happening. He ran as fast as he could, watching the stunned Fox stare at him for the first ten feet. By the time he decided to take action, Tommy Lee had him by the shirt and half pushed and half-carried him through the door. He crammed him up next to the wall and kicked the apartment door shut. He looked at the ashen and quaking Fox and said, "What did you do to me, Fox?"

"What ... what are you talking about?" he half gurgled in reply.

Tommy Lee looked behind him and saw a woman dash across a far hallway and into a room. She had a towel draped around her. He dragged Fox across the room and threw him onto a couch that occupied a wall of the medium-sized living room. He hit him across the jaw with a softened right cross that sent Fox on his side and caused momentary unconsciousness.

Tommy Lee ran to the door of what had to be the bedroom and could hear the bitch trying to throw a lock on the door handle. He could hear hyperventilating and sobbing. He turned the knob and threw his shoulder into the door, which flew open hitting the now-naked woman on her right toes and on the right side of her face. She tried to grab the towel that had fallen from her. She began to cry hysterically from the pain of the door hitting her, from her fear of the invader, from her nakedness, and who knows what else, Tommy Lee conjectured. She was too loud. Tommy Lee hit her with an open hand, hard across the face. She continued; he hit her again, harder still. He snarled, "Keep it up, bitch, and I'll keep hitting you."

She whimpered softly as she started the descension into shock. Tommy Lee said, "Now just lie there and shut up. Here's your towel, bitch." He picked up the hunter green bath towel and threw it at her. "If you try anything funny, I'll beat you to death- do you hear me?"

"Y—y—yes," she mumbled.

Tommy Lee went out to the living room and saw that Fox was groaning and beginning to come to. He picked him up and dragged him into the bedroom and hurled him horizontally onto the bed. He fell flat over the legs of his girlfriend, or whatever the whore was.

He went into the bathroom, which was no more than ten feet from the bedroom and filled a glass with cold water. He came back and threw it on Eddie Fox, who was making sly glances around the room and at Tommy Lee. He knew that he was had, Tommy Lee figured.

"Ok, Fox. I want to know, what did you do to me? Why are there people poking around on me?" The girlfriend started to sob more heavily now, so Tommy Lee belted her again with a resounding slap.

Fox yelled out, "You son of a ..." only himself to be hit openhanded with brutal force by Tommy Lee. "You don't understand me, fucker. I want to know what you did. If you lie to me, I'm going to kill you."

"They know about you. They know what you did to Tobin at the Quad Cities Oval."

"What do you mean, they know? Who're they?"

"Some friends of the old man." He took a handkerchief out of his pocket and spat out some blood. "They're not cops. I don't know what they are, but they know about you."

"And how would they know? You're the only connection to that. What did you tell them?"

"Look, they tortured me. What was I supposed to do?"

"You, fucker! How did they know that you were involved."

"I don't know."

"You're lying," Tommy Lee said and then proceeded to punch Fox in the stomach. He doubled over in pain. The girlfriend tried to get up and he pushed her back on the bed. "Now tell me, Fox, how did they know?"

"I don't know," he lied, "but I told them it was a mistake, that you didn't mean to kill her. They'll cut you a break, I'm sure."

Tommy Lee looked behind him and saw a chair. He sat on it and thought: this is the witness. I'll have to murder him, along with his bitch. There's no other way out of this. "What else should I know?"

"I'd get out of Chicago if I were you. Maybe it's just an Illinois thing and if you get to some far away state, they'll forget you," he said between a series of coughs and spasms.

Tommy Lee smiled at Fox and smiled at the girlfriend. He saw that they both showed expressions of hope that they might be safe after all. He held his left hand up in front of him and wiggled his index finger at the bitch who started to sit up in the bed as suggested by Tommy Lee's finger. She never saw the right fist nor would she ever be conscious again as she slumped back onto the mattress.

Fox said, "Jesus ..." as he tried to come to her assistance only to feel an ever harder right cross connect with his jaw. They were both unconscious. Tommy Lee looked at his watch. It said 3:35 p.m. He strangled the unconscious Eddie Fox until he knew that he was dead. He did likewise to the battered bitch, but only after having sex with her inert body. He was in his car heading back to Sportsman's Park by 4:00 p.m. He figured that the game was up and that he'd be on the run from here on in, unless there was some way to get to the very roots of the problem.

 **CHAPTER 18**

McAbee had been notified by Pat that she was failing in her effort to reach Augusta Satin. He called Jim Panayotounis.

"Jim, Bertrand McAbee."

"Yeah?" he asked warily.

"I need a favor. I think I know who the murderer of Erin Tobin is."

"I can't believe this, but go on."

"One of my people, a female, is, to the best of my knowledge, headed to Sportsman's Park. I think the murderer works there as a groom. I'm afraid that she might make contact and that scares me. Her phone is out of order. I need someone up there to intercept her and get her the hell out of there. I don't want her going near this guy. He's extremely dangerous."

"Well, Eddie Fox is up there. I got rid of him, but he is there."

McAbee was put off by this comment. He wondered whether Panayotounis knew anything of what had occurred. He dismissed it as coincidence. "Is he reliable?" McAbee asked with hesitation.

"Yeah. He oversees the grandstand. He's reliable if you

specifically ask him something. I'll give it a shot. It's 4:45 now. Call me in a half hour."

"Thanks, Jim."

McAbee wasn't happy with this scenario. He told Pat to call the stable gate at Sportsman's and leave a message for Augusta to call her at once. He told Pat not to leave the office until she was sure that Satin was out of harm's way. But he had ominous feelings about the situation, and they hung over him throughout the Barry Fisk questioning.

Augusta drove across Cicero Avenue and came to the track where she entered the gates and drove toward the grandstand, which was virtually empty. The harness card for that evening didn't start until 7:30p.m. It was now only 4:50p.m. She noted as she got to the grandstand, that some thoroughbred racing was showing on televisions that dotted the grandstand area; off-track betting, she surmised.

She went to a ticket window and asked where the security office was. A surly ticket seller said, "Go out those doors," he motioned his head to his left, "and go into the first building to the left." He looked down at his cash drawer in his practiced act of dismissal.

The building that she entered was clearly the racing office, with a large counter running the length of the open room before it found a hallway that held a series of offices. No one was there. She yelled, "Hello ... hello!" As she scanned behind the counter, she saw numerous files, computers, telephones, desks; and yet no one was there. She waited around, noting that it was just 5:00p.m. and perhaps that's when people came on duty.

At 5:05 p.m. she ventured behind the counter, picked up the telephone and dialed "0."

"Operator."

"Yes. Can you put me in touch with your security chief?"

"Hold on."

"Harris." She was elated. It was a nice bass voice - and black. It was almost always a hundred percent easier time when they were black.

"Mr. Harris, I'm Augusta Satin. I'm a PI and I need to talk with you right away."

"Where are you?"

"In the racing office."

"OK, just stand outside. I'll send a car over for you. I'm on the other side of the track - it'd take too much walking or driving to get to me from there and my times are tight." Because of this twist she missed the security gate of the backstretch and the message from Pat.

Melvin Harris was a retired detective who had worked with the Chicago Police Department for twenty two years. He had gotten the job at Sportsman's three years ago when a scandal broke about illegal drugs. He ran a pretty tight ship even though he had to report to Eddie Fox, for whom he had as much respect as he did for the omnipresent horseshit that was a constant feature of the backstretch.

Augusta Satin was one good-looking babe as he saw Jumbo leading her to his office. Jumbo had a smirk on his face, suggesting that he'd made inroads on her in the trip from the racing office to the security office on the backstretch. Looking at Jumbo, he said to himself, 'Dream on nigger.'

"What can I do for you?" He remained standing; so did she.

"I'm looking into a big-time problem with a honky. I mean first-degree murder stuff."

"Yeah?" He knew that these PI's would tell you anything when they were really after some deadbeat who wasn't paying his child support. "Who is this?" He still wasn't sure whether or not he was buying this sister.

"Tommy Lee. Heard of him?"

"No, but wait." He opened his door and saw Jumbo talking with another security man and giggling. He surmised that Jumbo was telling the other guy about how he'd already scored with the black sister. "Jumbo!" He nodded his head for him to come into the office. He came right away, smile gone. "You know a Tommy Lee?"

"Yeah. He just got here a few weeks ago."

"And?"

"That's about it. Keeps to himself. Weight lifter- big time. Never had any trouble with him. Pretty tough on the horses though."

"What does that mean?"

"Beats them." He smiled coyly at Augusta as if to say that he'd do the same for her. Melvin Harris glared at the dumb fucker in disbelief.

"OK, that's it." Jumbo left. "He give you any shit on the way over here?"

"The usual. No big deal. Listen, I just want to see this Tommy Lee, not talk with him. And I'd love to get into his room."

"What's it worth to you?" Harris had long ago adapted to the Chicago way, which in his view, was if you're in the right place at the right time, take advantage of it. Everything has a price.

"If you can get me ten minutes in his room- and a look at him- $500."

"Stay here. Let me find out what's going on with him."

It took him fifteen minutes. He found out that Tommy Lee had just come back onto the grounds through the back security gate and was taking a shower. He was expected in the security barn with a horse by 6:00p.m. By rule, he would stay with that horse until the pacer was taken over to the paddock at about 7:15 p.m. for the fourth race that went off at about 8:30p.m. Tommy Lee, therefore, should be nowhere near his room for about two-and-a-half hours. That's the window that he had for Satin. He came back, "You're on for both of your conditions. I want the money now."

Harris' office was located within 200 feet of the security barn where all horses had to be housed before they were eventually brought to the paddock in the grandstand area, and where bettors could observe their demeanor for upwards to an hour and a half before an actual race. At 6:05 p.m., Melvin led Satin into the security barn where the stalls were marked according to race number and post position. He knew that Tommy Lee's horse had drawn post position seven in race number four. This stall was on the other side of a divider of stalls that went through the center of the building. He said, "Wait here." He walked on to the other side and saw that stall seven for race four was occupied. He observed a heavy, well-proportioned man in his mid-thirties. He was a weight-lifter, all right. Melvin went back to Augusta and said, "He doesn't know you, right?"

"Yes."

"Well then, just follow me down the row. He's on the left side about midway down the aisle. He has a baseball cap on, a black tee shirt and blue jeans. He's built like a goddamned hulk. We'll just stroll through as if I'm giving you a tour. He's got no reason to even look at you twice, except that he might find you sexy."

Melvin led her down. Tommy Lee picked up his head and his eyelids came apart just slightly as he saw Augusta. Melvin Harris figured that the honky was impressed with Augusta. They walked on through and out of the building. He said, "Seen enough of him?"

"Yeah ... yeah. Now get me into his room."

Tommy Lee had limited choices in the interminable wait, during which he was expected to keep his pacer under surveillance at all times. During the time in the security barn, blood would be drawn for standardized testing which would rule out any substances that were deemed illegal by the Illinois Racing Board. The testing process was tightly administered and any infractions were dealt with harshly. The Chief Security Officer, Melvin Harris, wasn't someone to fool with, he had heard.

Trainers had lost their licenses for six months to a year if some major drug was subsequently found to be in the horse's bloodstream. Sometimes they could beat a pre-test, but could find their horse tested after the race and a positive would be had. When that occurred, not only did the trainer lose his license, but whatever the purse monies were that went to the owner had to be turned back into the track for redistribution. Trainers, therefore, were especially concerned that no foreign substance could be passed to a horse during the critical time before a race. The rule stated that if the horse was in your care, you were as responsible as the trainer of record.

Tommy Lee worked for a trainer named Carl Grandino who had been suspended twice, for six months each time, for using illegal substances. The Racing Board had told him that a third time would yield a lifetime suspension. That Grandino had enemies layered throughout the backstretch made him highly suspicious. Tommy Lee was always on his toes, consequently. Grandino was known to fire grooms on the spot who strayed from their horse.

Tommy Lee sat on a portable stool that he had bought on sale at K-Mart. He was directly in front of the horse's stall. It wasn't often that he would fraternize with the other grooms. Typically, he would read the Chicago Sun-Times or daydream and just wade through the process that required so much time for a simple two minutes-or-less race.

He first saw Melvin Harris looking down the aisle. He was alone, but he was clearly looking for something or someone, and that fact alone put Tommy Lee on alert. After all, he reasoned, he had just murdered two people a few hours ago. So, while keeping an alert for Harris, he thought through his options. If he stayed at Sportsman's, he would have to answer about the incident in the track dining room when Eddie Fox walked out on him. He shook his head in disgust with himself, because it was so unlike him to put himself on public display like that. The Chicago cops would be all over the track, but the track would discourage them because they didn't want any scandal around the shaky sport of harness racing; even so, he was in jeopardy.

And then, there was this black bitch being at Northfield.

What was that all about? Somebody was overly interested in him about something. He remembered Fox's words, maybe it was just some local thing in the Midwest; if he got to the south or the west, they'd forget him.

Then he saw them - Harris and the nigger woman. No way she wasn't the same bitch that Lynch had called him about. He struggled to control himself as he looked at them walking down the aisle, while Harris was pretending to be giving her a tour. Their eyes met... he knew then that she was on to something about him, and traveling to Cleveland meant this wasn't just some minor thing. They both left the security barn. Tommy Lee was now split in two- his job or his safety.

Within ten minutes, Carl Grandino came into the security area. He barked at Tommy Lee, "Let's get him hitched. I want to warm him up once before we take him to the paddock." Grandino had a perpetually sour expression on his dark face, along with a taciturn and abrupt speech pattern. Tommy Lee frequently desired to beat up the little Ginny bastard.

"OK."

Grandino, accompanied by Tommy Lee, led the horse from the security barn, outside of which they hitched the docile and experienced pacer to a sulky. Tommy Lee led him to the track where Grandino would warm him up and return him to the security barn, before still another warmup in anticipation of the paddock, and finally the fourth race. It would be the last time Tommy Lee would ever see Carl Grandino.

McAbee called Panayotounis at 5:15 p.m., but his line was busy. It wasn't until 5:45 p.m. that he could get through to Panayotounis' busy line and between his own strained efforts at trying to conciliate Barry Fisk, Agents Pauerhorst, Scorze, and Ledbetter.

"Jim? Bertrand McAbee."

"I've tried Fox at home. I keep getting his answering machine. I called the track. He's expected to be there by 6:00p.m. I left an urgent message for him to call me. Don't worry. I'll raise him."

McAbee didn't like the times; it was quite possible that Augusta was on the track ground right now. "OK, Jim. I can't go past 6:05. If that's not happening, I'll call security itself. After all, Fox oversees a lot of things at that track."

"Yeah, he does."

"Can you get me the name of the Chief of Security if Fox doesn't call you back?"

"Call me a little after six. We'll know a lot more."

McAbee went back to the negotiations. He was quite uneasy. He felt as though he was being victimized by circumstances beyond his control. Unlike Marcus Aurelius, he wasn't prepared to accept the inevitable.

Harris said to Satin, "So you want ten minutes in his room. I've got a master key and can get you in there, but I'm not going to stay with you. His room is over in Barn E. The rooms are on the second floor, with the stalls on the first floor. There are fifteen rooms on each side of a barn. His room is E6. It's going to be right on the end of the stairway that goes up the outside center of the barn. I'll go up and open his room, then I'm leaving. I could lose my job over this. When you're done, just turn the knob and the door will lock automatically. You don't have to worry about him. He has to be in the paddock, and his trainer is a real nut about it. When you're done, you'll notice that at about every 75-100 yards there's an opening in the fence around the track. Just stand near that opening. A bus owned by the Horseman's Association and going back and forth all the time will pick you up and bring you back to the grandstand where you're parked. Good luck!"

"Thanks. Are you sure about his not coming back?

"As sure as I can be. But- as they say around here- it's horses. Anything can happen, but it's 99-1 that you're safe. It doesn't get better than that."

They reached Barn E, a long rectangular building of dark tan brick. A bright blue staircase flanked either side of the long building. Harris climbed the stairs and then came down a few seconds later. He was upset.

"Goddamn it. He put a padlock on his door. That's strictly forbidden. I'm going to need a few more minutes." He dialed his cellular. "Yeah, Jumbo! What the fuck's going on, man? I thought I told you no padlocks on grooms' doors!" He listened for about three seconds and said, "Get your big ass over here with a lock cutter. Quick! I don't got time for this horseshit!" He looked at Augusta and said, "It's always something around here. Bullshit place!"

Augusta saw his eyes widen and turned around. She saw the track security jeep driving through the backstretch with its red lights blinking. Harris muttered, "Look at that crazy son of a bitch. There are horses on the road and he's going a fucking fifty-miles an hour! Je—-sus Christ! And I'm trying to do this real quiet like. Jumbo, one of these days I'm going to fire your fat ass right out of here."

Jumbo pulled up with a screech and flew out of the

truck with the lock cutter. "I'm sorry, boss. I just never saw it and nobody told me. I'm gonna kick some ass on this, let me tell you!"

Augusta thought of the small pond with the big fish, medium fish and little fish.

"Just give me the cutter and turn off your fucking lights. Every son of a bitch on the track is looking at us. Just what I don't want." He stormed over to the staircase and walked up. He gave a quick look around, cut the master lock and very quickly used his pass key to open the room. He put his arm behind the door so as to turn the knob and unlatch the door. He came down the stairs and said, "Jumbo, I'm getting in the jeep with you. I have to get back to my office. Sister, don't take anything, leave it the way you find it, and lock it up." He looked at Jumbo. "If he asks about his lock, just tell him that you cut it. We don't allow them. Go!" With that they left. Augusta thought it would probably be best to wait a few minutes before going up the stairs.

McAbee called Panayotounis at 6:15 p.m. Panayotounis was upset. Eddie Fox was nowhere to be seen. He even called the COO of the track, who told Panayotounis, "This is it. I'm going to fire him dead out when I see him. He's a pile of shit."

"Bertrand, here's the direct number into the Chief of Security- name's Melvin Harris."

"Jim, I just don't like this." McAbee sounded to Panayotounis like a man getting unstrung. He had gone from this cool inquisition the other day to a man with a sharp edge in his voice.

He counseled McAbee, "Just give Harris a call. The

COO told me he was really solid. Don't worry. Things will turn out for the best." McAbee hung up.

McAbee called Sportsman's Park and asked the operator for Melvin Harris. It rang for twenty times until McAbee hung up in disgust and re-dialed the track and pleaded with the operator to page Harris because this was an absolute emergency. After an indeterminable wait, a husky voice came through on the phone.

"Harris. Who's this?"

"My name is Bertrand McAbee. A woman is working a case for me by the name of Augusta Satin. Have you run across her by any chance?"

"Uh ... maybe. What's this about?"

"Look ... I've come across some things during the day that says she's in a dangerous situation over there. I want to get her off the track grounds and have her home immediately. This is really important, Mister Harris."

"Well, she'll be off the track grounds in about ten minutes. She's just ... completing a little project right now. You don't have to worry." McAbee felt that Harris was picking through his words too carefully.

"Is she alone?"

"Yeah. That's the way she wants it."

"Presumably she's talked with you about Tommy Lee. Look ... when she left Moline this morning, he was a high maybe- now's he's a certainty. Her life's in danger if she makes any kind of contact with this man. Please, find her and tell her I said to get away from there now and come right home. Would you do that, please?"

There was a pause. Harris was probably weighing the legitimacy of the call. "Where are you right now?"

"I'm in Davenport, Iowa. Let me give you my cellular number. If she'd call me, I'd feel a lot better." He gave him the number.

"OK, man, I'll try to hunt her down. I'll have her call you."

"I owe you. Thanks."

When he unbridled the pacer and saw Grandino move toward the track, Tommy Lee was within 200 yards of Barn E and the tight little room that they called grooms' quarters. One small window allowed the only natural light that came into the five-by-eight cell. Ex cons who worked on the track would remark that state prisons were better equipped than track housing, the track feeling that its obligation was met by not charging rent. Other than a sink, a bed, a small table, a chair, a row of three small shelves and an overhead light, you got what you got by having your own stuff and keeping the rest in your vehicle. If you were a groom, you traveled light. Anyone who tried to take a family through the experience was considered crazy. More and more, Tommy Lee saw Mexicans all about him. He figured that coming from where they were coming, this was plush living. He noticed glumly that most of the official signage governing backstretch life was in English and Spanish.

He moved quickly through the 200 yards, dodging through the backs of several stables to avoid any security. His intention was now to get to his room, grab his stuff and the cash that he had taped under the sink, head out to Sacramento and lay low.

Augusta Satin was surprised at how cramped the room was, but equally so by how neat the room was kept. The overhead light was far too bright for the small space. She went to the shelves and ran her fingers through his two carefully folded blue jeans, three sweatshirts and two tee shirts. She raised his mattress and looked under the single bed, but saw nothing. He was scrupulously tidy. She began to think that if he was hiding any incriminating material, it probably wasn't in the room. However, the fact that he used a padlock said that something was valuable. She found his money taped to the inside of the sink wall. Perhaps that explained the lock. She let it be. She turned to the desk. Just as she was about to pick up a pile of programs, a book and some loose papers, the door flew open. It was her worst fear - Tommy Lee filled the door. He said through tight lips. "Fucking bitch!" He slammed the door shut.

Her first thought was, "Who will take care of my kids?" She knew she had no chance against this maniac, but she tried to catch him with a kick to his groin as he tore toward her. She missed and he grabbed her outstretched leg and twisted it so hard that she felt it snap. The pain rushed at her as he threw her against the wall. As she rebounded from the force of the shove, he slapped her violently across her face. The blood was in her mouth as her legs gave way. He grabbed her by the hair and dragged her to the bed where he threw her diagonally across the thin mattress. He knelt alongside of her, his left hand on her throat.

"How did you get in here, you bitch?"

"They let me in."

"Who?"

"Security." The pain was unbearable. She just waited to die.

"What's this about?"

"Nothing. It's no big deal."

"Fuck you!" He slapped her brutally across the face. He backed away, looked around and saw her purse. He opened the wallet and saw her licenses. "A P.I. Who are you working for?" She didn't answer. He found McAbee's business card: "ACJ Investigation Services. Is that who you work for?" She still didn't answer. He grabbed her unbroken leg and began to twist it.

She yelled, "Yes ... goddamn it ... yes!"

"Is this about Tobin, the Tobin bitch?"

"Yes." She was crying in pain. He went to the sink and took his cash, grabbed an athletic bag, filled it with his shelved clothing and laid the bag down. He rushed at her and grabbed her by the neck. He started to strangle her.

CHAPTER 19

Melvin Harris left his office and saw Jumbo sitting in the security Ford Explorer.

"Jumbo! Get me back to this jerk's room. They're all worried about the babe." He jumped into the seat next to Jumbo who started up the sports utility vehicle. "And don't put on the lights, goddamn it!"

"Come up with me," Harris yelled to Jumbo. When they got to the top of the steel-grated stairway, the two-by-three glass widow, which was curtained, showed a figure leaning over and pressing down. Harris instantly knew from the build that this couldn't be Augusta Satin. "Big-time trouble - get ready!" He turned the door knob and got half way into the room when he heard a scream, "Son of a bitch!" Then, weight was hurled against the door. If Harris had been alone, he would have been ejected, but Jumbo threw his heft to the door and it flew open. The last thought Harris had was that Augusta Satin was probably dead. Tommy Lee had been strangling her. The right fist caught him flush on his jaw.

Jumbo knew his asset. It was his size which made the room so terribly tight. He watched Harris go down like a rock. He tried to move in close to Tommy Lee so that he couldn't have room to throw another one of those punches. He also yelled loudly, "Help ... help!"

He grabbed for Tommy Lee, trying to get him in a bear hug but instead he took four savage punches into his solar plexus. The big man backed away, catching his breath. Tommy Lee had a vicious snarl around his mouth, and he yelled out, "Get outta my way, you fat fuck!"

In between gasps Jumbo growled, "Mother fucker." Tommy Lee feinted with two left jabs, the second of which Jumbo made an effort to fend off. He never saw the right cross and was going down when the second hit him. In this maelstrom, Jumbo heard movement on the steel steps. Maybe some help was on the way.

Tommy Lee grabbed his bag and checked his cash supply in his front pocket. He cursed at his bad luck. He wanted to make sure that the bitch was dead, but instead, he ran out of the room, slamming his door. At the top of the stairs, he saw a Mexican groom who had probably come up in response to the giant nigger's yell. Before he could hit him, the Mexican ran down the stairs and out of the area.

In tum, Tommy Lee started to move toward the track gate by quickly going through the barns and staying away from the main road.

He was at his truck in less than five minutes. The parking lot adjoining the stall gate of Sportsman's was ill lit and served his purposes. Next to his pickup was a Dodge Ram pickup. He switched license plates. It took him about three minutes. Hopefully, the owner of the Ram wouldn't notice the switch for a while.

He made it to Interstate 55 within five minutes, determined to obey the speed limits and avoid mistakes. He felt that he had made enough of them for the day. Within 45 minutes, he stopped at a rest stop on Interstate 80. When he looked into the mirror of the empty rest stop bathroom, he saw that his face and arms were speckled with blood. He washed himself as best he could and dried himself in a stall with toilet paper. He noticed, with interest, that his right hand had a slight quiver to it. This was a new phenomenon for him.

As he was leaving the building, he remembered the card that he had retrieved from the bitch: "ACJ Investigation Services." It gave a phone number, an address and a name: Bertrand McAbee. Tommy Lee thought long and hard as he drove across Illinois on Interstate 80. As he was about to cross the Mississippi River into Iowa, he took the last exit in Illinois and drove north and east along Route 84 to Port Byron, Illinois, a small river town of about 1,500 residents. He had remembered a mom-and-pop motel that he had used a few times for trysts with married bitches from the Quad Cities Oval. Happily, it was still in business. It was the sort of place where you paid $30 cash and signed yourself in as John Smith. Everyone knew there was a reason behind the anonymity. When he got to his ill-lit room with the creaking bedsprings, lumpy mattress and snowy television, he laid down and turned out the lights, and wondered why he had not proceeded across Iowa on his way to Sacramento. Finally, he put it down to the business card. Here was the source of his trouble. It was as though fate demanded that he find the problem and eliminate it. If, in fact, his luck had run out and he was done, he would at least have the pleasure of eliminating the bastard who was taking him down. With that decision made, he went to sleep trying to picture who McAbee was and when he would be able to kill him. Then, he would make for Sacramento and hopefully lie low.

At the resolution of the Fisk interrogation at 7:30 p.m., McAbee asked Ledbetter to intercede at Sportsman's on behalf of Augusta Satin. He was furious with Melvin Harris, who would not respond to any phone calls.

At 7:40p.m., he was called by Pat who was still at the office. Jim Panayotounis needed him to call him as soon as possible. Pat had had no luck trying to catch up with Augusta.

McAbee got hold of Panayotounis by 7:45p.m.

"Yes ... Bertrand ... some problems. I was just called by the C.O.O. up there at Sportsman's. There are problems. Two security guys have concussions and are in the hospital, and a woman by the name of Augusta Satin is in the emergency room with a broken leg and a severely damaged windpipe, but she is expected to make it. That's the name you mentioned, isn't it?"

"What hospital?"

"Loyola in Maywood. It's right off the Ike on First Avenue."

"Where were they found?"

"Well, that's the funny thing. They were all in a groom's room- Tommy Lee!"

"Jesus! I'm on my way. Thanks, Jim."

"Don't mention it."

As he was leaving the courthouse, he saw Ledbetter and

told him of the situation. He called Pat, told her why he was headed to Chicago and that she should contact Augusta's ex and get those kids to Loyola by whatever means necessary.

McAbee spent the night in Augusta's room. Her breathing was being assisted and her leg was in a cast. Her face had taken a battering (the eyes were swollen and an outsized bandage rode her chin). She came to at about 6:00 a.m. She was in severe pain, so the nurse gave her a shot of percodan. She caught McAbee's eyes and he saw tears well up. She couldn't talk. McAbee knew that it was best that she try not to. He patted her on the shoulder and whispered in her ear: "It's OK, Augusta. We've got him in our sights. It's just a matter of time. Your kids are fine and will be up here this afternoon with Pat."

He could see that the percodan was taking effect. She went down again. After a while, McAbee realized that only a few miles east of here was the apartment of Eddie Fox. For no apparent reason, he failed to show up at the track last night and his so doing had almost contributed to the death of Augusta Satin. He decided to drive there and talk with him.

He remembered the Forest Park address and found himself in the Rockford Avenue parking lot within fifteen minutes of leaving Loyola Medical Center.

As luck had it, the vestibule security door was open with a wooden wedge. Someone was moving out and apparently found that to be a good reason to compromise the security of the building.

He walked up the narrow stairwell and found Fox's apartment. He rang the bell three distinct times, but to no avail. He turned the knob of the door and to his surprise, it opened. He yelled out, "Fox! Eddie Fox! Anyone home?" He saw a fairly spartan living room, a kitchen and dining room to his left. He yelled again, "Fox- anyone around?" McAbee saw the bathroom to his left and noticed that the light was on. He looked in there, but no one was there. He looked to his right and saw the bodies of Eddie Fox and what was probably his girl friend. Their bodies looked so small and insignificant. He whispered to himself, "Jesus."

McAbee found and took $40,000 of Tobin's money. He wiped the door handle of the apartment and left.

He reached Ledbetter with his mobile.

"Dan, I told you I was trying to get hold of this Eddie Fox guy. I have a feeling that something is wrong. I think that you might want to send someone over there to his apartment in Forest Park."

"Does that mean you've been there already, Bertrand?"

"No, my statement doesn't mean that. It means that there's no good reason for this guy to be so gone, so suddenly." McAbee didn't want to lie outright to Ledbetter. He felt Ledbetter's suspicions through the wires.

"OK. Where are you going to be?"

"Loyola, with Augusta, and then back home to Iowa."

"Stay in touch."

McAbee left the still drowsy and slightly incoherent Augusta Satin at approximately 3:00 p.m. Her kids and Pat would keep a vigil. They would head back to the Quad Cities when Pat and Augusta thought it to be appropriate. Ledbetter had come to the hospital to inform McAbee of the discovery of the bodies of Eddie Fox and Christine Healy. The coroner had given an estimate that death had occurred yesterday in the late afternoon. McAbee could sense Ledbetter's suspicions that McAbee had been to Fox's apartment, but he never asked him directly, much to McAbee's relief. The manner of death was strangulation; also, Ms. Healy had been raped. Fox had suffered jaw damage from a fist. Healy had been beaten with an open hand. Tommy Lee was the prime suspect. An all-points bulletin was out on him. They were particularly concentrating on upstate New York, Ohio and Florida, which had been his main areas of domicile. No mention was made of the West Coast, even though both men were aware of several suspicious murders that had occurred near Sacramento, Reno and Provo.

McAbee headed back to the Quad Cities, just beating the traffic rush out of Chicago. As he drove west, he called Orville Tobin and made arrangements to stop by the farm in Aledo on his way home.

Tommy Lee woke up hungry and angry. It was 8:00 a.m. He could hear some noisy bitch of a maid barking out a complaint about the weather and her stupid husband who didn't get home last night until 3:00 a.m.

After showering and shaving, he went to the motel office and paid out $30 for another night, just in case he needed to hang around for unfinished business. He had breakfast at a local cafe and bought a copy of the Chicago Sun Times. There was no mention of anything relative to him, or the murders. He decided to call McAbee's office when he couldn't find McAbee's residence in the telephone directory, which he had borrowed from the cashier. There was one McAbee in the entire Quad Cities - Irene - who lived in Green Rock, a small town on the fringes of the Quad Cities in Illinois. There was a public phone outside the cafe.

He took McAbee's card from his pocket and called the number.

"Hello. ACJ Investigation Services."

"Yeah, hi. I'm wondering if yuh can help me? I'm with Federal Express and I have a package for a Bertrand McAbee of ACJ Investigations. We know it's supposed to be delivered to his home address, but it's blurred and I can't read it."

"Well, you can bring it here to the office. The regular secretary isn't here today. I'm a substitute."

"Well, that's the problem. On my sheet it says home delivery and Federal Express is real fussy. Yuh can't break procedures. I know that sounds funny, but that's the way it is."

"Hold on, let me see if I can find it in Pat's Rolodex. Oh, here it is: 4543 Hayes Road in Davenport."

"Thanks. Do you have a phone number?"

"Sure, 319-355-3443. But I can tell you he's not around today. He's in Chicago, an emergency."

Tommy Lee felt three things: this was a really dumb bitch, McAbee and his secretary were in Chicago because of this case, and his luck was back.

"Thanks, ma'am."

Caryl Ford, the recently widowed, 58-year-old temp who had just returned to the workplace after thirty eight years went back to her crossword puzzle, happy for having been so helpful to Federal Express, a company for which she had great admiration. She had noted the call on Pat's list: "Federal Express- Package inquiry."

McAbee pulled up to Orville Tobin's farmstead at 6:45 p.m. The porch light was on. He saw Orviile's frame in the door.

"Come into the living room and sit down. Anything to drink?" Orville asked.

"No. I stopped and had some coffee in De Kalb on my way back from Chicago. How are you?" McAbee thought that Tobin's face was drawn, pale and his eyes slightly vacant.

"Not well. I had another bad go this morning. Shortness of breath, dizzy, the whole drill. You know, this thing about Erin is keeping me going. You said you had news."

"Well, first of all, I have $40,000 for you. This is extortion money from the man who called you. I think that you must treat it as though you never delivered it. You'll see why in a minute." Tobin didn't even look at the proffered bag, his eyes staying fixed on McAbee who continued, "Let me tell you what has happened."

McAbee gave him a detailed account of the progress of the investigation. At the end of it, Tobin said, "I'm very sorry about the black woman. When she was out here showing me how to use the tape recorder on that phone, I liked her. I think that she'd have a great sense of humor when she let her hair down. But that could never happen between us. I was sad about that. You know, you can take that $40,000 and just give it to her."

"Orville, think on that for another day, then tell me you feel the same way."

"Fair enough. So, now what happens?"

"Well, there are APBs on him. It's just a matter of time. My mission was to find the killer of your daughter. I have, but I know you want a prosecution or at least that there be justice. So, I'll stay on this and see if we can bring him in, but obviously the FBI and police departments are in a much better place on this than I am."

"Well, you've made my day. Even if I keel over dead tonight, I'll feel that I beat this rotten man. I'll think that Erin was vindicated somehow."

"And you should. But I'll say this, the case is like a tar baby, once you touch it, it sticks on you. Tommy Lee seems to have that curse."

At about the same time McAbee was discovering the bodies of Eddie Fox and Christine Healy, Tommy Lee went into the ACJ Investigation office. The knowledge that both McAbee and his regular secretary were gone, he saw as an opportunity. He figured, by lowering his voice a few octaves, that the dumb secretary would make no association between him and the pretended Federal Express employee.

"Yes, sir, may I help you?"

"Yes, I'd like to talk with Bertrand McAbee," he said, but all the while taking in the office in case he had to use it as a killing site.

"I'm sorry, he's not here today. He's expected back tomorrow or late tonight. What's this about?"

"Oh, yuh know, I'm having some problems with my wife and I need a P.l. McAbee was recommended."

"Well, I can make an appointment. How's that?"

"Uh ... sure ... why not." Tommy Lee was undecided. He thought that if he could murder this bitch, he could access McAbee's system and find out just what was known and by whom. But the presence of computers told him that there was no way he could access the data since he was computer illiterate. He wavered, then finally decided to spare her life.

She was looking at him, and he became aware that she must have asked him a question.

"Tomorrow? Sir, is there a good time for you?"

"Oh, sure. How about 10:00 a.m.?"

"That time is available. If there is a problem, what is your name and how can you be reached?" He saw a beginning look of suspicion in her eyes and thought it best to get out now.

"My name is Brad Connors and I can be reached at the Holiday Inn."

"Davenport? Bettendorf? Moline?"

"Ah ... Davenport. See yuh tomorrow." He left angry with himself for almost having blown the brief scouting mission.

For $10 he was issued a pass to the YMCA in downtown Davenport. He spent three hours there. He knew that people were watching him on the weights. He was doing things that normal people just didn't encounter often. He finished off his time there with a shower and a small lunch. It was 3:30 p.m. Then he set out to find McAbee's house, which he drove around three times, satisfying himself that no one was home.

He parked on the curb and rang McAbee's doorbell. He then walked around back and saw the dog run and the large, white German Shepherd who stood at full attention, ears pricked, eyes glaring and feet positioned for attack. The low growl started off his alert. Then, he proceeded to bark and jump at the fence gate. At this point, the back door of the house next to McAbee's was opened and a woman started to walk toward him. He smiled. He figured that he was being watched, a good six houses being situated to offer a view of him and this woman.

"Excuse me, sir, can I help you?"

"Yes, ma'am. I'm looking for a Bertrand McAbee. He was interested in using our lawn service. I just wanted to get a sense of what was needed so that I could give him a quote. Didn't mean to bother yuh, and I didn't know he had the dog. He never mentioned the dog when he called my boss." He thought she was swallowing his story hook, line and sinker. "How old is the dog? Is he as mean as he appears?" He smiled.

"He's four. His name is Scorpio, and he can be mean. But he never runs in the yard if that's what you mean."

"Well, I have to ask. We've had some of our men get bitten, and it doesn't go down well."

"OK, look around. He probably won't be back till late tonight."

"I'll call him with the quote."

She proceeded to put her fmgers through the wire fence and touch Scorpio's nose. "Nice dog, now. It's OK." She left and he pretended to look around as if making assessments. The filthy mutt started to bark again and wouldn't let up until he got out of his eyesight.

Tommy Lee went to the Northpark Mall, walked around and thought about what he would do. His sense of things told him to strike as soon as possible and get back on the road and out of the Midwest.

McAbee left Tobin's farmhouse at 7:30p.m. and decided to visit his office in Davenport before heading home. He called Gloria and told her that he'd be home at about 9:30p.m. and asked if Scorpio was OK. There was never a word exchanged about lawn service representatives.

McAbee was in his office at 8:20 p.m. He opened his

mail, read the telephone and visitor's log and saw nothing out of the ordinary. His appointment book was full for tomorrow. The 10:00 a.m. appointment was written in the following way: "Brad Connors: marriage troubles - edgy and uncomfortable. Referred." McAbee's mental take on her comment was that many husbands and wives come to a PI uncomfortable and edgy. He wished that the replacement had gotten the name of the referral, but he could get that himself. He had learned to have no great expectations about office temps. Otherwise, things looked to be in good order.

Tommy Lee had left Northpark Mall at 8:00p.m. After having driven around McAbee's neighborhood for fifteen minutes, had decided to drive to McAbee's office in downtown Davenport just on the off-chance that he was there. When he arrived at the fairly empty area, he looked up to the end office on the fifth floor of the building. To his shock, the lights were on in McAbee's suite of offices. Tommy Lee counted this as luck returning, but the superstitious part of him didn't want to make a move in the office itself since he had left the office earlier in the day, defeated and angry with himself.

He parked a block away and went into a yuppie micro-brew bar where he took a seat that allowed him a view of McAbee's office. Twenty minutes later, he left the bar at the instant that McAbee's light went out. He had an intense curiosity about what McAbee looked like. Three minutes later, a Ford Explorer pulled out of the parking ramp that was in the basement of the building. Tommy Lee started his pickup and began to tail the Explorer, fully expecting it to head to Hayes Road. Perhaps this was the time to take him out.

CHAPTER 20

McAbee drove into his long driveway and heard the staccato bark and the happy yip of Scorpio. He touched the switch of his garage door opener and parked his Explorer. It was 9:20 p.m. and a chill had set into the evening. He went to open Scorpio's gate with one hand and unclasp the leash that was attached to the run with the other when he heard a footstep. He was startled. It was Gloria. He hadn't heard nor seen her.

"Gloria, you spooked me. How are you?" He grabbed Scorpio's collar and attached the leash to the jumping and excited dog.

"Oh, fine. Now you listen here, Doctor McAbee, I have a meal for you; some good rich soup with just the tiniest bit of beef in it for flavoring. Let me bring it over. I don't like the hours that you're keeping. You'll get run down."

McAbee smiled and shook his head, but he thought the better of it because it sounded good, and he was hungry, tired and chilly. "OK, Gloria, it's a deal. Give me a few minutes to settle this guy down."

She looked up at the stars and said, "Thank God." While walking back to her house, she said over her shoulder, "And, I have a treat for Scorpio, of course."

McAbee walked Scorpio around the perimeter of his property and in the process picked up his mail and entered his house through the front door just as he saw a pickup drive by and down the street away from the house, a meaningless peripheral sensation to the occupied McAbee.

In a few minutes the house was lit up, Scorpio was loudly drinking water and glaring at the dried dog food that McAbee had put out for him. He would eat it, but only after he was totally convinced that nothing else was available. McAbee sat at his dining room table and scanned his mail: two bills, three catalogs, a credit card offering, a magazine and a subscription renewal; about par for the course, he thought.

When the doorbell rang, he remembered Gloria and the soup as he watched Scorpio hurtle from the kitchen to the front door barking with his full maniacal gusto.

"Come in." He had left the door unlatched in anticipation of Gloria's visit.

The knob turned as McAbee slit open the bill from the water company. But he didn't like what he heard and looked back up. An immense presence filled the entryway. Scorpio became quiet and backed away as this stranger pointed to McAbee and yelled, "Keep that fucking mutt down! We have business."

McAbee, up now and moving toward the door, said, "Like hell I'll call him off-get out of this house!"

"Have it yuh way, McAbee."

Only then did McAbee freeze, because now that he was within ten feet of the stranger, who wore a baseball cap that shadowed his face from a distance, he saw that it was Tommy Lee. McAbee's gun was upstairs. He'd have to move through this man to get it and that just wasn't going to happen.

"Scorpio, stay still!" McAbee yelled. "Come to me." McAbee backed away from Tommy Lee about five feet while Scorpio, all too willingly, came to his side. "Who are you and what do you want?" McAbee thought of Scorpio's guileful tendency to allow people into the house without a fuss.

"Yuh know who I am. I can tell it by yuh eyes. Why are yuh after me?"

McAbee was trapped by the architecture of the house. He couldn't make it to the back door and the front door was blocked by this giant athlete. McAbee saw that he had never appreciated the man's heft. He also realized that he had no chance against him. Gloria came into his mind. She would come to the door at any second, thereby endangering her life. He hoped that she would knock so that he could yell for her to leave the soup on the stoop. Perhaps he could get this maniac to relax, ever so slightly, by talking with him.

"Why am I after you? Specifically because of what you did to Erin Tobin, that's why."

"And who put yuh onto me? I was totally out of the circuit on that one."

"You know as well as I do," McAbee reached down and stroked Scorpio whose neck fur was raised and whose barely audible growl foretold an attack. He said to Scorpio, "Easy, Scorp, easy, it's OK." The dog relaxed about one degree in his vigilance, surely a concession to McAbee that ran totally against his canine instincts. McAbee looked again at Tommy Lee, "You killed him and his girl friend."

"I know. He got too cute. We were in the clear on this, but he decided on blackmail."

"Well, I think that you should surrender yourself."

"Is that so?"

"The FBI is on to you and you've been IDed in a series of murders. Out of curiosity, just how many did you commit?"

"Ah, who knows? Twenty-five or so. Who gives a damn."

"Maybe the friends and lovers and families of the victims do. Does that register?"

"Fuck that stuff."

"Listen, there's no escape for you. You're being hunted all across the country."

"Yeah, well, we'll see. But, yuh set this in motion and yuh going to pay."

Tommy Lee moved forward a few steps. At that instant, Gloria opened the front door. McAbee yelled "Gloria, run!" Tommy Lee turned and grabbed at her. "Watch out!" He let Scorpio go as he ran toward a closet where he kept a softball bat. Gloria threw the tureen of soup at Tommy Lee and hit him in the face with the hot supper before being felled by a right fist that caught her cheekbone and sent her to the floor unconscious. Scorpio was tearing flesh from Tommy Lee's knee as McAbee rushed to the scene. The ex boxer was trying to clean the thick soup from his face and kick away from Scorpio who had his kneecap in a vicious hold.

Just as he was trying to grab Scorpio by bending down to get at the dog's collar, McAbee swung the bat as hard as he could and caught Tommy Lee on the top of his head. He staggered back as Scorpio now went for his genitals. Tommy Lee blindly lurched for Scorpio's neck when McAbee hit him again across his face. Blood spurted from his nose and face. He tried to get out of the door with Scorpio in full bite. As he grabbed the doorknob, he tripped over Gloria. McAbee pounded his hand with the baseball bat and could hear the fingers break. Tommy Lee went down to his knees. He got ahold of Scorpio's neck, looking intent on breaking it, when McAbee, using all of his power, slammed the bat into his jaw. He fell back, not yet unconscious, but terribly dazed. McAbee stood over him and hit him two more times. He would not have stopped except for his concern for Gloria, and his absolute conviction that the man was unconscious.

AFTERWARD

Tommy Lee was ultimately taken by the Feds for interstate kidnaping and murder. He was given a life sentence in Leavenworth. That he was at peace with himself because of the severe brain damage caused by McAbee's bat, was neither here nor there to the prosecutor, who did wince, however, at the sexual mutilation that had occurred to the killer by McAbee's dog.

Gloria recovered with two teeth missing and a purpled left side of the face that found her reclusive for three weeks.

McAbee got the money promised to him by Tobin the minute FBI Agent Ledbetter presented him with the evidence against Tommy Lee. As a further gesture, he handed McAbee the bag with the $40,000 and told him to give it to Augusta Satin for her kids. Augusta recovered fully but needed two months before she felt ready for work again.

Four weeks after the arrest of Tommy Lee, Orville Tobin died in his sleep. People who knew him, said that in his last month, he was a changed man- for the better.

McAbee told his brother Bill about the incident with Tommy Lee at his house. He got a ten-minute lecture on preparedness.

Scorpio- is still Scorpio. However, McAbee couldn't

help but notice that he seemed to have an even bigger attitude about himself. It was almost like he thought he was in charge of things.

As for McAbee ... he continues to search for answers, and he likes the detective game. He argues to his friends that it's an existential morality play. And Beth? She's now free.

END

Printed in the United States
By Bookmasters